THE
Backup
BRIDE
PROPOSAL

JACI BURTON

BERKLEY ROMANCE
New York

BERKLEY ROMANCE
Published by Berkley
An imprint of Penguin Random House LLC
penguinrandomhouse.com

Copyright © 2024 by Jaci Burton, Inc.
Excerpt from *Housebroke* copyright © 2023 by Jaci Burton, Inc.
Penguin Random House supports copyright. Copyright fuels creativity, encourages
diverse voices, promotes free speech, and creates a vibrant culture. Thank you for buying
an authorized edition of this book and for complying with copyright laws by not
reproducing, scanning, or distributing any part of it in any form without permission.
You are supporting writers and allowing Penguin Random House to continue to
publish books for every reader.

BERKLEY and the BERKLEY & B colophon are registered trademarks of
Penguin Random House LLC.

ISBN: 9780593439654

First Edition: April 2024

Printed in the United States of America
1 3 5 7 9 10 8 6 4 2

Book design by Alison Cnockaert

This is a work of fiction. Names, characters, places, and incidents either are the product
of the author's imagination or are used fictitiously, and any resemblance to actual persons,
living or dead, business establishments, events, or locales is entirely coincidental.

If you purchased this book without a cover, you should be aware that this book is stolen
property. It was reported as "unsold and destroyed" to the publisher, and neither the author
nor the publisher has received any payment for this "stripped book."

Thank you to my readers for falling in love with the Bellinis. I hope you have embraced them like family and return to them often.

CHAPTER

. . . . . .

one

MAE WALLACE LOVED weddings, which was fortunate, since she was in the wedding business. She loved the flowers and the twinkling lights and the smiling faces of the wedding party, the way the groom teared up when the bride walked down the aisle, the way they clasped hands so tightly she just knew they were clutching each other at the altar out of sheer nervousness. It was adorable.

And receptions were the best. The food, the cake, the music and the dancing. And, oh, the men. This wedding in particular was blessed with a plethora of fine-looking men. Mae loved men. All men. All shapes and sizes and colors and all their vivid personalities. And by loved, she meant enjoyed, not love in the heart kind of way.

Because while men were fun and all, she didn't want to keep any of them. She was more of the catch-and-release type of woman. Date them once, have sex with one every now and then when the urge struck, then let them go. Because she'd caught one once, had almost married him, in fact. Until she discovered he was a serial cheater. Heart broken, end of love story. At least she'd found out before the wedding.

She was grateful, really, because it had taught her a valuable lesson.

Men couldn't be trusted. Sure, they were hot and great in the sack and fun to talk to and go out with. They were good for entertainment purposes. But marry them? Not on her life. After that colossal mistake she'd almost made with Isaac, she vowed to never fall in love again.

"Isn't this one of our wildest weddings ever?"

Mae looked over at Honor Bellini Stone, her friend and coworker, and smiled. "Everyone seems to be having a very good time."

Honor was the youngest of the three Bellini sisters. The sisters and their parents owned and operated both Red Moss Vineyards, where the weddings were conducted, and Bellini Weddings, which Mae was lucky to be part of.

Honor slipped her hand through Mae's arm. "And to think, after this wedding, the film crew arrives."

Mae wrinkled her nose. "Right. I hope they don't trample over everything that's beautiful about this place."

"I think we've made it very clear that they need to step cautiously around the vineyards and our wedding business."

"Let's hope so."

They walked outside the barn, where the reception was still going strong despite the late hour. Honor led Mae to the main house, where Honor's parents lived.

"Are you sure we should disappear like this?" Mae asked.

Honor shrugged. "Erin and Brenna have got it. And my feet hurt. I need five minutes with my shoes off."

Mae laughed and followed along. They stepped through the back door and Honor pulled out a pitcher of lemonade, pouring two glasses for them. They took seats on the back porch and Honor slipped her heels off, groaning at the same time.

Mae sipped the lemonade, enjoying its tart sweetness. "You know, you could wear flats."

"I could, couldn't I? Normally my feet are fine, but this wedding has had me running."

"It's a wild one, for sure. I'm pretty sure all the groomsmen are drunk."

Honor smirked. "They were drunk before the ceremony. I'm surprised the bride hasn't kicked the groom's ass from here to Texas by now."

"She's saving face. I don't envy that guy once the bride gets him alone later."

"Same." Honor wiggled her toes. "I guess it's time to get back there."

"Yes, before your sisters kick both *our* asses from here to Texas."

Honor laughed. "You're right about that."

They went back to the wedding party, which was in no way winding down. At least they were getting their money's worth, which Mae couldn't blame them for. Erin had charged the couple a premium for extra guests and longer reception time and they hadn't even balked. Mae was glad that they'd hired more than the usual amount of help, not only for wrangling the guests and serving but also for cleanup, because right now the barn looked more like the aftereffects of a major frat party than a wedding reception.

She wandered around, checking on the staff to be sure they didn't need any assistance. She also kept her eye on the guests because a free-for-all with a lot of inebriated people could get out of hand in a hurry.

"Anything going on?" Erin asked as they ran into each other.

"Nothing but a lot of heavy drinkers. Everyone's partying hard, but so far it's under control."

Erin wrinkled her nose. "I'll be glad when this one's over."

"You and me both."

They parted and Mae continued her sentry duties. She'd noticed a guy walking around. How could she not notice him? Extremely tall, well built, wearing a cowboy hat worn low on his face. As she wandered, she kept her eye on him, noting that he didn't interact with anyone, instead just wandered alone, a beer in his hand.

They'd had wedding party crashers before, people thinking they could slide in unnoticed, grab some free food and drink and slide on out. Big events like this one were popular with the interlopers, but they'd all learned to recognize the ones who didn't belong, because at weddings, you interacted with your friends and family members.

This guy? Mae would bet he didn't know a single person here. She intended to find out about him right now.

IF THERE WAS one thing Kane August had learned to do from an early age, it was to blend in without being noticed. And being an actor, and a fairly recognizable one? That not-being-noticed thing sure came in handy.

He'd gotten here to Red Moss Vineyards early, wanting to get a feel for the layout without people fawning all over him. Since he'd be filming here for a couple of months, he wanted to see how the staff operated, how they interacted with regular people. And, fortunately, this being Oklahoma and all, him sliding in wearing a cowboy hat that shielded his face came in handy. He'd shown up late to the reception and been able to blend right in without anyone recognizing him.

His agent had already given him the lay of the land as far as who was who. Brenna and her father, Johnny, ran Red Moss Vineyards; Erin was all about the business end; and Honor Bellini was the main wedding coordinator, assisted by Mae Wallace, who wasn't a member of the family. He'd asked around while grabbing a beer and both Erin and Mae had been pointed out to him, so he knew who to avoid and who to keep an eye on. So far, so good.

"Has anyone ever told you that you look an awful lot like Kane August?"

He cringed and turned around to see one of the bridesmaids, a pretty blonde who appeared to be extremely drunk.

He smiled and pulled out the Texas drawl he'd worked hard to lose when he'd started acting. "I get that a lot. I wish I was him. Then I'd have all his money."

She snorted, weaving unsteadily on her heels. "Yeah, I wish you were him, too, honey. But you're still hot as hell. Wanna dance?"

"Oh, thanks, but I'm here with my . . . wife."

"Too bad." She wandered off unsteadily and Kane relaxed.

"Are you friends with the bride or the groom?"

Damn. He'd gone this far without having to talk to anyone. He turned around and . . .

Crap. Mae Wallace. He offered up his most charming smile, hoping to keep his face partially hidden. "Groom. Steve and I went to college together." At least he'd remembered to read the names of the bride and groom on his way inside.

She eyed him suspiciously. "Really. And what college is that, exactly?"

"Uh, University of Oklahoma."

"Wrong. Steve and Evie met at Oklahoma State University." She reached up to tip his hat back and that was when he knew she'd recognize him. She blinked, but then shook her head. "Nice try, but you're done here, bud. You'll have to crash a different wedding."

"I was not—"

She gave him a critical gaze, and he had to admit that even frowning and irritated, she was beautiful, with brown curly hair, chocolate-brown eyes and the kind of curves that always set his pulse racing. And instead of squealing in excitement about who he was, she motioned for two burly-looking guys standing at the entrance to the barn.

Kane didn't know whether to be pleased or pissed. But rather than worrying about his bruised ego, he was focused on being thrashed by the two bodybuilders headed his way. He raised his hands. "Tossing me isn't necessary. I'm on my way out."

"Oh, we'll make sure you make it all the way out, won't we, guys?"

"You bet we will," one of the well-muscled guys said.

He turned and made a fast exit, getting into his rental at the far corner of the parking area and driving off.

So Mae had no idea who he was. That kind of thing rarely happened to him these days. Kind of refreshing, actually.

This shoot should be a lot of fun.

CHAPTER

· · · · · ·

two

THEY'D BARELY RECOVERED from the circus that was the giant drunken wedding over the weekend, and now the big circus had come to town.

A movie production, of all things. Trucks had begun to arrive early Monday morning. Johnny Bellini, along with several of the vineyard crew, had made sure they parked all their trailers—and oh, dear God, there had been so many—in the designated areas they'd carved out for them.

Who knew that making a movie took so many people and so much stuff?

"It's a nightmare out there." Erin bounced her six-month-old son, JJ, in her arms while staring out the dining room window. "An actual nightmare."

"I know we're going to regret this," Brenna said, reaching over to play with JJ, who giggled in response.

"It'll all be fine," Maureen Bellini said.

Honor sighed. "Will it, Mom?"

"Yes, it will. We were very clear in the contract about where the crew can and cannot be, including stiff penalties for any damages to the property. They've assured me they'll use utmost care while prepping and filming. Johnny and I went over earlier this morning to meet the director, the crew and the actors. We brought wine, and everyone was very nice and accommodating."

"Hmph" was all Brenna had to say in response.

"I'll be interested to see what changes they make to the wedding area," Mae said.

Four sets of eyes turned to her. She grimaced. Okay, wrong thing to say.

"Anyway," Maureen said. "Back to today's agenda."

Since this was the first week of the film crew being on board, they hadn't booked any weddings. Wine harvest had already been done, so the crew wouldn't be in the way other than people who wanted to book an appointment to tour the wedding venue.

"Honor and Mae will handle tours, mentioning that filming will be taking place," Erin said, handing off a suddenly fussy JJ to Maureen, who smiled and made baby sounds to him. "Brenna, you and Dad will fiercely guard the vineyards."

"As if I'd do anything else," Brenna said.

Louise brought out breakfast. JJ grabbed for a potato, so Maureen gave it to him to munch on. Mae was amazed how the whole eating-solid-foods thing was going. Young mister JJ was a champion at it. An expert with sliced bananas, too.

"I also think it would be a great idea if Mae acts as our official liaison to the production company," Erin said.

Mae blinked. "What?"

"Oh, excellent idea," Brenna said.

"Agreed," Maureen said.

"Uh . . . what exactly do I need to do?" she asked.

Brenna shrugged. "You know. Just . . . be our point person

with the production staff. Oh, and the actors. That way if they have questions . . ."

"Or if they step out of line," Honor added, "you'll be the one to tell them to knock it off."

Maureen nodded. "Agreed. I'll let them know to come to you with anything they might need."

"But . . ." She fumbled for some way out of this. "What about the Everson/Hones wedding? It's another large one. Plus, there's Brenna and Finn's upcoming wedding. I was going to handle—"

Honor waved her hand back and forth. "Don't even worry about it, Mae. I've got it all covered. And besides, the whole liaison thing isn't a full-time gig."

"It would be a huge help if you could handle it," Maureen said. "We need someone to get close to production, make sure they don't mess up our beautiful grounds."

"Or violate the contract," Erin said. "We know they'll try to cut corners."

"And there are so many people here already, Mae," Brenna said. "You're so good at managing. If anyone can do this, you can."

Well, crap. She knew this family. They weren't pushing this off on her, and they weren't blowing smoke. They trusted her to protect the vineyards and wedding venues. "Sure. Of course."

"Great." Honor smiled. "Though I will miss you at Bellini Weddings."

"Don't think you can get rid of me that easily. I can juggle all of my responsibilities plus this. Expect me at meetings. And weddings."

"We wouldn't have it any other way," Maureen said.

"Exactly," Erin said. "After all, we'll need regular reports about what the movie people are doing."

They put a plan together, and then Maureen contacted the director, Alexis Black, who set up a time today for Mae to meet with the team. After the Bellini meeting, Mae went into her office to go over her notes and plot her strategy. Also, to breathe, because she was nervous as hell.

She enjoyed the job she had, which allowed her to be more of a background player. She liked helping the wedding party with their special days, and also doing whatever she could to assist the Bellinis in whatever way they needed her. But this? This made her a key player, would put her front and center in a project that would give the Bellinis a serious amount of recognition.

She could not screw this up. She would walk over to the set, look around, start meeting people and get a feel for how it was going, and then she'd meet with Alexis Black and they'd gain an understanding.

She was so ready. Except she needed to step into the restroom and check her face and hair and outfit first. Hair, good. Face, outstanding. Outfit? Hmmm. It was a warm September day, and since it was Monday and meeting day, she hadn't planned to see any clients, so she'd worn capris and a short-sleeved top. It was hardly the outfit she needed to be wearing to meet a Hollywood director.

She knocked on Honor's office door.

"Come on in, Mae."

She stepped into the office, waiting for Honor to look up from her laptop, but she didn't, so she was obviously busy. Mae wanted to take up as little of her time as necessary since this was such a trivial thing. "I need to borrow a skirt and top for my meeting with Alexis Black."

Now Honor looked up. "Of course. Go on up and help yourself."

She was already halfway out the door. "Great, thanks."

Even though Honor had moved out and now lived with her husband, Owen, she, like both her sisters, always kept extra clothes at the house. Since they all spent a lot of hours there and sometimes had to adjust from casual office attire to meet prospective clients, changes of clothing came in handy.

Mae stared into Honor's closet, trying to figure out what the best outfit would be. She flipped through hangers over and over until she made herself dizzy. The problem was, she didn't know what the hell she was supposed to wear to impress Hollywood types.

"Go for the red skirt and the white blouse."

She turned around to see Brenna leaning against the doorway. "Red and white, huh?"

"Red screams attention, and the white silk top gives you that 'I'm damn serious, but also check how hot I am' look."

Mae laughed. "All from two pieces of clothing, huh?"

Brenna shrugged. "Hey, it's all about the ensemble. Oh, and here." She took off one of her bracelets, a turquoise beauty. "This'll look amazing against your skin."

"Thanks."

After Brenna left, Mae closed the door, changed clothes and slid the bracelet on, then checked herself out in Honor's full-length mirror. She always kept black heels in her car, so those would go well with this ensemble.

Okay, she did look professional. And hot.

Now all she had to do was impress the director so she'd think Mae was completely in charge of this thing.

And Mae could totally do that.

"WHY ARE YOU here? I don't want to see you yet."

Kane smirked at the aggravated look on Alexis Black's face. She was more of a big sister to him than a director.

They'd known each other for more than fifteen years. She was the star of the first movie he'd ever been cast in, when he had been only seventeen years old. He'd been terrified and unsure of himself and Alexis had befriended him, taught him everything he needed to know about the business, both the insides and outsides of it, and had gotten him roles he otherwise might not have gotten. Then, when he'd gotten his big break in that big-budget action movie directed by Oscar Valentine, Kane had brought Alexis as his plus-one to the premiere. Oscar and Alexis had fallen madly in love in one of the greatest Hollywood romances of all time, though Alexis still refused to marry him, calling the institution antiquated and unnecessary.

He leaned over and kissed her on the cheek. "How's Oscar?"

"In Switzerland filming. And here I am in Oklahoma." She patted his cheek. "Everly is still working on her film. She's going to be late."

Kane hated delays, but he'd been late to show up before, so he had to respect Everly being needed on one of her other films. "Of course she is. So what's the plan?"

Alexis shrugged. "No clue. We may need to get a stand-in to get early shots. Are you ready to film?"

"Like always."

"That's what I love about you, Kane. You're always prepared."

There was a knock on the trailer door. It opened, and Brian, Alexis's assistant, popped his head in.

"There's a Mae Wallace here to see you, Alexis. She said she has an appointment."

"Oh, right. Show her in, Brian."

"She's with the Bellini Weddings folks," Kane said.

Alexis arched a brow. "You've been doing your research."

"I like to get the geography down on a location shoot. And maybe check out the people I'll be working with."

She wagged a finger at him. "You will not be working with them. I will be liaisioning with them."

"Uh-huh. Sure."

"Hi. Hello. Are you Ms. Black?"

Kane turned around and smiled at Mae Wallace, who looked just as beautiful today as she had when he'd first seen her. Her wild curls had been somewhat tamed by pulling the upper strands back with pins, but Kane could imagine how lush and soft her hair was. Not that he'd ever get a chance to run his hands through it, which was a damn shame. He smiled at her.

She frowned at him. "Didn't I throw you out of the wedding the other night?"

"You did." He walked over to her and held out his hand. "Kane August."

She barely shook his hand. "Mae Wallace. What, exactly, are you doing here, Kane August?"

Alexis snorted out a laugh. "Kane is the star of our movie, Ms. Wallace."

She didn't look the least bit starstruck. "Oh. Sorry. Didn't recognize you. But you still shouldn't have been on the property, or at a wedding uninvited."

Alexis leaned back in her chair, her smirk evident. "Guess she laid those rules down fairly clearly, didn't she?"

"Yeah, well, I'm not much for rules."

"You should probably get used to them. We take pride in both the vineyard and our service to our wedding clients. We wouldn't want their privacy disrupted as they celebrate their big day."

Alexis stood and walked over to Mae, shaking her hand. "It won't happen again, will it, Kane?"

"Sure." He wouldn't promise anything, and he enjoyed the high color of irritation on Mae's cheeks.

"I won't take up much of your time," Mae said to Alexis. "I just wanted to meet you and let you know I'll be your primary contact during this shoot."

"Excellent. We'll trade numbers and I'll give you the production schedule. And if you wouldn't mind, could you give Kane a tour of your grounds? It'll help him get a feel for the atmosphere of the shoot."

From the grimace on Mae's face, that was the last thing she wanted to do, but she nodded and forced a smile. "Of course. I'd be happy to."

"Great. I've got things to do, so I'll email you the production schedule."

They exchanged phone numbers and email addresses.

"I'm looking forward to working with you, Ms. Black," Mae said.

"Same. And call me Alexis."

"Only if you call me Mae."

"Consider it done, Mae. Text or email if you have questions. And you're welcome to sit in on meetings or any of the shoots."

"I appreciate that." She turned to Kane. "Are you ready for the tour?"

"Ready when you are."

"Now works for me." He motioned toward the door, so Mae turned.

"Behave yourself," Alexis said, giving him a knowing grin.

"You know I will." He gave her a wink.

Behave himself? Not likely.

CHAPTER

· · · · · ·

three

W E HAVE SEVERAL acres of vineyards," Mae said, grateful for the overcast skies today as they walked among the grapes. "We just completed harvest so the vines are dormant at the moment."

She walked side by side with Kane, trying not to notice how tall he was, or how his dark hair rustled in the breeze. He'd casually tossed on a cowboy hat as if it were the most natural thing for him to do. He walked with that predatory manliness that made her insides quiver with sexual awareness. His dark sunglasses gave her no sign of his expression, and she was glad she'd tossed on her shades despite the overcast skies, because she was definitely feeling things she would not like showcased on her face.

"The vineyard is still beautiful, though," he said. "They need their rest. The vines work hard during the growing season."

She titled her head to the side, openly ogling him now. "Well, wow. That was deep. And pretty knowledgeable."

He laughed. "My grandpa has a small vineyard on the ranch. I spent my summers there."

"The ranch. You grew up on a ranch?"

"No. I grew up in the city. My grandparents have a ranch."

"Where?"

"Texas. North of Dallas."

"No shit?"

"No shit."

"Does your grandpa still have said vineyard?"

"He does. I figured if I get a break while I'm here, I'll drive down and visit him. I've done back-to-back movies so it's been about a year since I've been to the ranch. My gran died a couple of years ago and I'd love to see him."

"I'm sorry about your grandma."

"Thanks. She was pretty awesome. Made amazing pie. I miss her."

He sounded so sincere. She would not think about him having a family. Or grandparents that he might actually care about. She preferred to dislike him on the spot like she had the night he'd crashed the wedding.

"Anyway, Johnny and Brenna are now in the process of preparing the grapes for crushing and fermentation, while also processing other vintages for production."

"Sounds fun. I know the character I play is the best man in a wedding, and I know we got approval to do a chase through the wine cellar, along with my big fight with the groom."

She stopped, turned and faced him. "Really."

"Yeah."

She pulled out her phone and made a note to ask Brenna about that, because she couldn't imagine strangers being allowed in the cellars, let alone staging a fight there. "Anyway, on to the wedding venue."

She walked him through the vineyards and stopped at the arbor that looked out over the grapes. Seeing acres of vineyard never ceased to inspire her. "We perform ceremonies out here. It makes for spectacular pictures. We also do ceremonies in the barn during inclement weather."

He nodded. "We'll be shooting some scenes out here, including a big romantic declaration-of-love scene for the end."

"Huh." She would not ask, didn't want to know, didn't even care. He was just making a movie, so it would all be fake anyway.

Just like real love. Not that there was anything real about love. Or relationships. Or marriage.

She was much happier without any of those in her life.

"Anyway, if you follow along this path, it'll take you to the barn, where we typically hold receptions. Of course, you've already been there."

"Yeah. Sorry about that. I like to show up early to location shoots to get a feel for the places I'm going to be filming. I tried to stay out of the way and under the radar. No one even paid any attention to me and I didn't eat the food."

She couldn't hold back her laugh this time. "It's fine. Just don't wander in areas you're not supposed to be."

"Which are?"

As they walked up the steps of the barn, she pointed across the way toward the main house. "That's the Bellinis' private residence. You would definitely not be welcome there."

"Noted. And where do you stay?"

"I live off-site."

His smile was like lightning in a bottle, making his blue eyes sparkle. "Too bad."

She resisted shivering at his husky tone. Quite the actor, this one. He probably knew how to push all his leading ladies' buttons.

Her button, on the other hand, would not be pushed unless she wanted it to be. And the last person she wanted touching any of her buttons was some good-looking, sexy-as-hell hot-shot actor.

She might be their liaison, but she intended to keep her distance from Kane August.

"I'm getting hungry," he said. "Could you recommend some good places for lunch?"

"Oh, sure. But they're all in the city. Are you sure you want to risk being recognized?"

"You know, I'm pretty good about going places incognito. But I really could use someone to show me around."

She knew that GPS could show him around easy enough. But being new in town—and alone—also sucked. And she was hungry, so it was a self-serving gesture. "Sure. Let's go get some lunch. Anything in particular you want to eat?"

He shrugged. "Surprise me. I'm not a picky eater."

Their property was well outside Oklahoma City, and she intended to keep Kane from too many eyes that could recognize him, so she drove them to a place that had amazing barbecue. Of course, most of Oklahoma had amazing barbecue joints, but this was one of her favorites. She'd been coming to Ray's in Norman for as long as she could remember, and it was the best.

It wasn't fancy inside, and she was sure that Kane was used to high-class eateries, so she expected him to look down his nose at the place.

They walked in and he took a deep breath. "I can already smell those ribs. How did you know I love barbecue?"

Again, he surprised her. "I didn't. I just know that *I* love barbecue."

"Then let's eat."

She ordered a pulled pork sandwich along with okra and fries. Kane ordered a basket of ribs with the same sides. He tried to pay for her meal but she refused, insisting she pay for her own.

"Independent, huh?" he asked as they waited for their number to be called. "You did drive. The least I could do is pay."

"It's not a date, and I prefer we keep things between us—separated."

He shrugged. "Sure."

She was glad his ego hadn't gotten ruffled over something as simple as paying for a meal. Once their food was ready they grabbed a table and Kane dug in, slathering his ribs in sauce, uncaring that his face and hands got messy, which was exactly how you were supposed to eat ribs. She enjoyed watching him while she ate her sandwich.

"That was excellent," he said after he finished his ribs and wiped his mouth and hands with a wet wipe and a napkin. "I haven't had good barbecue since the last time I was at the ranch."

She wiped her hands and took a sip of her iced tea. "Your grandpa makes barbecue?"

"He and my aunt. They'll lay ribs out on the smoker and the smell will drive you crazy all day long."

She nodded. "The only way to make ribs fall-off-the-bone tender."

"Exactly." He popped the last bite of okra into his mouth, then took several swallows of tea. "Thanks for bringing me here. It's exactly what I wanted."

"I'm glad you liked it. Our area is filled with great food. You just have to search it out."

"I guess you'll have to show me around."

She absolutely did not intend to be his culinary guide. She

had too many other things to do. "I'm sure you have catering on location."

"Yeah, we do. But I like to get away from filming, get out and investigate my surroundings. Otherwise I feel closed in and that messes with my creative mojo."

She gave him a smirk. "Ooh, your mojo."

"Hey, it's a real thing."

She shrugged. "I wouldn't know."

"Sure you would. You do creative things all the time, don't you? With your weddings?"

She thought about it for a moment, then smiled. "You're right. Though Erin, Brenna and Honor are the creative ones. I just assist."

"I don't know about that. I watched you at the wedding the other night. The way you ran to help the bride when she had that issue with her dress, and then you stepped in with the bridesmaid who was having an argument with the maid of honor. You handled everything so smoothly. That was you, not any of the Bellini sisters."

He'd noticed all of that while he'd been wandering around the reception? "You have a keen eye for observation."

"It's my job to notice things. That's how an actor learns characterization."

"Really."

"Yeah. Movement, facial expression, dealing with conflict. Actors have to absorb all of that so we can use it down the line somewhere. Or at least that's how I do it."

"I don't watch a lot of movies. I'm more into books."

"This movie is based on a book."

She wrinkled her nose. "The book is always better."

He laughed. "I hear that a lot. And don't disagree. You can't possibly get every detail from a book into a movie. But I think this one's pretty good. It's romantic and funny, too."

"I guess I'll have to pick it up and read it, then compare. It will be interesting to watch it being filmed and compare it to the end product."

"Oh, so you'll actually go see this one, huh?"

She wouldn't commit. "I'll reserve judgment until I see how it goes."

They got up and left the restaurant, climbing into her car to head back.

"When do you start shooting?" she asked as they pulled down the long drive.

"Hopefully soon. We're waiting on Everly to show up."

She parked the car at the front of the security gate. "Who's Everly?"

"You really don't go to movies, do you?"

"Not a lot, no."

"Everly Sloane. She's the female lead in the movie."

"Oh. When's she due?"

"Tomorrow. So we should start costume and makeup prep, then be in rehearsals within a few days."

"Wow. Great."

His phone buzzed, so he pulled it out of his pocket, read the text message and frowned.

"Something wrong?" she asked.

"Yeah. Can you follow me into Alexis's office?"

"Sure."

She walked beside him, trying not to notice the way he walked, the way he looked or the incredible way he smelled.

Get it together, Mae. This guy is going to be around for a while and he is not going to be a plaything for you. You play and drop, and guys don't tend to linger in your orbit.

Excellent advice. She'd be sure to follow it.

They headed into Alexis's office. She was pacing the

length of the trailer, her cell in one hand, her other hand raking through the spikes of her silver hair.

"Might I remind you that Everly has a contract, Davis." She listened, tension evident in the way her shoulders tightened. "She's due on set tomorrow and her timeline for the other movie isn't my problem."

Figuring that she hadn't been invited to hear this, Mae tried to make herself as small as possible, hovering near the door. Meanwhile, Kane made himself comfortable on the sofa at the other end of the trailer.

"How long is it going to take for her to complete the movie?" Alexis asked, her pacing intensifying as she listened. Then she stopped dead. "Are you serious? Davis, you'd better have them step it up or we'll be looking for another lead for this movie." She clicked off and tossed her phone on her desk. "Dammit."

"So," Kane said. "Everly's delayed, huh?"

"Understatement. Her agent said three to four weeks until they wrap on her current film."

"Damn. So what are you gonna do?"

"I don't know. I need to have a conversation with the lawyers and see if we have an out clause with Everly's contract."

"And if we do, how are we going to book someone last minute? We're already set up here. Hell, I know almost all my lines."

"That's a shocker."

He frowned. "Hey. I'm always prepared."

She laughed. "Yeah, you are. And, hey, don't worry. We'll get something worked out. In fact, just hang around for a bit while I call Virginia."

"Virginia's the lawyer," Kane said as he looked over at Mae.

Mae felt like she was in the middle of something she wasn't supposed to hear. "I should probably go."

"No, Mae, you can stay," Alexis said, motioning to the sofa where Kane sprawled. "Make yourself comfortable. There are drinks in the mini fridge. Help yourself. This shouldn't take long."

Since she'd been given the invite, she made her way over to the sofa. Kane scooted over and she took a seat. Alexis was talking, so she kept her voice low.

"This seems very serious."

"It can be. Delays cost the production money. A few days, no problem. Several weeks? Big problem."

And delays would mean this whole production would be hanging out at the vineyard and wedding area longer, too, which could not happen. Mae pulled out her phone and made a note to discuss this with her people later. They needed to be kept informed, and this seemed like a major development.

"Okay," Alexis said as she turned to face them. "Everly has delays built into her contract, so we're screwed. We'll have to come up with a workaround until she's free. We can start shooting your scenes that Everly isn't in, but we still need to do a run-through of the entire movie and set up principal photography, which means we'll need someone to step into Everly's shoes, so to speak."

"Yeah. That's a problem." Kane looked over at Mae, staring thoughtfully at her. "Then again, maybe not."

He kept looking at her until she finally had to ask, "What?"

He stood. "Get up," he said.

She did. Kane looked over at Alexis. "You see it, don't you? The same height and build. Even the same hair. Eye color and facial shape is different, but as far as what the camera needs?"

Now it was Alexis studying her. She walked over. "Do you mind if I touch your hair?"

Mae had no idea what was going on. "Sure."

Alexis swept her hand over Mae's hair, pulled it up, then walked around and stared at her from the back before coming around between her and Kane. "You're absolutely right. She's perfect."

Mae had no idea what was going on, but whatever it was, she knew she wasn't going to like it. "Perfect for what?"

"You could stand in for Everly," Alexis said. "We could shoot you from behind for the scenes Kane needs to be in with her. And for the long shots. And then we'll fill in with Everly once she shows up."

"Fill in with . . . You want me in your film?"

"You won't need to do anything," Kane said. "Though it'd help if you'd learn the scene dialogue for flow, but not absolutely necessary."

This was going way beyond the scope of what she thought she was going to have to do. "Uh, thanks, but I don't think so."

Alexis nodded and held up one finger while she grabbed her phone. She scrolled and pressed a button, waiting a few seconds. "Hi, Maureen, it's Alexis Black. I'm fine, thanks. We have a small issue here. Our main actress is still finishing up a movie, which could delay production." She looked over at Kane and Mae. "I know, that's definitely a problem for both of us, but I have a solution. Mae is the same height and build and coloring as Everly and we were wondering if we could use her as a stand-in, allowing us to shoot a few scenes. I know it wasn't what we originally—"

Alexis grinned. "Pay her appropriately? Well, of course. We'll make sure she has the right credentials and get her on the payroll immediately." She paused and nodded. "I agree, we don't want any delays, either. Thanks, Maureen. Talk to you soon."

She clicked off. "Okay, so Maureen has approved us using you for the movie. We'll get you a SAG card and put you on the production's payroll."

Mae was at a loss for words. No one had asked her how she felt about it. Of course she wanted to help the Bellinis, and if it got this movie crew off the property sooner, she was all for it. But still, it would have been nice to be asked, to have a discussion with the Bellinis first.

"You do realize I'm not an actress," Mae said. "That I have zero training in this."

"You don't really need training to just stand on a mark and maybe do some hand or body gestures," Alexis explained.

"Still. This isn't my job. My job is to act as liaison between the Bellinis and the production. Not to help you out of a jam because one of your lead actors is delayed. I'm sorry, but no."

"Your boss has already agreed to let us use you."

"I know. And I can appreciate her willingness to be cooperative. But this is me saying no. I'm just not comfortable with this at all."

"But—"

Kane raised his hand. "Alexis. Hang on. Mae. I promise you that we won't put you outside your comfort zone. I'll be with you in every scene, and I'll help you in any way I can. You won't be in front of the camera since they'll be filming you from the back. You'll mostly just be standing there on a mark where Everly will be so they can film me, and then when Everly arrives they'll film her in the same scene."

She sighed. "You promise this isn't going to be a big deal?"

"I promise. And you'll get paid for your time."

She had to admit his smile was reassuring, making her slightly less terrified. Plus, she didn't want to let the Bellinis down.

"Fine. I'll do it."

Kane's smirk only irritated her further.

This was going to be a nightmare. And the sooner it was over, the sooner everything could go back to normal.

CHAPTER
......
four

"I DON'T KNOW, Mae. It sounds like all kinds of fun to me."

Mae shot Honor a look. "Sure, it sounds like fun to you because you're not the one doing it."

They all sat around the dining room table, the place where Bellini meetings were held. Louise, the Bellinis' cook and de facto member of the family, had made the most amazing cheese-and-fruit Danish for breakfast, which assuaged some of Mae's anguish at having been put in this position.

"If you really hate the idea," Maureen said, "I'll call Alexis and tell her you're unable to do it."

"Yeah," Erin said. "We can tell them you're needed else-where on wedding business."

"You absolutely shouldn't be forced to do something you don't want to do," Brenna said.

"I was only joking about the fun part," Honor said, look-ing apologetic. "Mostly."

She looked across the table at all of them, realizing how whiny and pathetic she must sound. It was her job to help out the Bellinis in their business. She felt that it was her business now as well, though it wasn't like she was an owner or anything. She was merely an employee. But she was a damn good one.

"I'm sorry. I didn't mean to complain. I'll be fine. And doing this puts me front and center in the production so I can keep an eye on things."

Maureen eyed her closely. "Are you sure?"

"Absolutely. Though the five a.m. calls will be interesting considering I live in the city."

"That's easy," Erin said. "You can temporarily move into one of our rooms here at the house."

"Absolutely." Maureen gave a short nod. "It's been so quiet here since Honor moved into Owen's house. With all three of the girls gone, it's like the house is too big. We'd love to have you stay with us for a while, Mae."

That would alleviate one of her concerns. "Thank you. I'd love that."

"Great. Move some things in tonight," Maureen said. "I'll alert Johnny not to walk around in his underwear."

"Mom," Brenna said, wrinkling her nose. "Ew."

Now all she had to do was read the script that someone from Alexis's staff had dropped off.

She'd always loved reading. So now she was going to be reading for work.

At least there'd be some fun part.

"What's Kane August like?" Honor asked.

Just the mention of his name made her blood boil. And her skin prickle, but not in the *Ugh* kind of way, unfortunately.

"Oh, you know, he's fine."

Brenna grinned. "I'll say he's fine. And I've only seen him from a distance."

Erin popped a strawberry into her mouth, chewed and

swallowed, then smiled at Mae. "Whereas Mae gets the up-close-and-personal experience. Do you get to kiss him?"

"No!" she said, probably a little too forcefully. Lowering her voice, she added, "There will be no kissing."

Honor gave her a knowing look.

Absolutely not. No kissing.

Ever.

KANE PRIDED HIMSELF on always being prepared and ready for a shoot. He read and reread his script, getting to know his character inside and out, understanding what motivated him. He'd create a backstory that wasn't included in the script so he could feel the character's depth. When the director said "Action," he was deep inside his character's head. He was ready to go right now. Which was why Everly being late to start this project was such a disappointment.

But that was the way this biz was sometimes. You had to learn to roll with it. And now he had play off Mae in his scenes. She wasn't an actress so he knew it would affect his performance, but there were always reshoots to consider once Everly finally made it to set. Hopefully Mae could handle this and there wouldn't have to be reshoots.

Mae was due to show up today for wardrobe, so he'd get to see her.

Not that he was interested in seeing her or anything.

He was being measured in wardrobe when she walked in, her above-the-knee dress swirling around her. He swore she walked in slow motion whenever he saw her. Her dark hair swayed around her shoulders like a soft breeze followed her. His stomach clenched and he forced his attention to Abigail, the costumer.

"Hey," Mae said as she came up to stand beside him.

"Oh. Hey," he said, trying to sound cool and unaffected when in fact he had started to sweat. Which wasn't great, because Abigail was currently handing him outfits to try on.

She stared at the pile of jeans and button-downs in his arms. "Those are your movie clothes?"

"Yeah."

"Huh. Sooo, pretty much what you wear every day, then."

"I guess so. Except for the tux."

She swallowed. "Tux?"

"Yeah, for the wedding scene."

"Oh, right. I read that last night."

"So you read the script."

"I did."

"What did you think?"

"It's . . . decent. Utterly preposterous plotwise, of course. But funny and filled with action. So it should be a good movie."

He noticed she hadn't mentioned the romance between the main characters. Maybe romance wasn't her thing.

"Mae, I'm going to give you these three dresses to try on," Abigail said. "Caroline, the character you'll be playing—or standing in for—is very feminine. So lots of dresses."

Mae nodded. "Got it."

"Dressing area is back here," Abigail said, leading Mae away while explaining what she needed to do.

She looked nervous. He could imagine she felt very out of her element. He'd been in the same position countless times when he'd first started out in the business. He'd have to remember to try to make her feel comfortable.

Of course she wouldn't have to go through full makeup and costume today. Today was just rehearsal, setting up camera shots for various scenes and the like. Hopefully she'd feel a little more relaxed for that.

He went into the other dressing area and tried on all the

clothes, letting Abigail mark whatever adjustments she wanted to make. Then he changed back into his own clothes while Abigail did the same with Mae. After Mae was done, they headed outside together. He stopped at the craft services table for a coffee and a croissant. Mae didn't pick anything up.

"You can have anything you want to eat or drink," he said.

She nodded. "Yeah, they told me. I already ate."

The way she was twisting her fingers together let him know that she was a bundle of nerves, which likely accounted for why she didn't want anything to eat. He also knew that an empty stomach wouldn't settle her, it would only make things worse.

He tore off a piece of his croissant as they walked and offered it to her. "This is pretty damn good."

Reluctantly, she took it from him and nibbled, then nodded. "It's from our local bakery. They make outstanding pastries."

"I'm kind of a sucker for croissants," he said, shoving a hunk into his mouth. She was right about the bakery. This croissant was melt-in-your-mouth good.

"Really." She looked him over. "How do you keep that body in such good shape?"

He tried not to grin at the compliment. "Lots of crushingly painful gym work."

She snorted out a laugh. "I can imagine."

"Worth it, though. Then I get to eat these." He tore the last of the croissant in half and handed it to her. This time she took it without hesitation.

"Kane and Mae, you're needed on set."

She nearly jumped at the loudspeaker calling them to set.

"They just want to do a scene setup," he said. He reached out to touch her, to ease her, but knew it wasn't the right thing to do, so he let his hand drop. Instead, he gave her a smile. "It'll be easy."

She gave a quick nod. "Sure. Right. Easy."

They walked over to where the cameras were set up outside in the bright morning sun.

Mae had a look of awe on her face. "It doesn't even look like the vineyard I know."

"That's the idea," he said as he walked alongside her.

"Oh, good, you're here. Let's get moving."

Alexis was in director mode, so Kane knew not to tease around with her. The assistant director got them into position, and then hair and makeup came in to do a minor brush and comb and touch-up since they hadn't been in for full hair and makeup today.

"Okay, let's do a run-through of scene six," Alexis said.

They walked onto the set. "Are you familiar with the scene?" Kane asked Mae.

"That's the one where he overhears her talking on the phone."

"Yeah, that's the one."

One of the production assistants handed Mae a phone.

"Now, in this scene, Mae, I want you pacing from that mark to this one while you're talking on the phone." She motioned for Kane, who came over. "He's going to be over there, but you aren't going to look his way. You're concentrating on that call, which is upsetting you. Kane, you're curious about who's on the other end of the call. Everyone got this?"

Mae nodded quickly. She wasn't an actress and Kane knew that. He hoped Alexis remembered that, too. Not that Mae would have to speak lines or anything. This was just for camera to mark the scenes today.

He walked over to the vineyard, crouched down, and readied himself for the scene.

Now he only hoped they hadn't scared the hell out of Mae, because they all needed her right now.

CHAPTER

. . . . . .

five

Mae had to go to the house and take a shower after they had run through a couple of scenes. She was a ball of anxious sweat and needed to wash it off. Plus, she was utterly exhausted.

She'd moved into Honor's room since they were friends and she knew Honor wouldn't care about Mae being in there. Not that any of the sisters cared since none of them actually lived there anymore. But she also knew that JJ's crib was set up in Erin's room and Brenna was still in the middle of moving things from her room to her and Finn's new house, so Honor's had been the best choice.

There was also a guest room downstairs, but Maureen and Johnny's room was next to it and Mae didn't want to infringe upon their privacy. Besides, having the entire upstairs to herself was almost like being back in her apartment.

Almost.

She felt a lot better after the shower, which had immensely cooled her overly heated body. Hopefully tomorrow would go better and she wouldn't have to spend the next few weeks in a sweat-soaked fever of nervousness.

She hadn't even had to directly interact with Kane in any of the scenes today. She'd met Sofie, the person who was going to play Amanda, her character's sister, for one of the scenes. She was a delight and funny as hell to bounce dialogue off of. Not that Mae was any good at it, but she'd read the lines, which she supposed was all they had asked of her. And Alexis had seemed fine with what she'd done. She'd call it a success. A semi-success since this wasn't her freaking job in the first place.

Tonight she had a date, which should help to relax her. She could blow all this off and go have some fun. She picked out a cute dress that felt nice on her body, slid into her sandals and headed downstairs.

"Someone has a date tonight." Maureen gave her a quick smile.

"I need it after today."

"Oh no. Did it not go well?"

"It went fine. It was just not what I'm used to, you know? I'll fill you and everyone else in at tomorrow's meeting."

"Okay." Maureen gave her a quick hug. "You go have a good time."

"Thanks. I won't be home late."

"We don't track your comings and goings, honey. You have a key and you can do whatever you want."

That was a relief. "See you later, boss."

She headed out the door, keys in hand. She walked toward the lot, which they'd moved near the movie production so they wouldn't have to move cars all the time while they were filming. She saw a few people wandering around, then spotted Kane stepping out toward the parking lot. She kept her head down in the hope he wouldn't see her.

He headed straight toward her, a big smile on his face.

"You look pretty," he said, stopping by her car. "Big date?"

"Not big. Just a date."

"Lucky guy."

Just get in the car. Don't make small talk. "What are you up to tonight?"

After she blurted that out, she wanted to kick herself.

"Nothing much. Where are you headed?"

"Having pizza."

"My favorite food."

Well, crap. "Why don't you come with me?"

He let out a husky laugh. "On your date? I don't think so."

"We're just friends. Trust me, I don't really date."

"Does this guy—or lady? . . ."

"It's a guy."

"Okay. Does this guy think it's a date? Just the two of you?"

She shrugged. "Maybe. Probably."

"Then it's a date. And I am not a third-wheel kind of guy. Go have fun. I'll see you tomorrow."

Now she felt guilty, though she had no idea why. She wasn't responsible for Kane August's social life.

"Great. See you later, Kane."

"Yeah, see ya, Mae."

She got into her car and started to back out. He turned and walked away and she couldn't help but scope out his very fine ass and his very sexy walk.

Damn.

She met Carl at the restaurant. He was nice enough, certainly fine looking. He could hold his own in a conversation, which was one of her top priorities before accepting a date. But her thoughts wandered to Kane throughout the meal, and she realized that no matter how attractive Carl was, or how engaging he was in conversation, there were just no sparks between them.

He had figured that out, too, because once she had boxed up her leftovers and they had walked out of the restaurant, he gave her a quick hug and told her this had been fun. Which it had. Nothing wrong with enjoying a nice meal with a good guy. But she knew she wouldn't be seeing him again.

Which was too bad. Not that she kept guys around for long, but she'd been really busy lately and a hot, steamy date was exactly what she'd needed. Unfortunately, this date had been neither hot nor steamy.

She pulled into the parking lot and grabbed the pizza box, intending to head to the house. Instead, for some reason her feet walked her toward the production lot where the trailers were located.

She searched out the names on the trailers, found Kane's name and started up the steps, feeling immediately ridiculous for even showing up here. What, exactly, did she think she was doing?

"Is that for me?"

She flipped around on the steps, nearly stumbling at the sound of Kane's voice behind her.

"Oh. Yes. I thought you might like to have this. I mean, you probably have better food here than any of our restaurants . . ."

"Like I mentioned earlier, I love pizza." He gave her a hungry look, a look she recognized. The kind of look a guy gave a woman—one that had nothing to do with food.

Yeah. Hot and steamy.

"Then I hope you like it." She made her way down the steps.

He walked toward her. "I'm sure I will."

She handed him the box. Their fingers touched and it was like she'd been zapped by electricity. Their eyes met and that zing between them was amplified by . . . well, by a lot.

"Thanks," he said. "You wanna come join me?"

Tempting. And a very bad idea. "I don't think I should."

He cocked his head to the side. "Why not? Nothing's going to happen."

She wondered why, then realized she should be relieved. Still, she felt sort of insulted. She knew she was hot. Not Hollywood hot, but she was pretty. Damn him for making her question it at all.

"What do you mean nothing's going to happen?"

He laughed. "Because we don't even know each other."

"Oh, right. And you don't pick up women and take them to bed without even knowing them."

"I didn't say that. But you're not the meet-'em-and-bed-'em kind of woman."

She was still insulted. "And why not?"

"Now I'm confused. And I'd really like to eat this pizza because it smells good. Why don't you come inside and we can argue some more."

He didn't wait, just turned and went up the steps to his trailer, opened the door and left it open.

If she was smart, she'd walk away. Actually, she was very smart. Smart enough to know nothing was going to happen between them. But she was invigorated by the conversation and nowhere near ready to go to bed, so she might as well.

She headed up the steps and found him sitting at the table shoving pizza into his mouth.

"Drinks are in the fridge," he said. "Help yourself."

This place was set up. Full fridge, a kitchen, comfy couches and everything. There was a closed door at the far end of the trailer that she assumed was a bedroom.

She'd wager that bedroom was something, too.

She opened the fridge, her eyes widening at all the water and juice and fruit. Glancing his way, she asked, "Health nut?"

He grinned, his mouth full of pizza. After he swallowed he said, "I eat healthy seventy percent of the time."

"And the other thirty percent?"

He held up a slice of pizza. She couldn't help but smile. She grabbed a bottle of water and went to sit at the table with him.

After he finished off the pizza, he wiped his hands with a napkin and took several swallows of water. "How was the date?"

"Oh, well. It was . . . uneventful."

"Sorry."

She shrugged. "I'm not looking for a relationship. Or love. Or anything, really. Just some occasional fun."

He leaned back in his chair and studied her.

"What?"

"Someone burned you."

"No, they didn't."

"Yeah, they did. Most of us are out there looking for that connection, ya know? That one person we click with. So when you say you're only out for fun, that leads me to believe you're afraid of commitment."

Oh, he thought he knew her after five minutes? The hell he did. "Maybe it's because I never want a relationship. Did that ever occur to you?"

"No, not really. So what's the real story? Some guy broke your heart?"

Damn him. "I don't want to talk about it."

"Well, whoever this jackass is, I'm sure he's regretting letting someone like you slip away."

"Oh, you're smooth. Does that usually work with the ladies?"

His lips curved. "Usually."

She rolled her eyes, finished her water and stood. "Too

bad it won't work on me. Thanks for the scintillating conversation, but I need to get to bed."

"Sure." He walked with her to the door. "Study your lines since we're doing a scene through dialogue tomorrow."

"Sounds delightful." She scooted past him, trying not to feel the heated effects of . . . whatever it was that seemed to emanate off him in waves. No such luck, though, because he smelled like something delicious and she paused, making the mistake of tilting her head up to meet his gaze.

And then she melted into the icy blue of his eyes. He raised his hand and laid it against the door above her head. Her breathing quickened and she'd never wanted to kiss a man more than she wanted to kiss Kane.

But she absolutely refused to allow herself to be tempted, especially not by some crazy-popular movie star who probably went through women like paper towels.

"Well, good night, Kane."

His gaze remained fixed on hers as he moved away to let her pass. "See you tomorrow, Mae."

"Right. Tomorrow."

She exhaled on a regretful sigh as she walked away. She headed toward the main house, then detoured, taking a stroll through the vineyards. It was a cool night and she needed that fresh air to clear her head.

There was something compelling about Kane August. It wasn't his celebrity because Mae didn't care at all about that kind of thing.

It was definitely the man. All of him.

She was going to have to watch herself. Or watch him. Or not watch him. Yes, definitely not watch him.

Or something.

CHAPTER

......

six

Iт was a hair and makeup day since they'd be filming a scene. Mae's back would be turned to Kane, so they'd be doing her up to look as much like Everly as they could. Alexis had been in makeup with them, talking her through the scene, since they arrived before dawn. Mae did a lot of nodding and sipping of her coffee, but otherwise she hadn't said much.

He finished up well before her, so he went to costuming to get into his jeans and button-down along with his boots, which would pretty much be his standard outfit for much of the shoot. Suited him just fine. Typically for movies he'd be in uncomfortable clothes that didn't suit him. That he got to dress in his normal clothes for this one was a bonus.

After dressing, he wandered off to talk to the cinematographer. While he enjoyed acting, he'd always been fascinated by how a film was made. Scene setup, direction, camera angles and all of the nuance was how you took an actor's *blah blah blah* and turned it into something incredible.

Someday he'd step away from acting and direct. Definitely produce. There were already projects he was interested in taking on from the production side. He'd been acting since he was a teen. He couldn't—didn't want to, really—do this forever.

He heard his name over the loudspeaker, so he headed over to the grassy area where they'd set up the scene. The main house was in the background and so were the vineyards. It was a great, beautiful background. The sun had risen and steam rose from the grass. It was outstanding for the scene they were about to play. He'd had a croissant for breakfast and was fueled with caffeine, so more than ready to lay into his argument with the character of Caroline—Mae's character. Well, eventually Everly's character whenever she showed up. But for now it would be Mae.

"Okay, I'm here—finally."

He pivoted and smiled. She was made up to look not at all like herself. Her hair was pulled back in a low ponytail instead of the loose, beautiful waves she typically wore. They'd put a hat on her, too. And the makeup was movie standard but so over-the-top.

"You look . . . nice."

Mae snorted out a laugh. "I look like I'm wearing funeral makeup. It's hideous."

He couldn't help but smile. "We all have to endure it."

She stepped closer, raising up to inspect his face. "You're wearing all that makeup and still, how can you look so . . . so . . ."

"Ruggedly handsome?"

She rolled her eyes. "Whatever. I don't even know why I'm made up, since no one's going to see my face."

He shrugged. "That's the way Alexis wants it. If we get a bit of a side view of your face, you won't be all pale and pasty."

She snorted out a laugh. "Gee, thanks."

"What I meant was, you need a lot of makeup for the camera. *You* are not pale and pasty."

"Okay."

Alexis came in, always a whirlwind of energy. "Okay, is everyone ready?"

"Yeah," Kane said.

"So ready." Mae offered up a tentative smile.

"Okay, everyone, let's get into positions."

They waited while makeup did a little touch-up and the cameras got repositioned to shoot Mae from the back.

"Do you know your lines?" Kane asked.

Mae nodded. "Yes, but I don't know why I'm saying them since I won't be the one on the screen when the movie comes out."

"That's true. Everly will dub her voice and then redo the scene from her angle so they can splice. But I need you to be here, to play off of me so I can get into my character."

"I'll do my best."

He felt the sincerity in her voice. "I know you will."

Alexis came in to give Mae movement directions. Kane already knew his marks, but Mae didn't know hers, so he figured this would require several takes. But as long as they could put something in the can today, it'd be worth it.

Alexis took her seat, the set went quiet and Kane and Mae stood on their marks.

"You ready for this?" he asked.

She gave a quick nod and blew out a breath.

"And . . . action," Alexis said.

"He'll show up," Kane said.

Mae tilted her head back and the look she gave him was filled with pain, just like her character would be feeling in this scene. "How do you know?"

"Because I know him. He's my best friend. I know he'll be here. He wouldn't bail on you, Caroline."

She inhaled a deep breath, held it for a beat, then let it out, shaking her head. "He told me last week that maybe we should rethink this whole big wedding, that maybe we should elope instead. He laughed when he said it, wanted me to think he was joking. But you know what, Blake? I think he was trying to tell me something."

"He wasn't trying to tell you anything, Care. He was joking."

She cocked her head to the side, and Kane realized she'd read the script perfectly. "You're lying. You know something. Tell me what he said to you, Blake."

"Annd, cut," Alexis said, coming off her chair with a bouncy step. "Mae, that was excellent. We'll do it again, but honestly? It was perfect."

Mae exhaled. "Thanks."

After Alexis left to confer with her staff, Kane looked at her. "You rocked that scene. You have a knack for this."

Her eyes widened. "Acting? Me? Oh, no. I've likely sweated through this dress. And who wears dresses to run a vineyard, anyway? That doesn't even make sense. And this hat I'm wearing is making my head sweat."

Her eyes were welling with tears, and he could see that she'd held it together to film the scene but now she was about to have a meltdown. She didn't realize how damn good she'd been during that scene.

He put his hands on her upper arms to get her to focus on him.

"Do you know how hard an actor works to get as good as you just were?"

She looked up at him, confusion written all over her face. "What?"

"You were brilliant, Mae."

"I was not. I just blurted out the lines."

"I could get a script assistant to blurt out lines. What you did was feel them as if you were Caroline, as if you felt her worry and anger. The way you made eye contact with me gave me everything I needed to do my part of that scene. Frankly, you're an actor's dream to work with."

She gaped at him, then finally laughed and jerked out of his grasp. "Shut up. I just read the lines. I'm not an actress, Kane."

She started to walk away, so he went with her. "Maybe not, but honestly? You could be if you wanted to."

"Well, I don't want to. I want to get through this scene so I can go do the other part of my job."

"Yeah? What's on the agenda for the other part of your job today?"

"We're doing a tour for a prospective bride and groom. And doing some planning for Brenna and Finn's upcoming wedding. Brenna is one of the Bellini sisters. She's getting married in a few weeks."

"That sounds important. I'll tell Alexis that the first take was fine and you can go."

She reached out to lay her hand on his arm. "No. What you do is important, too. I can stay until we get it right."

He wanted to let her go. He wanted her to stay. It wasn't his choice or his right to ask her.

"Whatever you want," he said.

"Then let's do this."

He nodded, happy to get to spend more time with her, and feeling more than a little guilty knowing that Alexis would have been fine if he'd told her that Mae had to go and they'd have to use the first take.

But he'd deal with the guilt later. Right now he was going to spend more time with Mae.

MAE WAS SO happy they had only needed her for one scene today. She was drained, physically and emotionally. She'd wanted to be good, or at least good enough that they wouldn't regret asking her to stand in for Everly Sloane.

She went back to the house, headed upstairs and took a quick shower, scrubbing off the heavy makeup and rinsing the sweat off. After drying her hair she put on a dress and sandals and felt much more like her authentic self again. She went downstairs, intending to park herself in her office until it was time for the tour.

She didn't quite make it to her office, because Brenna was hanging out in the doorway of Honor's office and spotted her.

"Hey, Mae," Brenna said. "Come on and tell us all about it."

"Sure. Let me grab a coffee first."

She'd missed coffee this morning—deliberately, in fact, because she'd been jittery enough with nervousness and hadn't wanted to add to it. So she went into the kitchen and poured herself a cup, adding a touch of cream.

"How did it go?" Louise asked. Though she was the cook for the family, Louise *was* family.

"It went fine. Thanks for asking."

Louise held out a tray. "I made cranberry muffins this morning."

Mae also hadn't eaten. "You always know exactly what I need, Louise. Thank you." She placed the muffin on a plate and went to Honor's office. Erin had just come in as well.

"I just put JJ down for a nap, so I'm all set to hear the juicy details," Erin said.

Mae couldn't help but smile. Working with Erin, Brenna and Honor had been a lot like having sisters. And being an only child had sucked, so she couldn't complain that they wanted to know everything.

They were in the midst of a conversation about Erin's baby, which gave Mae time to eat her muffin and take a few sips of coffee. So when they turned their attention to her, she felt almost like herself again.

"And how was it?" Honor asked. "Do you feel all Hollywood now?"

Mae let out a soft laugh. "Hardly. I was a ball of nervous sweat. My hair was weird and there was so much makeup. But Kane helped settle me and we got through the scene."

The sisters all exchanged glances with each other before turning their attention back on Mae.

"Ohhh, so Kane helped you, huh?" Brenna gave her a knowing look. "Was it a kissing scene?"

"Of course not. They're only filming me from behind. Remember, I'm just filler until the real actress shows up."

Erin rested her chin in her hands. "He's very attractive, Mae. Though I haven't seen him up close and personal like you have. Is he just as handsome?"

"Ridiculously good-looking. Like, it's a crime for a man to be that hot."

Honor leaned back in her chair, drawing in her notebook. "Hmm."

"No. There's no *hmm*. I just said he's hot. You know I don't go applesauce about celebrities. I was just stating a fact about his level of hotness."

"I have no idea what applesauce means," Brenna said. "Does that mean soft and liquidy?"

Erin snorted out a laugh.

"It does not mean that. I am immune to hot men except as a one-and-out."

"And by that she means in and out. Then she throws them out." Honor smirked.

"Honor!"

The sisters burst into a fit of laughter.

Mae rolled her eyes and got up. "You're all evil."

"Yeah, but now we know you like Kane August," Honor said.

Mae pivoted, glaring at all of them. "I do not like him. I mean, I don't hate him, but I don't like-like him. Not that way. What I meant was . . ." She realized she had run out of coherent sentences. "Whatever. I'll be in my office until it's time for the tour. And then I'll see you all at the meeting later."

Before they could make any other innuendos, she walked out, went to her office and shut the door. She sat at her desk, opened her laptop and checked her calendar to make sure there hadn't been any changes. When it was time for her to meet the prospective bride and groom, she headed outside to wait for them.

She walked the length of the front porch, her thoughts filled with that scene she'd done with Kane today.

He was a very good actor. She'd felt his angst and sincerity. She wasn't much for movies, but she made a mental note to watch some of his—just to get a feel for how he acted. She'd only do it to help him out, of course.

A car pulled up and a couple got out. She was gorgeous, with dark skin and beautiful braids. He was equally good-looking with the same beautiful skin, and totally bald. And when they took each other's hands and gave each other that love look, wow. Mae could swear the sun shone brighter.

This was what she loved about the wedding business.

She walked toward them and smiled. "Hello and welcome to Bellini Weddings. I'm Mae Wallace, one of the wedding coordinators. And you must be Rashida Rowell and Benjamin Davis."

"We are," Rashida said, beaming with excitement. "You have a lot going on here, what with the filming and all. I can't wait for our tour."

"I'm excited to walk you through and tell you all about what Bellini Weddings has to offer."

She started at the bride and groom private dressing areas, explaining how much space and privacy they'd have as they prepared before the ceremony. Then she took them to the arbor overlooking the vineyards.

"When it's weather appropriate, this is where your ceremony will take place."

"Oh, it's perfect," Rashida said.

"What if it rains?" Benjamin asked.

"We always take the weather forecast into consideration and will have the barn prepared just in case we need to switch to an indoor ceremony."

Rashida turned to Benjamin. "See. I told you."

"Hmm" was all he said.

Mae could tell right away that Benjamin would be the tough sell. She'd thoroughly read through their bios and their likes and dislikes, so she knew what would hit his hot buttons.

"You know, Benjamin, we also have a wine tasting room. In fact, we would be happy to incorporate that into your bachelor party if you'd like."

His brow rose. Just enough to know she'd captured his interest. "Really."

"Yes. Would you like to take a tour of the tasting room? I could arrange for Brenna Bellini, who manages the winery, to give you a personal tour of the vineyards as well."

Now both brows rose. "That would be great. Thanks."

"Follow me." She sent a quick text to Brenna, who told her she was already set up.

Perfect. She walked them across the property to the tasting room. She loved it here. It was always cool, slightly dark and atmospheric. Perfect for sipping Red Moss Vineyards's excellent wines.

"Now this is what I'm talking about," Benjamin said as they stepped up to the bar.

Brenna wasn't the only one in there. Kane was there as well. She hoped against hope that Rashida and Benjamin had no idea who he was.

"Oh my God," Rashida said, grabbing Benjamin's shirt. "That's Kane August. You're Kane August. I'm sorry. I'm fangirling. I can't help it. *Lone Stranger* was one of my favorite movies. Oh, and *Where He Roamed*. You gave a fantastic performance."

Mae tried not to grimace, but Kane just turned and smiled, shaking Rashida's hand. "Thanks so much. What's your name?"

Rashida and Ben introduced themselves, and then Brenna interjected with some wine offerings, so they got down to tasting. Kane joined them and talked about his favorites, but once Benjamin and Rashida's attention had turned fully to the wine, he stepped away.

"Sorry. Brenna didn't tell me you were expected in here with your guests."

"I didn't know, either. I had to think on the fly."

"Does that happen a lot during your tours?"

"Not all that often, but sometimes if I have a semi-reluctant bride or groom, I have to do something to entice them. With Benjamin, it was wine."

"I see." He leaned against one of the tables. "How about dinner tonight?"

"What? Why?"

"Because you had a date last time and couldn't go with me. I thought you could find a fun spot for us to eat."

"Oh." She supposed it wasn't a date, that he just wanted to get out and around the city. "Sure. How about seven?"

"Sounds good. Give me your phone."

She handed her phone over and he put in his number, then handed it back to her. After that he took his phone out. "Now give me your number."

She did, realizing a movie star now had her phone number.

No. Kane had her phone number. She still didn't think of him as some big-time movie star. He was just a guy. Some guy who wanted to go to Oklahoma City for dinner. That seemed normal to her. If she kept him in the "just a guy" category, everything would be fine.

He straightened. "I'll get out of your way. Text me when you're ready to go."

"Will do. See you later."

He walked out and Rashida turned around. "Oh no. He left before I could get a pic with him."

"Yeah, he had things to do. Sorry."

"Oh well. At least I got to meet him."

"Very true. Are you ready to continue the tour?"

Benjamin nodded. "Yes. And then we'll talk about adding the tasting room to my bachelor party."

She looked over at Brenna, who gave her a double thumbs-up.

Boom.

CHAPTER

......

seven

KANE WAS LOOKING forward to getting out tonight.

He had a car of his own. It was one of the things he insisted on, contractually. Unless they were on some remote island where transportation was impossible, he couldn't handle being stranded on a location shoot and forced to stay in his trailer. One or two days he could deal with. Months? No way.

Besides, he could easily throw on a ball cap, T-shirt and jeans and blend in. He'd been doing it for years. It helped that he was just an average-looking guy.

Tonight he just wanted to eat a meal in a restaurant with a beautiful, intelligent woman.

She'd texted him at six thirty to say she was ready, so he drove over to the main house to pick her up. She walked outside and got in the car.

"I'm surprised you don't limo everywhere."

He shook his head. "You have the wrong impression of actors. At least of this actor."

"So some of them do limo everywhere."

"Some. Not many. Most of us drive around like normal. Unless you live in New York. No one wants to drive there."

She laughed. "I wouldn't know. I've never been there."

"Amazing city. Lively and friendly and so much to do. The shows are amazing if you like music or theater."

"I enjoyed the plays in high school and college, so I probably would."

He pulled onto the highway and headed north toward the city. "Okay, so you're not a movie fan. Tell me what you do like."

"Oh. Well. I like a lot of things. Museums and art, and I love to read, so I spend a lot of time in bookstores or the library. I love sports, both watching and playing. I also enjoy boating and hiking and I could swim all day long. I was on the swim teams in high school and college."

He cast a glance over at her. "I could see that. You have the body for it."

Her lips curved into a half smile. "Actually, I don't. I'm short and a little chunky, whereas most of my teammates were long and lean. But I made up for it with sheer determination because I loved it so much."

"Sometimes that's all it takes. No one ever thought I'd be good at acting. I was kind of a slacker in high school and college."

"I could see that about you."

He laughed.

"Hey," she said. "Do you have any idea where you're going?"

"I figured we were headed to the city for dinner, right?"

"Yes."

"I mapped it so I know where it is. I figured you could choose a restaurant and give me directions while I drive."

He felt her gaze on his. Then she said, "Okay, that works."

They ended up at a place called Bricktown, which seemed touristy but was actually pretty cool. Awesome brick buildings and walkways along with water and bridges and lots of things to do. They walked along the path next to the water.

"Okay, so," Mae said. "Fancy or regular or a bar or down home?"

"That's a lot to choose from. What do you like?"

"Hmm. Let me think a minute." She pondered as they walked along the tree-lined walkway. He could see why she liked this place. It might be commercial as hell, and it was probably crowded in the summer, but there was something peaceful about it. He really wished he could take her hand while they walked, but they weren't there.

Not yet, anyway. He'd like to get there with her. He liked her sharp wit, her beauty and, God, he really liked the way she smelled. All he could think about was getting closer to her.

But he was a patient man, and he could wait.

"Bricktown Brewery," she finally said, making an abrupt turn. He followed.

"Yeah?"

"Great food. Awesome beer. TV screens for sports. Nice, relaxed atmosphere. Really, there's nothing better."

"I can't think of anyplace I'd rather eat."

They made it to the restaurant, which was exactly the kind of place he needed. Filled with couples and families and had TV screens all over. They were seated at a booth and, though their server did a double take, she didn't say anything to him.

"You think she recognized you?"

He shrugged. "No idea. Sometimes people think it's me, but they don't want to say anything only to find out it's not. Then they'll look foolish, and no one wants to look foolish. And I try not to give them that sly 'Yeah, it's me' kind of smile."

"Low profile, right?"

"As much as I can."

He ordered a specialty beer, a dark ale that looked really good. Mae ordered a blueberry ale and then they perused the menu.

"The burgers here are so good," Mae said. "And order the sea salt caramel sweet potato fries. They're incredible. Sweet and spicy because they add jalapeño."

His stomach growled at the description. "Oh, yeah. We need those."

Their server brought their beers and set them on the table. She hovered and Kane thought that maybe she was going to say something about recognizing him.

"Do we know each other?" she asked him.

"I don't think so."

"Are you sure? My older brother went to college with a Clyde McKellum and you look just like him."

He wanted to sink with relief. Instead, he shrugged. "Oh. Sorry. That's not me."

"Damn. You two could be twins. Anyway, are you ready to order?"

She took their food orders, then wandered off. Mae snorted out a laugh. "Clyde?"

"What? I could totally pull off Clyde."

"Sure you could."

He leaned forward. "Have you ever been mistaken for someone else?"

"Just once, in a store when I was about ten. Some woman thought I was her daughter and started screaming at me from across the store. I knew that wasn't my mother so I stood there and then the woman started walking fast in my direction. My mother saw her and was convinced the woman was trying to kidnap me, so she threw herself in front of me. Then

THE BACKUP BRIDE PROPOSAL

there was a very loud confrontation between my mom and the other lady."

"So where was her daughter?"

"About ten feet from me, giggling in one of the clothing racks."

"Bet that mom felt awful about arguing with your mom. And yelling at you."

"Not really. She was pissed at us for keeping her from looking for her real daughter. As if we'd been the ones to hide her in the clothes rack."

"She sounds like a piece of work. No wonder her daughter was hiding."

Mae laughed. "Right? But that was my one and only brush with being confused for someone else."

"That's because you're beautiful and unique."

She took a sip of her beer and cocked her head to the side. "Do those lines usually work for you?"

"I don't know. I'm not one to use lines unless I'm working. Do guys hit on you with cheesy lines?"

"More often than you'd think."

He shrugged. "Some men have no game."

She took a swallow of her beer. "Oh, and you do?"

"Of course I do. I'm suave and sophisticated and know how to talk to a woman by being honest and sincere."

She gave him a look, then laughed. "Come on."

"Hey, I gave it my best shot."

"Try not to be so nauseating next time. You almost ruined my appetite."

Their server brought their meals, and Kane figured that all conversation would stop while they shoved food in their mouths. But it didn't. They ate and argued baseball—games and teams as well as individual players. Since it was nearing the postseason and both their favorite teams were likely going to be in it, they both had a stake and staunch opinions as to who was best. His team, obviously.

But he liked that she knew her sport and argued it so passionately.

"These sweet potato fries are good," he said. "But this spicy caramel sauce? I want to bottle it and take it home with me and eat it every day."

"Right? It's so good. Though I couldn't eat it every day. My ass would be huge."

"Your ass is outstanding."

He saw the way her cheeks pinkened and thought about how rare that was. Most of the women he knew accepted compliments like it was their due. Mae, on the other hand, was like a rare gem.

"Well. Thank you. And where is home?"

"Right now? On the Bellini property."

She slanted a look at him.

"Fine. I've got a place in L.A."

She popped a fry in her mouth, chewed and swallowed, all the while studying him. "Condo, town house, home, or sprawling mansion?"

He laughed. "Definitely not a sprawling mansion. Just a small house with some privacy."

"Do you like living there?"

"I don't really live there. It's just a place where I stay when I'm filming at one of the studios."

"So you don't consider it your permanent home."

"No."

"What would you consider your permanent home, then?"

"Texas."

"Do your parents live there?"

"No. They live in Arizona now, though I was raised in Dallas. The ranch is close to there. But I've only ever felt really at home on the ranch."

"The ranch where your grandpa lives?"

"Yeah. That's home. Always has been, always will be."

She leaned back, took her beer in hand. "I'd like to see you on that ranch."

He'd like to see her on the ranch. In tight jeans and a T-shirt, wind blowing through her beautiful hair. Just the visual of it . . . His lips curved. "I could make that happen."

"Oh, sure. You just head on down to Texas in the middle of filming a movie."

"We get breaks, Mae. We don't work seven days a week."

"Well, anyway, that'd be interesting. Do you have horses?"

He nodded. "Yeah, it's primarily a horse ranch. We do have some cattle. Also have chickens. Some goats, too."

"Nuh-uh. Really?"

"Really."

"And your grandpa takes care of all of them himself?"

"No. He has help. It takes more than one person to run a ranch."

"That's good. I can't imagine someone at his age trying to wrangle all those animals by himself."

Kane smirked. "You haven't met my grandpa. He's probably in better shape than I am. He'll go to his grave training horses."

"If that's what he loves to do, then that's the way to go, right?"

He liked that she understood. "Yup."

They each had another beer, and then Mae insisted on paying the bill, which Kane thought was ridiculous because after all, he made a ridiculous salary. But he also understood fairness, so he stepped back and she paid. They took a walk again and it was even nicer now that it was dark.

"Thanks for taking me to this place. Food was great."

"My company was even better," she said.

He didn't disagree. "Yeah, it's nice having you around. You're like . . . like . . ."

She was waiting for him to say something, he knew. The problem was, every time he looked at her, stared into the depths of her liquid brown eyes, he had a tendency to lose himself.

"I know," she said, shooting a crooked grin at him. "Men are dumbstruck with awe over me."

"Hell yes we are." He stopped, then moved in closer, unable to help himself. He slid his hand around the side of her neck, nearly trembling at the feel of her skin against his palm.

He waited for her to pull away, to shove him away, actually. She didn't. Instead, she tilted her head back and her glossy lips parted in invitation.

Unable to resist her delicious mouth, he put his lips to hers.

MAE HAD LOST track of place, or time, or even what planet she was on. All she knew was that Kane was kissing her, his hands sliding over her skin, and this was delicious, dangerous territory. She should stop him right now.

But how could she when his lips were soft yet his intent so strong as he slid his tongue inside, making her feel simultaneously hot and shivery cold? She couldn't help herself. She had to explore, so she slid her hands up his arms to his shoulders while he moved that fantastic mouth of his over hers. She could just imagine his mouth would be magical on her—

Someone coughed loudly, a clear signal that this volcanic kiss was not for public viewing. Kane was the first one to pull away, his breathing harsh as he licked his lips and dragged his hand through his hair.

"Sorry," he said. "I kind of got carried away."

"Yeah, me, too." Too carried away. She didn't even know this guy. And she also had to work with him.

The one thing she prided herself on as far as her romantic life was always making good decisions. Well, at least after Isaac, anyway. That had been a disaster. But after him? Always good decisions. With dating she kept it light and easy and never set up any expectations. She was also honest with any guy she went out with, letting him know she was in it for fun and nothing long term. That way if some man was looking for the love of his life, he'd know right away that it wasn't going to be her.

She'd met and dated some amazing, beautiful men. And then promptly dropped them—amicably, of course. For the past couple of years it had worked out perfectly.

She wasn't dating Kane, so she had nothing to worry about. It had just been one kiss between them.

But when she lifted her gaze to his, the heat in his eyes nearly melted her to the walkway, making her want to feel his mouth against hers again. And again.

"We should probably go."

Those words were the cold slap of reality she needed. "Yes, we should."

They started back toward the house, Mae's thoughts a jumbled mess the entire drive back.

She shouldn't have kissed him, because now his full lips and his strong hands and the way his hard body felt against hers were all she could think about.

And once she set her sights on a guy, she wouldn't be satisfied until she had him. But she was absolutely not going to have Kane August. He wasn't even her type.

Liar.

Okay, she didn't actually have a type. She liked men of all different shapes and sizes and colors. As long as there was an attraction, she'd move forward with a guy, knowing it was only a temporary thing anyway. It wasn't like she was looking for forever.

She figured Kane August wasn't a forever kind of guy. He was actually kind of perfect for a fling except for one thing— he was famous. And she wanted nothing to do with being in the spotlight.

"You're quiet," he said as he exited the highway. "Are you okay?"

She pulled her gaze away from the passenger window to smile at him. "I'm great. How about you?"

"Also great. I was just wondering if you were upset about the kiss."

He had to bring it up, didn't he? "The kiss was also great. And I'm not upset about it at all."

"Good. I wouldn't mind continuing where we left off when we get back."

"Yeah, that's not going to happen. Look, there's no doubt we have chemistry, Kane. But you're . . . not really my type."

Again—liar.

His lips curved upward as he turned off the street and headed down the back roads. "Yeah? What is it about me that you find repulsive?"

"Now you're being ridiculous. I never said you were repulsive. But you are an actor, and I can't do that."

"You were acting just fine."

"Not what I meant. I meant your celebrity. I don't want to be a part of that."

"I don't know if you paid attention, but we had dinner at

one of your tourist spots tonight and not a single person noticed me."

"Our server did."

"Yeah, she thought I was Clyde."

She let out a frustrated breath. "I'm not looking for any kind of relationship, Kane."

He turned up the drive leading to the main house. "Great. Me, either. We're like perfect for each other."

Dammit. She should have just told him the kiss sucked.

He pulled up to the front of the house and stopped the car, walking around to her side to let her out.

"Hey, thanks for having dinner with me," he said, taking a step toward her. She thought for sure he was going to pull her into his arms for a kiss. And, honestly? She wasn't sure she'd want to push him way.

But, instead, he held out his hand, a smirk on his face. "Good night, Mae."

Now she was irritated, though she had no right to be. She gave his hand a quick shake. "Night, Kane."

She stomped up the steps, knowing he stood there and watched her. When she got inside, she refused to look out to see if he drove away.

Kane August was the most annoying man she'd ever met.

CHAPTER

· · · · · ·

eight

"OKAY, TODAY, MAE, we're going to be in the vineyard," Alexis explained. "We've cleared the area, but as you know we only have the location for a brief time."

Mae looked over to the edge of the vineyard, where Brenna and her father, Johnny, watched. Glared, really. She couldn't blame them. The vineyard was their baby, and the idea of strangers trampling on the family livelihood had been a source of contention ever since the production company laid out the plan for filming. But they'd promised Brenna that the few scenes taking place in the vineyard would be short.

Mae was nervous on about twelve levels. For the scene today, which required touching. For the vineyard, which meant there'd be oversight from the Bellinis. The whole family was out there watching.

She hoped they could get through this in a hurry. She'd studied her lines, though they weren't her lines, but she had to work through them for Kane so he could do his part.

After makeup and hair finished their touch-up, she was told where to stand. Kane was going to approach, but her job was just to stand there as if she were inspecting grapes, though she knew nothing of grapes or how to inspect them. Fortunately, Brenna had given her some quick instruction on what to do so she looked like an expert.

As was typical, her back would be to the camera so that Everly would fill in when she showed up. She shouldn't be nervous because her face and voice would never be on camera. And this wasn't her first time, so, dammit, Mae, relax already.

If only she could forget about that kiss.

"And, action."

Immediately pushing everything else from her mind, she got into the head of the character, studying the vines as if they were the only things that mattered. When Kane stopped in front of her, she looked up in surprise, just as the script said she was supposed to do.

"What are you doing out here?"

"Looking for you."

"Have you heard from Brian?"

"Not yet. I'm sure he'll be here soon."

She tilted her head back to meet his gaze, remembering all the body cues. "Will he? Or has he changed his mind?"

Kane picked up her hand. "He loves you, Caroline. You know he'll show up."

"You didn't. Not when I needed you." She shook her head. "I'm sorry I said that. This isn't about you."

He ran his thumb over the top of her hand, making her shiver. "Maybe it is."

This would be where the character would turn away, where the camera would see her face.

"Annd, cut," Alexis said. "Good job."

They ran through it a couple more times until Alexis was satisfied, and then they broke to set up for the next scene.

Mae walked toward the craft table to grab some water, her throat so dry she could barely swallow.

"You did great," Kane said, coming up beside her to grab a glass of iced tea.

"Thanks." She started walking. He walked with her.

"Is it getting easier?"

She laughed. "No. It'll never be comfortable for me."

"It should. You're a natural. You could be an actress. You really get into the character. I wish the camera could pick up your expressions, the emotions you convey. You're good, Mae."

"Thanks. If I ever decide to become an actress, you can write me a letter of recommendation."

He laughed. "I'd definitely do that."

They'd stopped at his trailer, and he walked up the steps, opened the door, his expression one of invitation.

Since she had no intention of kissing him again, she figured she could hang out for a few minutes with him. She walked up the steps and he shut the door.

"Make yourself comfortable. You want something else to drink? I have tea, fruit drinks, sparkling water."

She held out her bottle. "I'm good with this, thanks."

He flopped onto the sofa, so she took a seat in the cushioned chair across from him.

"Afraid I'll bite you?" he asked with a smirk she wanted to slap right off his face.

"No. This chair looked comfortable. And we . . . should keep our distance."

He shrugged. "Sure. If that's what you want."

"It is."

"Fine."

"Fine."

Then there was silence. She shouldn't have come in here.

Now she was stuck. Though she could just get up and walk out.

"So what do you want to do with your life?"

Her gaze shot up. "What?"

"I mean, you're a wedding assistant, right?"

"Yes. What's wrong with that?"

"Nothing. But you're smart and I think you can do so much more. Be so much more. What do you want to do?"

Anger coiled inside her. "I'm happy doing what I do. I love it, actually."

"Yeah, I'm sure you do. But you could do anything."

"I see. So you see me as something less because of what I choose to do for work."

"What?" He frowned, a look of confusion crossing his face. "That's not at all what I said."

"It's exactly what you said." She stood and walked over to him. "You think you're so important because you're an actor, when in fact you're not doing anything more important than I am. Your paycheck might be a lot bigger, but if you're totally fulfilled in your job—which I am, by the way—then it's good enough, no matter what the job is. So how dare you assume that I'm meant to do something more just because you see it as less. Asshole."

She turned and walked out. After stopping at costuming to change out of the character's clothes, she stormed over to the house, fuming the whole way. Her pulse still raced and her blood pounded in her veins.

She threw the front door open and ran straight into Honor. "Oh, hey, how did the—"

"Not now, Honor." She went upstairs to Honor's room and brushed out the tons of hair spray from her hair, winding it up into a bun on top of her head. She scrubbed her face clean and changed into leggings and a T-shirt.

Then she sat on the bed and pulled her knees up to her chest, wrapping her arms around her legs. She dragged in a deep breath.

Five minutes. She just needed five minutes to calm down, and then she'd be fine.

Maybe.

There was a knock on the door.

"Mae? Honey? Are you okay? Can I come in?"

She knew eventually Honor would make her way up there. Honor wasn't one to let things slide.

"Come on in."

Honor came inside and quietly closed the door. Mae thought for sure that all the sisters would be there. She was grateful it was only Honor.

"You're upset," Honor said, grabbing a spot next to her on the bed. "Talk to me."

"Kane August upsets me. No, that's not right. He pisses me off. He thinks what I do is of no importance." She leaned forward. "Do you know he basically asked me today what I want to do when I grow up?"

Honor frowned. "What?"

"Yeah, like what I'm doing now is some stopgap on my way to some sort of greatness that I haven't discovered yet."

Honor stared at her for what felt like an eternity. "Well, fuck him to the moon."

Mae snorted out a laugh. "My thoughts exactly."

Honor stood and began to pace the room. "How dare he say that what you do isn't important. So he pretends to be other people and he thinks . . . what, exactly? That he's God and he created rain? He's nothing. Nobody. And we love having you here. You've saved weddings for us, Mae. You are the most organized and efficient person I've ever met, and that's saying something, because the Bellinis are incredibly efficient and organized. You have people skills that are beyond compare. You can handle angry mothers, crying brides, stressed grooms and drunken guests with grace and finesse. Those skills don't come easily."

Hearing Honor list her skills warmed Mae in ways she couldn't explain. "Thank you. I wasn't fishing for compliments, by the way."

Honor waved her hand. "Of course you weren't because you never seek out accolades. You just do the job that you are good at without complaint." She turned and glared angry eyes at Mae. "I want to go kick his ass right now."

Honor's tirade had helped a lot. "Thanks, but I think we'll avoid that. I yelled at him."

"Good for you. He deserved it."

The door opened and Brenna came in. "What's going on?"

"Kane August was an ass to Mae," Honor said.

"He was not. Want me to kick his ass?"

"Unnecessary," Mae said. "But thank you. I handled him—it—the situation."

Brenna sighed. "I could still kick his ass anyway."

Honor snickered.

"Hey, what's everyone doing up here?"

Brenna looked at Erin over her shoulder. "Mae's upset because Kane's being a jackass."

"Oh, do tell. Mom has JJ and I've got some free time for gossip."

Mae filled them in on what exactly transpired.

"Wow," Erin said. "What. An. Ass."

"I'm fine, really. But thank you all for supporting me."

"Hey, you're part of our family, Mae," Honor said. "Of course we support you."

She'd never felt so warm and accepted like this. She didn't have siblings, didn't know that this was what it felt like. This overwhelming feeling of protection, of occasional teasing, of love.

"I love you all," she blurted, then realized they probably didn't feel as deeply as she did.

"We love you, too, honey," Honor said, wrapping her arm around Mae's shoulder.

Erin nodded. "And if someone hurts you, they hurt us."

"And we don't stand for that," Brenna said. "We'll always have your back."

Mae took in a breath. "And I'll always have all of yours."

It had started out a shitty day, but things were looking up now.

CHAPTER

· · · · · ·

nine

SOMETHING WEIRD WAS going on.

Kane had gotten used to wandering the grounds of the Bellini property, and so far everyone had been friendly.

Until today, when he started getting glares from almost everyone he walked past. He said hello and got polite nods, but not the typical gregarious greetings he'd grown accustomed to.

What the hell had happened? Because as far as he knew, group grumpiness wasn't a thing.

They were setting up in a makeshift house that had been hastily built to be the homestead for Caroline's family, since the Bellinis had refused to let them use their main house. Not that he could blame them. Using their property was inconvenient enough. Shoving them out of their home and place of business was something else.

Still, Kane wasn't the one who'd done it, so he had no idea why everyone on the site was mad at him. Unless . . .

It was Mae. He'd upset her with what he'd inferred, even

though that hadn't been at all what he'd meant. He'd only meant to ask if she had other plans for her future, but he'd bungled the question and she'd been insulted. He should have gone after her and apologized right away, but he figured she'd get over it once she realized that hadn't been his intent.

You'd think after all these years and a few fucked-up relationships that he'd have learned to be clear with his words. Apparently he hadn't learned a damn thing.

Clearly, he was still a work in progress, which meant he owed Mae a big apology.

She wasn't due on set today so he couldn't talk to her there. Which meant he'd have to go find her. He made his way toward the house, hoping he could find her there. He passed a couple of vineyard workers, including Johnny Bellini.

"Why are you here?" Johnny asked.

"I'm looking for Mae."

All he got was a grumble and Johnny turned away, so he made his way to the main house and rang the bell.

Brenna Bellini answered the door. "What do you want?"

"I'd like to see Mae."

She gave him a look that would make anyone take a step back. "You can't be serious."

"I am very serious."

"Well, she doesn't want to see you."

"Did she tell you that?"

"She didn't have to. And besides, you hurt her, so you're not welcome here."

"Look . . . I know I did. And I'm sorry. But I have to apologize, and in order for me to do that you have to let me see her."

Brenna opened her mouth to retort, then closed it again. "Wait here."

She shut the door in his face. He turned around, taking in

the grounds from the view of the front porch. There was a nice-looking chair so he took a seat, figuring he might be here for a while.

No wonder the Bellinis loved this place. From here you could see the vineyards, pond and rolling hills beyond, along with the walkway leading to the barn. The subtle whinny of horses could be heard behind the house, making Kane ache to be on the ranch in Texas.

He missed home, his grandpa, his horse. The dog, too, though if you asked Lucky, he'd tell you he was Grandpa's dog now. That was Kane's fault for being gone so long. He'd been traveling a lot doing back-to-back-to-back films, coupled with promotional work. But at least Lucky had Shadow to keep him company, and a lot more space to run on the ranch than at his place in L.A.

Sometimes he didn't love this job. Today was one of those times, because he could sit here on the porch and listen to the sounds of the vineyard and workers and be perfectly content to not move for the rest of the day. Or if he hadn't pissed off Johnny Bellini, he might have gotten a chance to ride one of the horses. He propped his booted feet up on the porch railing and sighed.

"Playing a part?"

He stood when he saw Mae. "No. Just enjoying the amazing view."

"It is nice. You can sit."

He waited until she took a seat in the chair next to his before he sat again, and then he swiveled to face her, figuring the longer he waited to say something the worse this was going to get, so he might as well start talking. "I'm sorry for what I said. It was insensitive and I didn't mean to imply that the work you do isn't important. I had only been curious about your plans for your future. If this is your plan, it's an awesome one. Who wouldn't want to be around all this, making people's dreams come true?"

She didn't answer right away. He didn't expect her to. In fact, he hoped she didn't toss him off the porch immediately.

"Most people rarely get to do what makes them happy. If this job puts a smile on your face and brings you joy, then it's the career for you."

Finally, she said, "Thank you. As apologies go, that sounded pretty sincere."

"It was. I feel shitty for what I said. For making you feel as if what you do isn't valid. It was thoughtless of me and I'll work on thinking before dumbass comments fall out of my mouth."

Her lips quirked. "Think you can do that?"

He shrugged. "No fucking clue. But I'll give it a try."

His phone buzzed. He pulled it out of his pocket and read the text message. "I'm due on set."

"Okay." She stood and he did as well. "Thanks for coming by."

"I'll . . . see you later?"

"Hmm. I'm around, you know."

She smiled, the kind of smile that was hot and made sparks dance in her eyes. He wanted to grab her and kiss her and find a place where they could be alone so he could explore every tempting inch of her.

But it was daylight and he could hear voices inside the house, and there was someplace he needed to be. So, despite what he wanted to do, he'd go do what he had to do.

"I'll see you later, Mae."

"Okay. See you."

He walked away and it sucked.

• • • • • •

MAE WENT BACK into her office, gathered her things and checked her phone. Fortunately, she had five minutes before the meeting, so she had time to go into the kitchen to grab a cup of coffee. She made her way into the dining room and laid her things down on the table.

It took her a few minutes of organizing her notebook, laptop and pens before she looked up and realized that everyone at the table was staring at her.

"What?" she asked.

"You know what," Erin said. "Hot hunk of cowboy on the front porch. Did he apologize?"

"Profusely and eloquently."

"Dammit." Brenna tossed her notebook on the table. "How are we gonna talk shit about him if he's out of the doghouse?"

Mae gaped at her. "I'm . . . sorry?"

Honor glared at Brenna, then smiled at Mae. "No, don't be sorry. It's good you got things worked out with him."

"I think so, too. Otherwise acting as the stand-in would be awkward."

"Because that's all you're doing with him, right?" Brenna arched a curious brow.

"Of course it is. I mean, what else would we be doing? I did take him out to eat and show him around town a little, but that's just me being friendly. Nothing else going on."

She could hear herself blabbing incoherently. *Oh my God, girl, shut up already.*

"Anyway, things are fine and I can get back to work—both here and on the set. So what's on the agenda today?"

She was glad when Erin took control of the meeting so they could talk Bellini Weddings and Red Moss Vineyards business instead of about her and Kane.

Once they'd gone through the agenda, Mae intended to hide out in her office for the rest of the day.

"Oh, and before you all leave," Brenna said, "Finn and I are having a housewarming party tomorrow. You're all coming. That wasn't a question."

Mae looked over at Erin and Honor, and found they were both looking around as well.

"I . . ." Erin paused, then said, "Yes. Jason and I will absolutely be there."

"Ditto," Honor said.

"What about you, Mae?"

"Of course. I've been dying to see the new house."

"Awesome." Brenna gathered up her things and started to head out, then turned and said, "Oh, and bring Kane August with you. He probably wants to get outside the compound here. He can meet the guys."

"Sure, I can . . . wait. What?"

But Brenna had already disappeared, as had her sisters.

Dammit.

CHAPTER
· · · · · ·
ten

K<small>ANE WATCHED THE</small> play of emotions cross Mae's face as she drove them to Brenna and Finn's house. One minute she looked calm and relaxed, the next like she might need to pull over and be sick.

You'd think he would be the nervous one, not her. But clearly something was bothering her.

"We don't have to go. What I mean is, I don't have to go if you don't want me there."

She made a turn onto another street, not bothering to look at him as she said, "I asked you to come with me, didn't I?"

"Yeah, and it seemed as if it pained you to ask. So this wasn't your idea, was it?"

"I . . . no. Brenna was the one who invited you. She thought you might want to get out."

"That was nice of her. I do like people."

"I'm sure you'll be awesome with the family."

He laughed.

"What was that for?"

This time she shot a glare his way. At least that was something.

"I think you're worried that I'll put on my 'actor' persona for the day and do . . . I don't know . . . something to embarrass you."

"That isn't at all what I think."

"Then what's making you so nervous?"

"Nothing I want to get into while I'm driving."

"Okay, I'll wait."

They drove out to where the houses were farther apart, where there were land and trees and a huge two-story brick house with a dark roof. Mae pulled up the long driveway, where several cars were already parked. She turned off the ignition and they got out.

"I have a housewarming gift in the trunk," she said, walking around to the back of the car.

"Wait a minute," he said. "Let's talk first."

She shook her head. "That's not a good idea."

"You said you couldn't tell me what's bothering you while you were driving." He reached for her hand, took the keys from her and slid them into his pocket. "You're not driving now, so tell me why you didn't want to bring me today."

She inhaled, then let it out. "You make me nervous. And being with all these people—my people—with you—will make me even more nervous."

He took one step closer, brushing an errant hair away from her face. "I make you nervous?"

"No guy has ever made me nervous. But you. Whenever I'm around you, Kane—"

He swept his hand along the side of her neck and pressed his lips to hers, sliding his arm around her back to bring her against him. He kept it loose, kept the kiss as easy as it was possible for him to do given how much he wanted her, so she wouldn't bolt. But when she sagged against him and flicked her tongue against his, he groaned and slid his hand down her back, grasping a handful of her sweet a—

The cry of a baby made them pull apart. Erin stood there, holding a gift box while a tall guy he assumed was her husband stood there smirking.

"Oh my God, Mae," Erin said. "At least do it in the car instead of on the front lawn." She laughed as they headed inside.

Mae covered her face with both hands. "This isn't happening. She'll tell her sisters, and they'll tell their guys. Oh, God, and Maureen and Johnny, too. And then everyone will know."

"We were just kissing. It's not a big deal." He reached for her but she slapped his hand away.

"Maybe not to you. But I take my job seriously and I'm supposed to be monitoring you."

He arched a brow. "Excuse me?"

"Not monitoring you like watching you, but keeping an eye on the production to make sure things run smoothly. And so far all I've been doing is making out with you. Which makes me look opportunistic."

"Opportunistic how, exactly? Are you trying to get a leg up in the entertainment industry?"

"Of course not."

"You want exposure on entertainment sites, get your face on social media and television by being seen with me?"

She looked horrified. "I'd rather have all my teeth pulled."

"Do you want to get me to marry you so you can get half of my money?"

She snorted, then laughed. "Marriage? That's the last thing I ever want."

"Then there's no opportunity here for you." He brushed his knuckles down her cheek, along her neck and across her bare collarbone. "Except kissing, and what comes after that."

She shuddered and tilted her head back. "Now I wish we weren't standing in the middle of Brenna and Finn's driveway. Table that thought for later, okay?"

He wished they were somewhere else more private right now, too. "Consider it done."

She grabbed the gift bag out of the trunk and they went inside.

The house was big and spacious, with high ceilings and wood beams and a plethora of tall windows that let in light.

He saw the bar in the corner of the living room and headed straight for it, mainly because that was where all the guys hovered.

He met Jason Callum, Erin's husband, who he found out was a veterinarian, and Owen Stone, Honor's husband, who owned a microbrewery. He also met Finn Nolan, the owner of this house and Brenna's fiancé. Finn worked as a carpenter at the vineyards and also brewed whiskey. Clay and Alice Henry arrived. They owned the property adjacent to the Bellinis. Alice was a matchmaker and Clay ran their ranch.

Wow. They were such interesting people. He could spend a lifetime talking to all of them and still not learn everything. No wonder Mae liked living and working around them. Kane couldn't wait to talk to everyone individually.

"So you're the movie star, huh?" Jason sipped whiskey while leaning against the bar.

"Actor. Not a star of anything."

"I don't know, bro," Finn said. "I really liked that action series you starred in. You gained a lot of muscle for that role, didn't you?"

"Yeah. Months of eight hours a day doing grueling squats and bench presses, and more protein than I ever want to take in again."

Owen grimaced. "That's a lot of gym time. But in your job you probably have to do that a lot."

"Not as much as you think, except for that action series. And, honestly? It was brutal. I don't ever want to do it again."

Jason poured him a whiskey. "Here you go."

"Thanks." He took a sip. "Excellent whiskey. You make this?"

Finn grinned. "I did. Thank you."

"Great house, too."

"Thank you. It took a while, but it's got four bedrooms and three bathrooms plus an office. It has enough space that Brenna can get away from me whenever she wants to. There's a big yard for whatever we want it to be. It has everything we'll ever need. This is our forever home."

Finn's Irish lilt lit up with happiness as he described the house, then walked them through for a tour.

What must that be like? To be so happy in love and looking forward to a future.

Kane had had a happy enough childhood, had awesome parents, though there were some question marks about what was going on with his mom and dad right now. The problem was he'd tried to address it and neither of his parents had been forthcoming with answers, so he'd tabled it for now. All he could fathom was that they were busy doing their own thing, just like he was doing his own thing. He supposed that was what adulthood was about. His parents had always been happy for his life but had focused on living theirs separately. He'd never seen that as an issue because he'd been happy as hell to have his own independence.

He'd lived a nomadic lifestyle ever since he'd started this life as an actor. It had kept him busy, though not exactly fulfilled.

But watching Finn right now? The way his face lit up when Brenna walked into the room and he slid his arm around her and smiled? Kane might not know a whole lot about love, but he could tell when feelings were genuine.

"You do realize that you all can't hide out in a testosterone herd all night long," Brenna said.

"Why not?" Finn asked. "There's whiskey here. Plus, I'm giving house tours like you asked me to."

Brenna opened her mouth to object, then shook her head. "Fine. But do mingle with everyone else, okay?"

"You got it, babe." He leaned over and kissed her.

When they got back where they started, Kane searched the living room and kitchen area but didn't see Mae. He really wanted to see Mae. Why, he didn't know. He had always been comfortable in a room full of strangers, so it wasn't like he "needed" her.

He wanted her, wanted to be near her, to breathe in that sunshine-and-lemons scent that always seemed to linger around her. He wanted to get her naked and slide his hands over the buttery softness of her skin, and make love to her until neither of them could breathe.

Yeah, he had it bad for this woman, which was so damn unfathomable to him he didn't know what he was going to do about it. And though she had kissed him back, and oh fuck it had been good, the only thing she'd admitted was that he made her nervous.

He couldn't wait to talk to her again and see if they could pick up where they'd left off outside.

MAE STOOD IN the kitchen with Erin, Alice, Brenna and Honor, listening to all of them talk while surreptitiously stealing glances at Kane. She couldn't help herself. Despite standing among a crowd of amazingly handsome men, she only had eyes for Kane. How could she not with all that thick dark hair, broad shoulders and lean waist and those long, long legs. She could already imagine how he'd look—

"And then we're going to get some pigs for the backyard."

Her gaze shot to Brenna. "Wait. You're getting pigs?"

Brenna laughed. So did her sisters, who were both staring at her.

"You weren't listening because your attention is laser focused on Kane August," Erin said.

"Oh, it's his eyes," Honor said. "She's lost in them."

"It's . . . no. I was admiring this beautiful house."

"Oh, honey." Honor put her arm around Mae's shoulders. "Yes, Brenna and Finn's house is utter perfection."

"Not as perfect as Kane August's ass, I imagine," Brenna said with a smirk.

Erin sputtered a laugh. Mae gasped.

"I am not . . . I didn't notice . . ." Mae finally raised her hands. "I give up."

"Hey, we're just teasing," Erin said. "Plus, he's hot as hell. How could anyone not notice him? I did. And I'm married to a hot-as-hell man."

"You can trust us, Mae," Brenna said. "We think of you as one of our sisters, which means we're going to tease you."

Honor nodded. "Mercilessly sometimes."

Erin shrugged. "You get used to it. I'm surprised you haven't yet."

She looked at all of them, unable to speak.

Brenna elbowed Erin in the ribs. "Now you've hurt her feelings."

Erin glared at Brenna. "You talked about his ass."

Honor lifted her chin. "I didn't say anything."

"Oh, you're far from innocent," Erin said, with Brenna

chiming in, and suddenly all three of them were sniping at each other.

Mae hated being the cause of the three sisters at war with each other.

"Oh, please stop," she said, but since their argument had gotten louder, they didn't hear her. She finally stepped into the fray—physically.

"Stop!"

They did, gaping at her.

"I wasn't complaining about you teasing me. I was momentarily stunned at the thought of having sisters. As an only child, one who craved siblings my whole life, you can't even imagine the spark of warmth, of joy I felt at having you think of me as family."

Suddenly she was surrounded by three pairs of arms, holding her tight.

Her sisters.

They broke the embrace and Brenna poured glasses of wine for everyone. They went outside and gathered around the fire pit. Brenna and Finn had purchased land outside the city, so the lack of lights showcased the clear night and amazing stars.

"Where's JJ tonight, Erin?" Mae asked.

"We have an awesome babysitter who lives on our street. She's sixteen, CPR certified and JJ adores her. This way he can stay home and sleep in his bed and I get a night out."

"Oh, you know Mom and Dad would love to keep him anytime," Honor said. "So would any of us."

"And they have. You all have, and Jason and I appreciate that so much. But since Mom and Dad are coming tonight, and family is not always available, we knew we'd need backup. Backups, actually. Between Jason's job requiring him to be on call and my involvement in Bellini Weddings on the weekends, we need lots of options."

Brenna wrinkled her nose. "Babies screw up your entire life. Not that yours isn't adorable, Erin. And cuddle-worthy. But I'll be glad to hold off on having my own for a while."

Erin laughed. "Totally understandable."

Mae noticed Honor looked a little pale. Plus, she hadn't touched the wine Brenna had poured. She wanted to ask if Honor felt all right but didn't want to be intrusive while they were in a group, especially knowing just how intrusive the sisters could be. She made a mental note to follow up later.

KANE GOT TO spend some time talking to Clay Henry, discussing all things ranching.

"You have horses and cattle?" Kane asked.

Clay nodded. "And you live on a horse ranch in Texas, huh?"

"Not as much as I'd like to. My grandpa runs the ranch, and I try to spend as much time there as I can. In the meantime I have a small house in L.A."

Clay wrinkled his nose. "You must hate that."

Kane laughed. "It's not ideal, but it serves a purpose."

"Not to be intrusive, but you probably make enough money to buy yourself a spread, even in Los Angeles."

"I could. I'm just not there enough to enjoy it. I travel a lot on movie shoots, so the house I have now suits me for a place to stop off and do laundry every now and then."

Clay nodded. "Makes sense. Tough lifestyle, though, not being able to live at the place you love."

"Yeah." Kane appreciated that Clay understood, something not many people did. Most people thought that the jet-setting, moving-around life that Kane lived was exotic and exciting. He knew how lucky he was to live this life, but it was often exhausting. And lonely. He missed home.

The grill masters—aka all the men and a few of the women, too—were hard at work over at the outdoor kitchen. The smells drove Kane crazy. He looked around and saw Mae standing off by herself sipping on a glass of wine, so he made his way over to her.

"I don't know about you, but I'm starving."

She looked up at him and smiled. "They're torturing us with cooking smells."

His lips curved. "Nothing like the aroma of a steak on the grill."

"It's one of my favorite scents."

He turned to her, picked up her hand, his thumb drawing circles over her skin. "You want to know my favorite scent?"

"Shrimp? Scallops? Pork chops?"

He laughed. "Not quite. You smell like fruit. Sometimes it's lemons. Sometimes peaches. Very subtle. Drives me crazy."

He felt that slight shiver. Since it was overly warm today, it wasn't because she was cold. "So, more torture?"

"A better kind of torment, I think." He leaned in, pressing his lips against her neck. "I could return the torture, you know."

"Yeah? How's that?"

"Licking all this delicious skin. Starting right here." He flicked his tongue along the column of her throat, making him want to do so much more. She started to reach for him but he stepped back, remembering where they were. "But I can wait."

"Right." He caught the reluctant look before she took another sip of wine.

Yeah, him, too. This crowd of people didn't mesh with what he wanted tonight. He craved some alone time with Mae.

When the food was ready, Kane had something else to focus on besides his constant attraction to Mae. There were barbecued ribs and chicken, along with potato salad, corn on the cob and grilled vegetables. There were various fresh salads and fruit and frankly it was all overwhelming, especially since Kane wanted some of everything. He piled it all on his plate and followed Mae to a table where other people were seated.

"This is quite the haul," Kane said as he took his seat, his plate overflowing with food. "Thank you for all of it."

"Hey, dig in and enjoy," Finn said, grabbing some ribs and taking a big bite.

"This is what the guys have been discussing all week," Erin said. "The food."

Brenna nodded. "No kidding. I tried to get Finn interested in setup and décor and all he wanted to do was talk to these jackasses about meat."

"Hey," Owen said. "Meat choice is important. It defines the whole meal. You build your sides around meat choice. It's everything."

Honor gaped at him. "Who are you?"

He laughed and put his arm around her. "Hey. You married me."

"I'm beginning to have second thoughts."

"Is this weirdness what I have to look forward to after Finn and I get married?" Brenna asked.

"Hell no," Finn said. "We live together. You already know all my weird quirks."

Erin lifted her chin. "My husband doesn't have any weird quirks."

Jason tilted his head back and laughed. "Woman. You know better than that."

Kane liked these people. A lot. He wanted to spend more time with them, getting to know them.

But first, he intended to get to know Mae a lot better.

CHAPTER

· · · · · ·

eleven

MAE HAD AN off day today—at least from filming—which meant she could actually do the job for which she'd been hired. The one she loved that made her happy.

Sort of. After spending the day in meetings followed by planning sessions with Honor, she found herself staring out the window of her office to see if she could catch a glimpse of the goings-on over at the movie location. In other words, she was trying to see Kane, which of course she couldn't do because the production was secluded from the house and vineyards.

Dammit.

They'd had a good time at Brenna and Finn's housewarming the other night, but then she'd driven him to his trailer and he'd said good night and walked away with a smile and a wave.

No kiss. No . . . nothing. After all his teasing banter and the kiss in the driveway? She'd kind of expected something more. She wanted more, even though she knew she shouldn't. Then again, Kane was exactly the type of man she wanted to date. He'd film here and then he'd leave, with zero expectations of a relationship.

If she was looking for a perfect man—at least a perfect man for her—Kane was it.

Her phone buzzed, drawing her away from the window. She was surprised to see a text message from Kane.

Filming till about six but free after that. Dinner
tonight?

Annoyed by the flutter in her stomach, she thought about saying no, then wondered why. She wanted to see him.

Before she could overthink this any further, she texted him back.

Dinner sounds great.

She spent the rest of the day trying to concentrate on work, but all she could focus on was her date—no, it was just dinner—with Kane.

After staring at her paperwork for fifteen minutes, reading the same wedding couple's menu over and over again, she decided to step out of her office and go for a walk to clear her head.

It was a sunny, cool afternoon, a breeze slipping through the strands of her hair. She breathed in the freshness of the air, observed the changing foliage from green to beautiful golden colors.

She walked the property, thinking about absolutely nothing, which, it turned out, was exactly what she needed.

Until she ran into Brenna, who was out in the vineyards.

"Taking a late afternoon stroll?" she asked.

"Yeah. Clearing my head."

Brenna stepped out from the vines and swiped her hands together. "Stuck in dreamland over Kane August?"

"No. Just a full schedule of to-do's today. This has nothing to do with Kane." She pivoted and walked away, knowing Brenna would follow, which she did.

"You realize I don't believe you."

Mae started to object, then shrugged. "So I was thinking about Kane. He's hot. Who wouldn't? And before you ask any more invasive questions, we're having dinner together tonight."

Brenna looked over at her, brows raised so high they practically disappeared into her hair. "He asked you to dinner? And I heard about the hot makeout sesh in my driveway."

"Dammit, Erin," she whispered.

"So this means things are getting serious."

"Things are absolutely not serious. There is nothing between us. We haven't even—"

Brenna stopped, turned to face her. "Ohhh. You two haven't done it yet, huh? What the hell are you waiting for, Mae? He's hot, he's available and he obviously wants you."

She stared at Brenna, her mind racing with thoughts. So. Many. Thoughts. "Yeah, that's under consideration."

Brenna shook her head and started to wander off. "Girl, get on that man ASAP, 'kay?"

Mae laughed as she made her way back to the house. She looked at her phone, realizing it was time to get ready for her date with Kane.

And now all she could think about was expectations. Which was kind of unexpected because she was always so laid back about dating. Ever since Isaac, she'd taken dating as fun and frivolous. Catch and release was her motto. And Kane was the perfect man for that.

So why was she suddenly so damn nervous? She needed

to get her shit together, because if nothing else, she'd get a nice dinner.

As far as expectations, she had none. She reminded herself of that as she picked out what she was going to wear.

She decided on a warm nicely burnished caramel cotton dress since the nights were cool, then put on her ankle boots. She brushed out her hair and pulled it into a high ponytail, then added a long necklace and earrings.

She answered the knock at her bedroom door to find Honor standing there.

"You haven't had sex with him yet?"

She rolled her eyes. "Brenna told you that?"

Honor walked in and sat on the bed. "Of course she did. You know we don't keep things to ourselves. Well, at least Brenna doesn't. Erin doesn't, either. I'm a vault, though, so spill."

"Nothing to spill, obviously, since there's been no sex."

"How come? Knowing your propensity for loving and leaving, I'd have thought you'd have tried out the goods on the first day."

She shrugged. "I don't know. Because he's not someone I can have sex with and then dump. He's going to be here a while, you know?"

"You've been thinking about this," Honor said, cocking her head to the side. "Debating the pros and cons."

"I very rarely debate sex. I'm either in or out." She thought about it for a few seconds, then said, "But, yeah. This one? I've been debating."

"So he's different from all the other guys."

She shrugged. "There haven't been that many guys."

Honor shot her a look. "Honey. Since Isaac, you've gone through so many men we've all lost count."

"I wasn't aware you were all counting. And I don't have sex with every guy I go out with."

"Just a figure of speech. Of course we weren't counting. But seriously, there've been a lot. Which just means you've been having fun. Nothing serious, right? That's your motto."

"Yes, it is."

"And who cares how many men you have sex with? That's your business. As far as Kane?" She blew out a breath. "So hot. Definitely add him to the who's-counting list. Or no-one's-counting. Whatever you call it. Won't that be fun?"

She wasn't certain. "Absolutely. I'll get right on that."

Honor pursed her lips, giving her a thoughtful look. "Now you're mad. I'm sorry. I didn't mean to imply anything. I was actually kind of jealous you were having so much fun. You're so free and open to possibilities in ways I never could have been. I don't want you to lose who you are. Not for any man ever again."

Tears filled her eyes. "Thank you, Honor."

Honor, her eyes teary as well, stood. "Well. I hadn't ex-pected this conversation to turn emotional. So I'm going to leave and you're going to go have some fun tonight, got it?"

Shaking off the emotion, Mae nodded. "Got it."

After Honor left the room, Mae stared at her reflection in the mirror.

She looked good. Damn good. Except for one thing.

She took her hair out of the ponytail, brushed it out until it was flowing and glossy, then looked again.

Yes. Much better. Before, she looked cute. Now, though? Hot. Definitely hot. And she was in the mood for hot.

Now she was ready for tonight.

CHAPTER

· · · · · ·

twelve

KANE STOOD AT Mae's front door—or the Bellinis' front door—suddenly nervous to ring the bell.

This was a date. Not a hookup, not meeting at a bar or someplace neutral. He knew the Bellinis weren't Mae's parents. Hell, he didn't even know anything about her parents. There was so much more he wanted to know about her.

Like, everything.

The door opened and Mae stared at him.

"Are you planning to stand out here all night or were you going to knock?"

"Sorry. I was thinking."

She arched a brow. "Change your mind?"

"About dinner? Hell no."

"Great. Let's go." She grabbed her bag off the table and he stepped aside so she could walk out the door. She pulled it shut behind her.

"I was going to say hello to the Bellinis."

"They're not here."

"Oh. Okay."

He led her out to his rental and held the door for her. He programmed the restaurant's address into the GPS and they headed out.

"Tell me about your family," he said as he pulled out onto the main road.

"Oh. Well. Not much to tell. My father died when I was little and my mother and I are no longer close."

"I'm sorry. You don't have to talk about it if you don't want to."

"No, it's fine. My mom was very close with my ex-fiancé. When I broke up with him, she was angry with me."

He turned onto the highway, merging with traffic. "Why would she be mad about that? Isn't that your decision to make?"

"I think it was more about the lifestyle he could afford me. He came from money and we don't, so my mother thought I should overlook Isaac's infidelity and move forward with the wedding. She knew how much he had hurt me, but for some reason she didn't care."

"The idea of the money and the lifestyle was more important to her than your heartbreak."

She nodded. "That's something I can't ever forgive."

"Don't blame you for that." He couldn't imagine finding out your fiancé cheated, calling off a wedding and then having your mother against you as well. "That must have been devastating for you."

"It wasn't a fun time. Anyway, after I realized my mother would take the side of the man who cheated on me rather than see how much he hurt me, that she valued financial security over the feelings of her own daughter . . . well, that was the end of our relationship."

Kane blew out a breath. "I'm sorry."

"Thanks. Me, too. But I'm over it now."

He didn't think a person could ever get past a betrayal like that. First by her fiancé, then by her mother. Two people who were supposed to love her. Damn.

He was sorry he'd brought up the subject of family. He was going to have to try to make this night fun for her, to hopefully take the sorrow away.

"Anyway," she said. "Tell me about your family. You've talked about your grandpa and the ranch. How about your parents?"

"They're fairly normal. Dad worked the ranch when he was a kid, then he went to college and now he works in financial services and Mom's in tech."

"Really."

"Yeah. They're both busy, dedicated people who love their jobs."

"And how do they feel about you being an actor?"

"They said as long as I'm happy doing what I do, then they're happy for me. But they don't pay a lot of attention to it, honestly. They kind of live in their own world, ya know? Sometimes it's hard to get them to even answer the phone when I call them. At least recently."

She frowned. "Is everything okay?"

"I don't know. I mean, I'm sure it is. For all I know they're on a cruise and don't have cell service. It's just . . . well, nothing."

"No, go on. Tell me."

"I don't know. It's a gut feeling that something's wrong?"

"Have they told you something?"

"No. That's the issue. They haven't said anything. I can barely get them to talk to me."

"I'm sorry. That must be frustrating."

"Yeah. Kind of. But like I said, they're both very independent and our lives are very separate. Which is okay. I don't need to know everything going on in their lives. Just like they don't need to know everything about mine."

"That's probably a good thing for them, not to be so invested in what you do."

He almost sighed in relief when she didn't push about the "problem" part he'd brought up about his parents. He didn't even know why he'd said anything, other than because Mae was easy to talk to.

"I think so. They celebrate my successes but otherwise they're totally removed from this crazy business. I invite them to all my premieres and they've been to a couple, though they mostly save their vacation time for trips abroad."

"Does it bother you that they don't come to see your movies?"

"Nah. They see the movies, just on their own timetable. The glitz of premieres isn't their thing."

"I can understand that."

He pulled into the parking lot of the restaurant. He'd chosen this place because it looked like a fun location to walk around after dinner. There were several restaurants, walking paths, even a pumpkin patch since it was nearly Halloween, and there was a pond with lights and waterspouts. Plus, he liked the ambience of the restaurant and the menu looked amazing.

They walked in and he gave his name. Not his real name, but a made-up one. Fortunately, it was dark inside and crowded and the hostess was busy so didn't pay them any attention as she led them to a table near the back of the restaurant, just as he'd asked. She handed them menus and promptly disappeared.

"Perfect spot for dinner," Mae said.

"It looked good. Have you eaten here before?"

"I have, but it's been a while. I think you'll like it."

He studied the drink menu. "Would you like some wine?"

She studied the menu thoughtfully. "You know, I think I'll have a cocktail tonight."

"Okay, sure."

When their server returned, he ordered a whiskey on the rocks and Mae ordered a flavored martini. She took a sip and he saw the delight on her face.

"Yum." She held up the glass. "Want a taste?"

He shook his head. "All for you."

"Fine, then." She took another sip, then studied the menu. "The salmon looks good to me. How about you?"

"Steak, of course."

"Of course." She laid her menu to the side and took another sip of her cocktail. "How did filming go today?"

"It went fine. Not as much fun without you."

She laughed. "You mean without your real leading lady."

"Everly's fun, for sure. We've worked a lot together, came up in the business about the same time, so we shared similar trials."

"How did you end up a big movie star, anyway?"

"I took a liking to drama in middle school, which surprised the hell out of me, since I was a big jock who thought sports were my future. I did all the plays in high school, and got noticed by a talent agent who got me a small part in a TV movie. I guess I did well, because I got booked on a series. After that, I moved to L.A. and got a few roles here and there while I went to college, working some side jobs in between gigs. Then I got a part in a movie, then another movie, and my career just took off."

"Huh. It's like it was meant to be." Their server had brought warm bread, so Kane sliced pieces for both of them, sliding one onto her plate. She grabbed a pat of butter and slathered it onto her bread, taking a big bite.

"You like food," he said.

"No, I *love* food."

"Yeah, me, too. It's refreshing to be out to dinner with a woman who likes to eat."

She waved her bread at him. "I'm not even going to ask."

"Best not to."

She smiled. "No worries here. I eat all the time. I like all food. There's nothing I won't eat, and if I haven't eaten it before, I'll try it at least once."

"That sounds promising. We'll have to explore more food."

"Sounds fun."

Their food was great and they talked through the whole meal without any awkward silences. She talked about her education and friends she had growing up. She asked him all kinds of questions about himself and none of them were movie related, which was refreshing. That didn't happen all that often when he was out on a date.

After their plates were cleared away, Kane ordered coffee and Mae wanted a cappuccino.

"Are you sure you don't want cheesecake?" Kane asked.

"I do like food, but I have my limits, and the bread was very filling. I'm good, thanks."

"Okay."

He paid the bill and they stood. Mae started to put on her cardigan, so Kane stepped in to help.

They walked outside and he breathed in the cool night air, took in the sounds of laughing kids, watching them run so freely. He wished he could remember that far back—how it felt to be that carefree. It was awesome to watch those kids.

He took Mae's hand and they walked the grounds, moving

toward the pond where dancing spurts of water put on a light show.

"Want to take me through the pumpkin maze?" she asked.

"Are you sure we'll make it out alive?"

She snickered. "I don't know. But if we get lost in there . . ."

She let that thought trail off and smiled. He squeezed her hand. "Let's take our chances."

They wandered in and he could tell right away that this had been set up for the kids. You could easily see where you were going and how to get out, but still, it was fun to walk through with Mae while littles zoomed past them. Hearing their giggles and squeals made Kane's stomach tighten with a need for something he'd never felt until just now.

"A lot of kids here," he said.

Her happy smile was infectious. "I know. Aren't they great? Noisy and messy and running around squealing with joy."

"And you like that."

"Of course I do. Who wouldn't? I mean, I guess if you don't like kids it might bug you." She paused, looking over at him. "Does it bug you?"

"Hell no. I love kids."

She looped her arm in his. "Good to know our date can continue, then."

He laughed, realizing he felt more at ease with Mae than he had with anyone in recent memory.

After winding their way out of the maze, they stopped in at a pizza place for glasses of iced tea, found a bench to sit and watch the kids play on the ropes and slides. He put his arm on the back of the bench and Mae leaned back as if instinctively searching for his touch. He didn't want to presume, but he couldn't help but reach out to play with a strand of her hair. Since she didn't shrug him off—or punch him—

he continued, letting his fingers wander over to her shoulder, keeping his touch light and easy, though the feelings that touching her evoked were anything but light.

"Can I ask you a question?"

She looked at him and nodded. "Of course."

"You mentioned in earlier conversation that marriage would be the last thing you wanted. I wondered why."

"Oh, that. I told you I was engaged once. It didn't work out."

He took her hand in his and squeezed. "Right. You mentioned that when you talked about the falling-out with your mother, though you didn't get into detail. Want to tell me about it?"

"No."

"Okay."

They went silent then, so he resumed watching kids and parents chasing after kids.

"He cheated on me," she said, her voice a low whisper. "Repeatedly. Even after we were engaged."

He turned to look at her. "What? What kind of guy cheats on the woman he's going to marry?"

"A jerk. Asshole. Scum-sucking jackass. Reprehensible piece of shit. A lowlife loser with no sense of honor."

Impressed, he nodded. "You seem to have summed up his character well."

"Yeah, but what does that say about me? I didn't see it coming."

"Maybe he didn't let you see it. Some people are good at hiding who they really are."

"I don't know." She took a sip of her tea before continuing. "I should have seen it. As the wedding date drew closer, he was disappearing more and more, canceling out on more dates with me. He's a musician, so I knew he was busy, and I thought he was just trying to fit in more bookings since we'd be taking off a couple weeks for the honeymoon."

"Wasn't gigs, huh?"

"Hell no. He was seeing another woman—multiple women, in fact. And when I found out and confronted him, he acted like it was no big deal. He told me he loved me and he was marrying me and I should be flattered. That he'd always be there for me, and I shouldn't be upset about the small issue of him having a few, as he called them, fun pieces on the side."

Kane blinked. "Well, fuck that. And you didn't kill him?"

She laughed. "Surprisingly, no. But after I got over the cancellation of the wedding and the heartbreak, I did some digging and found out from former girlfriends that that was who he was. Who he always was. A serial cheater. And I never knew."

He rubbed her arm. "You know who really lost out on that relationship? He did. You didn't lose anything other than some asshole who didn't deserve you."

She nodded. "I know that now and believe me, I'm grateful I found out before the wedding. But seriously, what kind of person does that?"

"I'm sorry to say that there are people out there who only think of themselves and their own version of happiness. I see plenty of it in my business. There are some people who buy into their star images and believe they're deserving of being put on a pedestal, thinking that no matter what they do or who they hurt, they're never in the wrong."

"That must be a lonely existence."

"You'd like to think so, but if they have a big enough entourage, with assistants and hangers-on who continually stroke their egos, then they don't feel lonely. It's all fake, of course, but they don't realize it."

"I notice you don't have an entourage."

He grinned. "Yeah, that's not my thing. I do fine on my own."

"And yet you're a big movie star."

He shrugged. "It's all an illusion. I'm surrounded by plenty of people on set and at premieres, plus when I have to do promotion for a film. The last thing I need is more people following me around when they don't have to be. I have an agent and a publicist and they take care of the business that needs taking care of. Otherwise, I'm good."

"Yeah, you are." She laid her head on his shoulder and continued to sip her iced tea.

That felt good. She felt good sitting next to him. All in all, this night was going well.

When they finished their drinks, they headed back to the car. Kane had been careful tonight, had kept his head down in order to avoid being recognized. He didn't see any cameras or gawkers, so hopefully he'd been successful. Not that he was worried for himself. He was used to being in the public eye. But the last thing he wanted to do was to expose Mae to this lifestyle he'd signed on for.

They drove back to the main house. He got out and walked over to open her door, wishing he could find someplace private to be alone with Mae. He thought about asking her back to his trailer, but for some reason that wasn't the place he wanted to bring her.

"Do you want to come in?" she asked. "Johnny and Maureen are out of town visiting friends for a couple of days, so I'm in this big house all alone."

And, jackpot. "Yeah, I'd like that." He followed her up the stairs, unable to keep from focusing his attention on her amazing legs.

She used her key to open the front door of this incredible

farmhouse, then walked inside, closing the door behind them.

He started to ask for a tour, but then Mae pushed him against the wall just inside the door. Her hands crept along his chest, snaking along his stomach, sending his dick into rock-hard mode.

"We're alone," she said. "And we've danced around this attraction long enough, don't you think?"

He smoothed his hand over her back, eager to feel more of her, all of her. "Bold approach."

She shrugged. "I go after what I want, and you know as well as I do that there's this smoking hot chemistry between us."

He picked her up, scooping his hand under her butt, then shifted around, pressing her against the wall. "Chemistry, huh? Let's set it on fire and see what happens."

He put his mouth on hers. The explosion of heat ignited a desire he'd never felt so intensely.

Yeah, they were gonna burn it down tonight.

CHAPTER
· · · · · ·
thirteen

K ANE'S KISS INCINERATED her, made her feel as if she were melting from the inside out. Mae rocked against his erection, needing his touch, his mouth all over her, his cock inside her. She needed him right now.

Someone was moaning. Loudly. Were those sounds coming from her?

"Your room," he groaned.

"Upstairs. Second door on the right."

Without taking a breath he carried her up all those stairs, his mouth on her neck, licking and sucking until she thought she might come from the sheer pleasure of it. He shoved the door open and laid her on the bed, then pulled his shirt off while he toed out of his boots, then began to unbuckle his belt. She leaned forward and removed her boots and socks and was about to get up so she could get undressed.

"Oh, no," he said, kneeling in front of her. "Stay right there."

She leaned back on her elbows, anticipation flaring as he swept his hands along the length of her legs from her ankles to her thighs, taking his sweet-ass time doing so. He paused, smiling at her as he grasped her thighs and spread her legs, leaning down to press a kiss to each thigh.

"You smell good here," he said. "Everywhere, really."

She shuddered as she inhaled, as she watched him lift her dress over her hips, grateful that she'd worn her pink lacy underwear. He teased the top of her panties, then pressed a kiss there, making breathing difficult.

He grasped her underwear and pulled it down. His warm breath caressed her sex, followed by a slow, delicious lick. She shuddered, enveloped in delicious sensation as he licked and sucked her in all the right places until she thought she might die from the sheer pleasure of it.

She writhed, totally out of control, having given it up to Kane, who had cupped her butt in his hands and delivered exactly what she so desperately needed. When she orgasmed, it was the sweetest release, a giant quake that rolled on and on until all she felt were the tiny pulses of postrelease.

She blew out a breath as Kane hovered above her. She smiled at him and cupped the back of his neck, bringing his lips to hers for an incendiary kiss that had her climbing right up that mountain of desire once again.

He pulled back.

"What you do to me," she whispered.

"We're just getting started." He stood, unzipped his jeans and let them drop to the floor along with his boxer briefs. Naked, he was spectacular, all lean muscle and angular planes. All she wanted to do was map every inch of his incredible body.

He pulled her to stand and she turned so he could unzip her dress. She slid out of it and he unhooked her bra, tossing it to the side.

He shook his head. "You are so beautiful," he said, cupping her breasts to tease and stroke her nipples, sending waves of pleasure throughout her body.

"You know," he said, "I want to take the time to worship your entire body the way you deserve."

She placed her palm on his chest. "That sounds nice and all, and I'd like to do the same to you." She wrapped her hand around his throbbing shaft. "But what I'd really like is this hard cock inside me."

He shuddered in a breath. "Yeah, let's do that."

They climbed onto the bed and he bent over to reach into his jeans at the same time she opened the drawer of her nightstand, both of them pulling out condoms.

He grinned. "Ever prepared?"

"Always."

"Same," he said. "But I'll let you be in charge."

"I like the sound of that." She pushed him onto his back, removed the condom from the wrapper and enjoyed the hell out of the feel of him as she rolled it on. And since he gave her freedom of exploration, she intended to use it, straddling his hips and sliding his cock inside her. She paused, quivering with pleasure as her body wrapped around all that delicious steely flesh.

Unable to control the pulses, she began to move, sliding forward, then back, all the while using her hands to explore Kane's magnificent body. She swept her fingertips across his chest, teasing his nipples until he gasped and gripped her hips, dragging her clit across his flesh.

Now it was her turn to gasp, to scrape her nails along his chest as with every one of his movements she climbed ever closer to climax.

Kane must have felt it, too, because his breathing sharpened to go along with the quickening of his thrusts. Mae tilted back, her hips arching so he could go deeper, so he could get her there, so he could get them both there.

He dug his fingers into her hips, that slight pain taking her right over the edge. She let out a loud moan with her climax, the pulses grabbing on to his cock and plummeting him over as well. The two of them shook with the force of it, like an erotic earthquake that made her reach out for him to help her balance. He grasped her hands and she held on while she rode it out, soaking in every delicious tremor until there was nothing left but heavy breathing and lingering peaks of pleasure.

Mae fell forward, stretching her legs on top of Kane's and resting her head on his chest. He rubbed her back and shoulders and she swore she was going to stay just like this for the remainder of her days. Naked, languorous, her body aligned with this studly man.

It would be the perfect way to go.

But she figured that Kane might go numb with her body weight on top of him, so she rolled off. He got up from the bed and stepped into the bathroom for a minute. She turned onto her side, still feeling lazy and satisfied. When he came out, she couldn't help herself—she ogled him. Fortunately, he took his time sauntering back to bed, crawling over to her, letting her enjoy the way his muscles flexed as he made his way to her.

He bent and brushed his lips over hers, then trailed his lips across her jaw and neck, making her shiver with delight.

"Remember when I said I wanted to take the time to appreciate your glorious body?"

"Mmm-hmm."

He blazed a trail of heated kisses from her neck to her breasts to her belly, heading south. "Let's do that now," he murmured against her skin.

As he spread her legs, she said, "Yes, let's."

CHAPTER

· · · · · ·

fourteen

THERE WAS NOTHING worse than being on a location shoot and having nothing to do, but apparently the crew had some technical glitches to work out before they could resume filming, so Alexis had told Kane that they'd resume within a couple of days.

Which would have been great if he could have spent that off time with Mae, especially since it was Friday, which would have meant an extended weekend. But she had left early this morning and was now off in Vegas doing the bachelorette party thing with Brenna and her family and friends. So now he had no idea what he was going to do. Go exploring in the area, he imagined. He was fine going off on his own, but hanging out with Mae would have been a lot more fun.

Someone knocked on his trailer door. Figuring it was Alexis or one of the crew, he hollered for them to come in.

He was surprised to see Finn, Brenna's fiancé.

"Hope I'm not bothering you," Finn said, hovering on the stairs.

He got up from the sofa and made his way over to him. "Not at all, Finn. Come on in."

"I've just got a minute, actually, but tonight's my bachelor party and I thought you might want to join in, if you're not busy doing something else."

"I literally have nothing else to do, so thanks for the invite. I'd love to come."

Finn gave him a wide smile. "Great. You need to be back on set early tomorrow?"

"As of right now? No."

"Good. Because we're heading out of town."

Kane shrugged. "Sounds good to me."

"Okay. Meet us over at the main house around six. We're not doing fancy shit, so dress casual. And pack an overnight bag."

There was nothing Kane enjoyed more than an adventure. "Sounds perfect. And, Finn?"

"Yeah?"

"Thanks again."

Finn smiled. "You bet. Later."

After Finn left, Kane had a surge of renewed energy. He did a satisfying workout at a local gym, keeping his hat on and his head down, then came back and studied his lines, talked to his agent, then called his dad. The phone call went the way most of the calls with his dad had gone lately. Short. Curt. Dad said he was busy and didn't have time to talk, but everything was fine. And that was it. After he clicked off, Kane stared at his phone for a long minute. That just wasn't like him. Something was up, he just couldn't put his finger on it. He tried his mom but got her voice mail.

Whatever.

Fortunately, he had a long phone conversation with his

grandpa to see how he was doing. Grandpa was doing great and asked when he'd come visit. He told him soon. Then he checked in with Alexis to get a more firm timeline on the resumption of filming, to which she grumpily replied, "Eventually," which wasn't helpful at all. Not that he was some stickler for schedule, but he liked to be able to make a plan.

Not wanting to bother Alexis when she was irritated, he let the assistant director know he was going to be away from the site overnight. They had his cell if they needed to get in touch, but the AD didn't think it would be a problem since it might be a couple of days' delay before filming would resume.

By the time he'd made a few scene notes and read several chapters in a book, it was time to shower and get ready for tonight. He put on a nice pair of jeans and a black button-down, slipped into his boots and packed a change of clothes. He walked over to the main house, enjoying the cool night air.

Just as he got to the house he saw a shuttle pull up. No, not a shuttle, it was a party bus. The door opened and the sounds of raucous music blasted from inside.

Kane walked over and peered in.

"Kane!" they all yelled in unison.

When he stepped onto the bus, Kane saw Finn, Jason, Owen, Clay and a few people he hadn't met yet, so he introduced himself while the bus took off.

"Drink?" Clay asked.

"Definitely. What do you have?"

"Beer. Whiskey. Wine."

"Let's start with a beer."

Clay pulled a beer out of the cooler and handed it to him. He twisted the top off and took a deep swallow, letting the liquid cool him off. "Thanks."

"Got some time off from filming?" Clay asked, leaning back against the seat and sipping his beer.

Kane took a seat next to him. "Yeah. A couple of days, apparently. Some technical stuff with the equipment."

"I'm surprised you didn't hightail it down to your family's ranch to spend time with the horses."

Kane grinned. "A couple of days isn't long enough. I'd just get settled and then have to leave."

Clay nodded. "Understood. You gotta be able to soak it up. I'm sure you miss it."

"You know it."

"So, why acting?"

Kane shrugged. "Just got a feel for it and ran with it."

"Havin' fun?"

"So far."

"Good." He reached for a bag and tossed it at Kane. "Chips?"

Kane laughed. "Yeah."

One thing about cowboys. They were men of few words, but it was always a great conversation.

Eventually, the two of them joined in with the rest of the guys, talking about their jobs, their women and where they were headed.

"Where are we headed, anyway?" Kane asked.

"Tulsa," Finn said. "Dinner, drinks and the casino."

This was going to be fun.

It took about two hours to get to Tulsa. The party bus pulled up in front of the casino hotel, which was a lot bigger than Kane expected. Inside reminded him of a Vegas casino, which meant he felt right at home.

They headed to the registration desk, where Jason arranged their rooms.

"Kane, you'll be sharing a bed with Owen."

Yeah, that wasn't gonna happen. He hadn't shared a room with anyone since college. "Uh . . ."

Owen laughed and slapped him on the back. "You should see your face, bro."

"Oh, don't worry," Clay said, sliding his phone into his jeans. "I got a pic."

He cracked a smile. "You guys are all assholes."

Jason handed him a key card. "That much is true." He handed another card to Finn. "You get the fancy room."

"Hey, thanks. What's that gonna cost me?"

"First round of drinks at the craps tables tonight."

"You got it."

Jason gathered the group. "We'll meet in Finn's room in ten."

Kane went up to his room, surprised to find out it was a damn nice suite. Great shower, too, and a big bed. He had a queen bed in his trailer, which wasn't bad, but he was a tall guy. So he was looking forward to sprawling out in this over-sized king bed tonight.

He used the bathroom, washed up, brushed his teeth, then put on the ball cap he'd brought along. Not the best of disguises, but it was surprising how well it worked to hide his face. Plus, he tended to find that, outside of Hollywood or New York, he could easily disappear in a crowd. It wasn't like people were on the lookout for celebrities in places like this. He went to the elevator to head up to Finn's room. Two young women got into the elevator one floor up from his, giving him a lot of stares.

"Hey," one of them said, eyeing him close. "Did anyone ever tell you that you look a lot like that movie star Kane August?"

He frowned. "I get that a lot, though my girlfriend thinks I'm prettier than that guy."

The other woman laughed, and the one who asked the question looked him up and down again, then said, "Tell your girlfriend she's right."

They got off on the next floor, and Kane breathed a sigh of relief. That line didn't always work, but he was relieved it had just now.

He got to the top floor and searched out Finn's room, then knocked. Jason answered, a glass of something in his hand. "Finally. Come on in, the party's getting started."

Finn's suite was . . . well, sweet. It had a huge living room with a fireplace, along with a dining room table that right now was loaded with food.

"Figured everyone would want to eat so we could get to drinking," Owen said. "There's steak, salmon and all the sides."

Kane was hungry, so he joined the guys and they dove into the food, talking while they ate.

"It must be fun working with animals all day," Kane said to Jason.

"It's like living the dream, man," Jason said, sliding a piece of steak into his mouth. "Kind of like what you do."

"Except you're saving lives. I'm . . . popcorn entertainment. Not exactly the same thing."

"Hey, don't underestimate popcorn entertainment," Owen said. "It's vital to our survival."

Finn raised his glass. "I'll drink to that. Where would we be without our favorite movies?"

"Hail to *Gladiator*," Jason said.

"Nuh-uh," Clay said. *"Tombstone."*

"Oh, please," Owen said. "We all know it's *Batman*."

"Which one?" they all asked, almost in unison.

And then they began to argue the various nuances and merits of which *Batman* was the best, which took them through the rest of the meal and continued as they made their way downstairs to the gaming area.

Kane liked these guys. They were genuine, no bullshit, and they treated him like one of them, which he appreciated more than he could say. It was hard for him to make friends in his business. Some people wanted to be his friend for the potential connections or the perks, but honest friendship because they liked him? Just Kane August the person? Yeah, that didn't come around all that often. Even some of his friends back home treated him differently these days, and that hurt.

Acting was his job, not who he was. Which was why getting to hang out with an awesome group of men like this charged him up.

They set up shop at the craps tables, one of Kane's favorite things to do. He got on a winning streak but then bowed out once a crowd started to gather. The last thing he wanted was to call attention to himself, and the ball cap only went so far, so he let Clay take over while he enjoyed himself on the sidelines. They drank, won some, lost some, and Kane had an awesome time.

They all took a break and sat at the bar to chill.

"So," Jason said. "One more week and it's your turn, Finn."

"Yeah. I can't wait to marry Brenna. Plus, you know it's gonna be a party."

"And you know how much we love a party," Clay said.

"Hell yeah we do." Jason's phone lit up so he grabbed it, looked at it and laughed. "Looks like our ladies are having a good time. Check out this pic Erin sent."

He passed the phone around, everyone grinning. When Clay handed it over to Kane, he smiled.

Brenna was in the middle in a short white dress with her

Bride sash and a tiara, surrounded by the other women all dressed in black. And there was Mae, looking sexy as hell in a short black dress and silver stiletto heels, showing off her incredible legs. He let out a sigh and handed the phone back to Clay.

"You like her, huh?" Clay asked.

"Yeah."

"That's good, right? Having fun with someone while you're here filming?"

"Sure. I mean, we're both on the same wavelength. Neither of us wants a relationship, so it's all good, right?"

Clay cracked a smile as he lifted his glass to his lips. "Right. That's how it always goes."

"What do you mean?"

"Nothing, man. Other than sometimes the longer it goes on, the harder it gets to make it just about the fun. Then feelings get involved and then you're in too deep to just walk away."

"Oh, I don't think so. Mae seems pretty adamant about keeping things between us free from any emotion. She told me about her ex-fiancé."

"Yeah, that was rough on her. We all rallied around her after that. But she's tough and she recovered and now she's living life on her terms. Which doesn't mean we don't still protect her."

"Understood. I don't intend to hurt her."

Clay nodded, and then they resumed drinking. But Kane took out his phone and sent a quick text to Mae.

Saw the pic. Hope you're having fun.

A half hour later she replied: We drinkin and dancin. You with the guyses huh?

He typed back: Yeah. They're good guys. Be careful and have a good time.

She sent back all emojis of kissy face, laughing, champagne and lips.

He grinned and slid his phone back in his pocket. Looked like they were both having fun tonight.

But he was still looking forward to seeing her again.

CHAPTER

· · · · · ·

fifteen

THIS WEEK HAD been a flurry of work and prep for Brenna's wedding. Along with that, Mae had some stand-in duties to perform with Kane, which was about all she had time for as far as seeing him.

They'd filmed two scenes together, one where they were in conversation in the garden, and the other where all she had to do was stand in a field a ways away while he filmed with another actor. Of course they filmed her from behind while he and the other actor spoke their dialogue, but whatever. She positioned herself wherever they told her and she no idea how they put the film together.

They did manage to eat lunch together one day in his trailer, catching up on each other's activities, but it was brief because he had a scene to film and she had a to-do list ten miles long, so there hadn't been enough time to do much other than chat, shove food in their mouths and say a quick goodbye.

And then he'd had to leave for a couple of days to do some location shoots outside the vineyard. Mae wouldn't be needed for those, thankfully. The other good news was, the entire crew had disappeared as well.

"It's so blissfully quiet here with the film crew away," Brenna said as they sat at the table during their morning meeting.

"Isn't it?" Erin held JJ on her lap, and he happily played with a toy while simultaneously sucking his fingers.

"Now that they're gone for a couple of days I've rearranged several appointments for tours for prospective clients," Honor said. "I hope we can get quite a few through before filming restarts."

"They weren't exactly in the way of that, though, were they?" Mae asked, tapping her pen on her notebook.

"Well, not exactly. But they were here, and then there's the curiosity factor and having to explain the whole thing to prospective brides and grooms."

"That's true. If there's anything I can do to facilitate tours, let me know."

"I think I have it covered, Mae, but someone needs to handle Brenna."

Brenna's brows rose. "Excuse me? What about me needs to be handled?"

"You are getting married this weekend," Erin said. "There are still a million things that need to be done."

"That's true," Honor said. "Plus, we're all in the wedding, so there are a lot of details to be handled related to the event while the rest of us try and do our other jobs."

"I have the list," Mae said, grabbing the book for Brenna and Finn's wedding. "I think we're on track so far, though you all have mani-pedi appointments tomorrow at ten, so you need to make sure you're all available for that, along with your mom."

"I'll remind her right now," Erin said, sending a text with one hand while juggling JJ.

Mae perused the list. "Jason said he'd pick up the tuxes tomorrow after work. Brenna, your mother is picking up all the dresses and shoes tomorrow afternoon."

Brenna nodded, marking things off of her master list.

"I've spoken with the caterer, the florist and the deejay," Honor said. "Everything is in order there."

"And tomorrow I take over everything from all of you," Mae said. "Starting then, you're bridesmaids and I'm the wedding planner. No arguments."

Honor looked over at Erin. "She's so pushy."

"Kind of perfect for a wedding planner, actually," Honor said. "Especially since she has to corral all of us. Plus Mom and Dad. And all the guys."

Erin nodded. "True. And don't forget dealing with Brenna."

"Hey!" Brenna glared at them. "I am the most relaxed bride ever. I've totally got this."

Erin snorted. "Right. That's what I said. Until the day of. Trust me, the panic will set in."

Brenna shook her head. "Nope. I've got the man. Everything else is cake."

Mae made her own mental note to keep a close eye on Brenna over the next couple of days. Sometimes the most calm, confident brides were the ones who totally lost it on wedding day.

Her list was getting longer. She was going to be incredibly busy.

But she still couldn't wait for Brenna and Finn to get married.

CHAPTER

······

sixteen

KANE LOOKED IN the mirror, adjusting his tie and making sure his hair looked good.

He sat and put on his dress boots, then checked the mirror again.

Suit looked great, and he had to admit he could dress up well. He'd been to enough premieres to know how to do it. But this was a wedding, and he wasn't the star tonight. Thankfully.

Still, he had a date, even if said date had already told him she was going to be busy working.

Finn had already invited him to his and Brenna's wedding, which Kane appreciated. But the text from Mae asking if she'd be his date for the wedding had been even better. They'd hardly had any time together other than filming a few scenes, and he missed talking to her, touching her, and oh, man, did he miss kissing her. He knew he wouldn't get a lot of time with her tonight, but even a little was better than none.

He put on his cowboy hat and headed up to the wedding area to see that guests had already started to arrive. It was a nice fall day, the sun shining and the weather warm enough to have an outdoor wedding. Each row of chairs was decorated by flowers. Dropping his hat low over his eyes, he took a seat in the back, hoping to be as invisible as possible.

He sat back, crossed his arms and watched as the chairs were filled with happy, smiling people.

Finn and Brenna were really popular. It made him wonder if, when he got married someday, there'd be anybody to show up for him. His parents. His grandpa for sure. Definitely his aunts, uncles and cousins. Alexis. Everly. They were as close as family to him. Some of the Hollywood types would show up for the photo op. But who else could he count on?

He watched as the groomsmen all walked up to the arbor. Finn, Jason, Owen, Clay.

He'd made friends with genuine, honest guys while he was here. But were those lifelong friendships or just temporary ones? He didn't know the answer to that yet. All he knew was that he was happy for Finn.

The arbor was decorated with flowers, and Kane imagined that—if he were the marrying type—this whole day would make him pretty happy.

The bridesmaids started walking down the aisle. Erin, Honor, Alice, then everyone stood while Brenna was escorted by Johnny. All eyes were on her as she made her way to where Finn stood waiting for her. Kane caught sight of Mae, dressed in a beautiful burgundy dress, standing off to the side as she watched the wedding ceremony take place.

Mae might be the wedding planner at this shindig, but to Kane she was the most beautiful woman in the room.

Finn and Brenna spoke vows to each other about love and commitment, and Kane could feel the emotion in their words. And when they kissed to seal the deal, he was happy for them.

Afterward, everyone filed out of the vineyard and headed toward the barn, where drinks and appetizers awaited them.

The wedding party stayed behind for photos, so he'd get to talk to them later. Kane decided to search out the bar, found it easily and got a beer, then made his way inside.

Of course, he didn't know anyone, since everyone he knew was outside getting photos taken. But he wandered, keeping his head low in case anyone recognized him.

"Excuse me. You're Kane August, right?"

He pivoted to find a very attractive, very pregnant woman smiling up at him. "I might be."

She laughed. "Don't worry. I won't blow your cover. My name is Rebecca Simmons. I'm a friend of Mae's. And the Bellinis. Mae asked me to drag you over to our table so you wouldn't skulk around looking gorgeous and obvious."

Gorgeous and obvious? "I don't even know what that means, but thanks."

She looped her arm in his and started walking. "It means you kind of stand out in a crowd. Come meet my husband. Kane, this is George."

He shook hands with George and they sat at the table. George owned a car repair business and obviously couldn't care less about movie stars, while Rebecca worked as a preschool teacher. They'd been married for three years and were expecting their first baby in a couple of months.

"Excited about becoming parents?" he asked.

"Very," Rebecca said. "We've waited a while for this little miracle, so we can't wait until he makes his appearance."

George had his arm around Rebecca's shoulders. "He'll be the best Christmas present I've ever had, that's for sure."

They asked him a few perfunctory questions about the movie business, but obviously they weren't starstruck, which he appreciated. They mostly asked about where he was from, and they were way more interested in the ranch, which he was always happy to talk about. More people joined the table and he finally relaxed when he discovered that people here were just people, happy to get to know someone new, and if they did recognize him they didn't make a big deal out of it. The ones who knew his movies well told him how much they enjoyed them, and then the conversation moved on. No one bugged him for selfies or squealed when they met him. This was probably the most enjoyable large gathering he'd ever attended. Maybe he could finally let his guard down.

And when the bridal party was announced and everyone cheered, he did, too, grinning when Finn and Brenna had their first dance, followed by the bridesmaids and grooms-men. They all looked good out there.

Arms went around him and he nearly jumped, but then Mae slid around to his side. He instantly relaxed.

"What do you think?" she asked.

"I think you should direct movies. It went off without a single problem."

She laid her head against his arm. "Thanks. Though I have to give a lot of credit to Brenna and Finn. They really held it together, nobody panicked and everything went so smoothly. And all the vendors showed up on time and noth-ing was screwed up. It made my job look easy."

"I'm sure it's not as easy as you'd like me to think. Do you get a break now?"

She nodded. "For a bit. Dinner is next, and I just need to make sure the photographer and videographer stay on track, but they're pros and know what shots to get."

"Then come sit with us," Rebecca said. "You probably need a glass of wine."

"That does sound good."

"I'll get you one," Kane said. "I need a refill myself."

He started to walk away, but Mae stopped him. "You didn't ask what I wanted."

He grinned, bent and brushed his lips across hers, whispering, "I know what you want."

She sighed and swept her hand across his jaw. "Yeah, you do."

He grinned as he walked toward the bar.

"GIRL, YOU DIDN'T tell me things between the two of you were so hot."

Mae pulled her gaze from a disappearing Kane and back to Rebecca. "Didn't I?"

"You did not. Wow. Tell me everything."

Mae looked over at George, who was busy in conversation with someone else at the table, so she shrugged and said, "Not much to tell. We're just having fun. Hot fun."

"That's good. I mean, I understand you not wanting to get involved. His time here is temporary, and you're very much a free spirit these days. No entanglements, right?"

"Right. Exactly." She looked over at Kane, who was at the bar deep in conversation with someone he absolutely did not know at all. He wasn't obsessively clinging to her, nor was he pissed off that she hadn't stuck to his side when he didn't know anyone here. Instead, he'd made friends and seemed utterly at ease. Which in turn made her feel at ease.

This man constantly surprised her.

She got up and walked over to him, leaning in to speak to him in a low voice so as not to interrupt his conversation. "I have to go do some work things."

He reached for her hand, giving it a squeeze. "Go do your thing. I'll be around."

Yeah, just like that, she thought as she made sure dinner

went off without a hitch, and that all the appropriate photos were taken and Brenna and Finn had everything they needed. After everything ran smoothly, she could finally exhale.

"Hey," Brenna said to her after the cake-cutting photos were done. "It's time for you to take the rest of the night off and have some fun."

"I *am* having fun. Are you kidding? This is the best wedding I've ever been involved with. I'm so honored you let me take the reins on it."

"Okay, honey. I appreciate that, and yes, it is an awesome wedding. Everything is handled now, so you're officially off duty. As the bride I demand it."

Mae sighed. "You are a beautiful bride, too." Her silk organza gown with tiny, beaded sequins made Brenna look like a stunning, red-haired fairy princess.

"Aren't I, though?" Brenna winked and looped her arm in Mae's as they strolled across the barn. "Now. As your last official duty of the evening, you can help me find my husband."

"How does it feel saying that?"

Brenna gave her a curious look. "Saying what?"

"Husband."

"Oh. It feels . . . I don't know, Mae. It feels kind of awesome."

"Aww." Mae laid her hand on Brenna's arm. She'd been fighting back tears all day and wasn't about to start the waterworks now.

"Though, to be honest, the minute I moved in with Finn at the cabin we both said we felt like that was our forever. So, this? Just a formality to make it official."

Mae squeezed her arm. "And that's how it's done when you meet your soul mate."

"It sure is."

They found Finn sharing his own brand of distilled whiskey with the groomsmen. Kane had joined them.

"I still can't believe you make this," Kane said.

"I do."

"It's damn good, Finn."

Finn grinned. "Thanks. Remind me when I get back from my honeymoon and I'll give you a tour of the distillery."

"I'd like that."

"I hate to break up this guy gathering," Brenna said, walking into the midst of the guys to take Finn's hand. "But I need to dance with my husband."

"See ya, mates," Finn said, immediately tuning out everyone else to focus his attention on Brenna.

Just as it should be.

Everyone else wandered off, leaving her with Kane.

"Guess what?" she asked him.

"What?"

"I'm finished working for the night."

"I saw you running nonstop. Did you even eat?"

"Of course I did. The food was too spectacular to pass up."

"Yeah, it was." He took her hand in his and led her toward the dance floor. "I guess that means you're ready to dance with me."

"Oh, I'm ready to do a lot more than that, but we can start with a dance."

He pulled her into his arms and they glided across the floor. Dancing with him was as easy as everything else they'd done together. They fit, his body aligned with hers, his touch eliciting sensations, his eyes locking with hers. It was . . .

Perfect.

But only for now, she told herself. And just for fun. Because emotions and attachments could only lead to pain and hurt.

Honor and Owen danced over to them, Honor bumping against her. "Having fun?" she asked.

"I don't often get to dance at the weddings," Mae said. "Okay, never. So, yes, definitely having fun."

"I know, right?" Honor tilted her head back. "This is one of the best ones ever."

"Except for ours, of course," Owen said.

Honor winked at Mae, then laid her head against Owen. "Of course."

After the dance they started to make their way back to the table, but Brenna grabbed her arm and dragged them over to the bridal table. "Come sit with us."

"Oh, no. Your table is full."

"Please. I'm the bride. I get what I want and we'll make room."

In typical Brenna fashion, she asked people to shift, which meant her sisters and brothers-in-law and best friends, so of course everyone did. Mae shook her head, hating to disrupt the wedding party, but when Brenna had an idea, one should get the hell out of her way.

Everyone seemed good natured about it, and the meal was over anyway, so chairs and drinks were moved and extra chairs were brought in.

"People always do your bidding like this?" Kane asked Brenna.

Brenna shot Kane a smirk. "I wish. But they have to today and I'm taking every advantage."

Kane laughed and held out a chair for Mae to sit.

"I'll get us drinks," he said.

"Okay, thanks."

He disappeared and Mae noticed he was immediately waylaid by Owen, the two of them leaning on the bar carrying on an intense conversation. She figured it would be a while before she saw him again.

Honor leaned over to whisper in her ear. "The two of you together are so hot."

She sighed as she watched him tilt his head back and laugh at something Owen said. He'd discarded his suit coat, and she couldn't help but notice his shoulders, and his forearms, since he'd rolled up his sleeves. "He's hot, for sure."

"You're enjoying him."

She tore her gaze away to smile at Honor. "If by enjoying him you mean sex, then yes, I've indulged."

Honor let out a loud sigh. "Good for you. I'm a little jealous."

"Please. You have Owen, speaking of hot men."

Honor grinned. "This is true."

"You look beautiful, by the way."

"Thanks. Luckily my sister knows how to choose good dresses." She took a sip of something that was definitely nonalcoholic.

"Are you feeling all right?" Mae asked. "I noticed you haven't been drinking alcohol lately."

"Yes, I'm fine. And, no, I'm not pregnant."

Mae's eyes widened. "Oh, Honor, no. I wasn't . . . I wouldn't ever presume. I'm so sorry if you thought I was asking—"

Honor waved her hand. "It's okay."

"It's not okay. I only thought you might be sick. There's a virus going around and I thought you might have caught it."

"Which I did, and then it led to bronchitis, which sucked right before the wedding. So I'm on antibiotics and off alcohol for the time being."

"Ugh. I hope you're feeling all right."

"I feel fine now. And thanks for checking in."

But she had thought . . . "Honor, I am so sorry. I would never, ever ask something so intrusive. It's not my business what you choose to do with your life or your future. I hope you know that."

Honor reached out and touched her hand. "Of course I do. I'm just being sensitive." She took a sip of her drink. "My mother is being somewhat pushy in the baby department. The thing is, Owen and I aren't ready. Not right now. Or maybe not ever. We haven't decided yet. We're both very career focused and we're not sure that's the direction we're headed in."

"Hey, it's no one's business but yours and Owen's, and whatever you two decide, it'll be what makes you both happy, right?"

"Exactly. And thank you for noticing. And caring."

"Always, honey." She was happy that Honor was all right. Her friends meant everything to her, and the last thing she'd want to do was hurt their feelings. "And as far as mothers, well, I didn't have the best one, but yours? She's pretty stellar. And understanding. Maybe tell her how you feel and ask her to back off?"

Honor sighed. "You're probably right. Thanks."

Mae breathed a sigh of relief. She would never want to upset Honor. Hopefully, Honor would get things straightened out with her mother, and all would be well.

Kane and Owen came over to where they were seated. Kane placed a glass of wine in front of her, so she took a sip. Owen dragged Honor away to dance, and Mae watched them, realizing how happy the two of them were with each other.

Just each other.

"Sorry I was gone so long. Owen was telling me about his brewery. It's an amazing enterprise he has going."

"It sure is. You need to check it out."

"I'll do that. Or maybe you can take me."

"I can definitely do that." She kept her eye on Honor.

"Something on your mind?"

"Oh . . . just . . . nothing, really. Marriage. Family. Children. Or not."

He turned her in her chair to face him. "Nothing, huh? Care to expound on those nothings?"

"Just a conversation I had with Honor and a discussion about whether to have children."

"Ah. And what's your take on that?"

She frowned. "On what?"

"Kids? Yes or no?"

"Oh. Definitely yes. I love kids."

"Me, too. I want tons of them."

For some reason, that surprised her, though she had no idea why. Preconceived notions, probably. "Define tons."

He looked up, thinking. "I don't know. Three or four."

"You'd better get started. You're not getting any younger."

Now it was his turn to laugh. "Hey, I'm only thirty-two. I could have four by the time I'm forty."

"Uh . . . Does the future Mrs. August know she's going to be popping out four babies in less than ten years?"

"Huh. Okay, you have a point. Though there have been twins in my family."

"So, two at a time, then. How lovely for her."

"Hey. I plan to help."

"You won't be the one carrying or birthing them, bud. That's on your wife. Or girlfriend. Or whatever you have in mind."

"Actually, until we started this conversation, a wife and kids wasn't even on my mind."

"But now it is?"

He shrugged. "Maybe. As you mentioned, I'm not getting any younger."

"I know a lot of awesome single women. Want me to set you up with some?"

He picked up her hand, rubbing his thumb over it. "Trying to get rid of me?"

With the way her body reacted like a sizzling strike of lightning had hit her, just because he was rubbing her hand? Not a chance. "I can give you a few more days, but only because you seem so desperate."

"Appreciate that." He stood, pulling her up. "Slow song's playing and I want to feel you up close to me. How about a dance?"

"How could I say no? Lead the way."

She was in deep, deep trouble with Kane August. Because he said all the right things, he got her motor running in all the right ways and he made her feel like when it was time to walk away, it was going to be the most difficult thing ever. And she hadn't felt that way since the last time she loved someone.

That just couldn't happen.

CHAPTER
· · · · · ·
seventeen

KANE HAD TO fly to Los Angeles to do some quick re-shoots for the movie he'd completed prior to the one he was working on now in Oklahoma. He left before dawn, slept on the plane and landed early. A car was waiting for him to take him to the studio.

This wasn't the first time he'd had to do reshoots, and they could take either days or not much time at all. Since he'd worked with this team before, he knew they were quick and professional. He went into hair and makeup, got into costume and met with the cast he was shooting with. He hit all his marks and then they broke for lunch.

Since he didn't have a lot of time before he was due on set again, he decided to hit the studio's commissary. As he walked out of the production stage, he ran smack into—

"Everly." His eyes widened as he saw his leading lady for the current movie. More than his leading lady, Everly was one of his best friends.

"Kane!" She threw her arms around him and hugged him. "What are you doing here?"

"Reshoots."

"How long are you here for?"

"I'm just in for the day. We just broke for lunch."

"Same. Have lunch with me?"

"Sure. I was just heading for the commissary."

She wrinkled her nose. "Please. Walk across the street with me. I'm dying for a soup and salad."

Now *that* he had time for. "Sure."

They walked arm in arm across the street and were seated immediately at a table near the window. Their server came by and they ordered drinks and their meals. The one great thing about this place—besides the food—was the fast service, which was critical for an actor who had to be back on set.

"I'm really happy to see you," Everly said. "And I'm so sorry about delaying our shoot. I had no idea this was going to take so long."

"It's okay. We've shot around you on a few scenes with a stand-in. She actually lives on the property and has the same build and coloring as you."

"Outstanding. Still, I hope to be done here soon. Geoffrey is never happy with a scene and takes forever to call a shot right. You know how he is." She rolled her eyes.

"I do. But he's also an incredible director, so it's worth it."

"Thanks for your patience." She laid her hand on his arm. "I know it's tedious and irritating waiting on a co-star."

He laid his hand over hers. "You're worth waiting for."

She smiled. "You always say the right things."

Their server brought their drinks and food. Kane dug into his salad.

"How's Ethan?"

She looked around and leaned in. "Shh. No one knows

about us yet. Except you. And my parents. And my sister. And my best friend."

He snorted out a laugh. "Right. But no one else knows."

"Hey. You're in my trust circle. That says a lot. And he's a hot commodity. Plus, if it gets out about the two of us, the paparazzi will be staked out at my house."

"Photographers follow you around anyway. You being so gorgeous and perfect and all."

She took a stab at some lettuce and waved her fork at him. "And you have always been like my annoying big brother, ever since we starred in that juvenile TV show together."

"Love you, too, sis."

She laughed and they spent the rest of their lunch reminiscing about old times. The good times. The naïve times.

The one thing he loved about this business was that occasionally you made connections and friendships with people that would serve you for the rest of your life. Everly was one of those people. They'd started out in the biz together, had clung to each other when neither of them knew one end of a camera from the other. They'd gotten through some rough times together. They were family and always would be.

He valued his friendship with her. She'd been through a tough divorce, some awful relationships, and this new one she was in? Yeah, it was good for her. He knew Ethan, had worked with him on a couple of projects. He was a damn fine actor, and an even better person. Kane couldn't think of a nicer guy for Everly, and he understood why she wanted to keep this relationship a secret for as long as she could. Nothing could destroy a new relationship quicker than the media.

As her friend, he intended to help her keep that secret, no matter what.

CHAPTER

· · · · · ·

eighteen

M AE WAS UP to her eyeballs in to-do list items in their morning meeting when Erin nudged her.

"Did you see this?"

She looked up from her list. "See what?"

"Kane and some actress looking cozy and intimate together in a coffee shop in L.A."

Her heart lurched. She took Erin's phone, zooming in on the pic of Kane and Everly Sloane looking very cozy, their hands entwined. Her stomach lurched and she wanted to expand the pic, to search every plane and angle and nuance. But then she reminded herself that Kane wasn't hers, so she handed the phone back to Erin.

By then, everyone else had looked at the pic. Everyone but Brenna, anyway, since she was off on her honeymoon with Finn. At least that was one less person to see her embarrassed.

"No big deal," Mae said. "They work together a lot and they're friends."

"Of course," Erin said. "I'm sure it's nothing."

"Even if it is, it wouldn't matter. It's not like we're exclusive or anything."

"Still, it has to bother you, honey," Honor said. "He could have told you."

"But he probably didn't even know someone was taking their picture," she said, immediately realizing she was coming to his defense. Why would she defend him when it was obvious what was going on?

Her phone pinged and she picked it up to see a message from Kane.

Just saw the pic of Everly and me. We ran into each other at the studio and had lunch. Nothing happened. Can we talk about it?

She stared at the message, searching for clues to the real meaning of that photo and finding nothing.

"Is that from Kane?" Maureen asked, a look of concern on her face.

"Yes. He wants to talk about the photo."

"Is that good or bad?"

"I don't know. I guess we'll talk. But later." She laid her phone down. "Right now we have things to discuss, so let's get to it."

Fortunately, they all got back to the items on the agenda, and Mae's drama was forgotten, at least for now. After the meeting she went back to her office to deal with her to-do list items.

Honor poked her head in. "Hey. Are you all right?"

She nodded. "I'm fine."

Honor tilted her head.

"Okay, not totally fine. You know, I have a past with a man who wasn't honest with me, so I'm wondering if this is a repeat of that. Plus, the whole Hollywood angle."

"It's a valid concern," Honor said, stepping in to take a seat. "You have to be able to trust the guy you're with."

"Which is why I've never wanted a serious relationship with any man since I broke off my engagement to Isaac. I'm not about to put my heart out there again, only to have it trampled. Again."

"Noted." Honor shifted, laying her stuff down on the edge of Mae's desk. "But, honey. No one deserves love more than you. Eventually you're going to find someone who loves you back. Wholly. Completely. Honestly."

Not if she didn't let them.

"Maybe. We'll see." She tried to be nonchalant, but she still felt that sting.

Honor stood and gathered her things. "You know I'm always here if you want to talk."

"Thanks."

"And, Mae?"

"Yeah?"

"Don't judge prematurely. Kane, I mean. That photo could be nothing. You might want to give him the benefit of the doubt."

She gave a quick nod. "I will."

After Honor left, Mae dug into her list, checking off several of her top items before taking a break to go grab a glass of iced tea. When she got back, she intended to continue on with her list, but she glanced at her phone, realizing she'd never replied to Kane's text message.

She picked up the phone and sent a reply.

Let's talk tonight, if you're available.

She laid the phone down, figuring he was busy filming, but then he texted again.

I'm available anytime. Dinner at my trailer?

She thought about it for a few minutes, then replied: That works. See you around seven.

Now that that was done, she could get back to work.

It was after six when she finished up for the day. She had done a tour for prospective clients who seemed way more interested in the movie action beyond the vineyard, so keeping their focus on wedding planning had taken longer than she'd expected. But they loved the venue—of course—and said they'd have an answer for her by the end of the week. She went back to the main house and realized everyone had left for the day, including Maureen and Johnny. Louise told her they had gone out for dinner tonight, which meant Louise and her husband, Marcus, also had the night off, though Louise offered to make her something for dinner. Mae declined with thanks and dashed upstairs to her room to change clothes.

The temperature had dropped throughout the day, and the forecast called for rain, so she washed up, fixed her makeup and changed into leggings and a long-sleeved shirt, then added her ankle boots. She finished the look off with one of her long silver chains, brushed her hair and went downstairs. She grabbed her keys and her phone and headed toward the trailers. It was dark, but the path was well lit so she had no trouble finding her way.

She'd noticed throughout the shoot that most of the production staff and actors left the site to go out for dinner. She couldn't blame them for that, plus there were some awesome places to eat in the city and a lot of fun things to do.

The lights were all on at Kane's trailer, so she went up the steps and knocked. He opened the door and smiled down at her. "Come on in."

"Thanks." She entered, immediately assailed by something that smelled amazing. She laid her phone and keys down on the table by the door and followed him farther into the trailer, realizing he hadn't had something delivered but had stuff going on his stove.

"You're cooking."

He nodded and smiled. "Well, yeah. I invited you here for dinner. Wine?"

"Yes, please. And I just figured you'd have food delivered."

"Nah. I get tired of restaurant food and I like to experiment." He poured a glass and handed it to her.

"Thanks. So what are you fixing?"

"Chicken piccata with rice and asparagus."

Her stomach shouted for joy. Rather loudly, in fact. "That sounds delicious. What can I do to help?"

"Uh . . ." He looked around. "You can slice and season the asparagus and put it in the oven for me."

"I can do that." She washed her hands, then rolled up her sleeves and got to work on the asparagus.

It wasn't a huge kitchen, but roomy enough that she could work side by side with Kane. It also gave her the opportunity to watch Kane work. He seemed comfortable and confident as he cooked the chicken and worked with the other ingredients.

"You like cooking?" she asked.

He nodded. "It relaxes me. Plus, I can fix food the way I like it."

"Same. I mean, don't get me wrong, I love a good restaurant meal, but there's something about creating something yourself."

"Exactly. And I like making up my own recipes. Trying new things. Though sometimes I fail."

He laughed after he said that, and she appreciated that he didn't take himself too seriously.

Once the oven was at the right temperature, Mae slid the asparagus in and set a timer on her phone. Kane had put a lid on the chicken, so they took a seat in the living area. She sipped her wine, taking in how sexy he looked in jeans and a long-sleeved shirt, the sleeves pushed up to his elbows.

The man had very fine forearms. What was it about a man's muscular forearms that could make a woman swoon? Not that Mae ever swooned, but those forearms made her heart rate tick up. She breathed out a contented sigh.

"How was your day?" he asked.

"It was good. Hectic, but good. Yours?"

"Fine. Finished off a couple of scenes with some of our other actors, so those can actually be finalized since they didn't require Everly. And before we get any further, Everly was doing her reshoots at the studio and we ran into each other. So we had lunch. That's all it was. All it could ever be, really. We're just friends, Mae."

"Okay."

He laid his glass down on the table and shifted to face her. "I know you have no reason to believe me—or trust me—but I'll tell you right now I don't cheat. I've never cheated. When I'm seeing a woman, I'm only seeing that woman. No one else. I'm seeing you. No one else."

Whoa. That was some declaration, and now she did feel swoony. "I believe you."

"Good." He took her glass and set it on the table next to his, then pulled her into his arms and laid one hell of a kiss on her, the kind that made her feel hot and desired, the kind that made her want to slide her hand under his shirt to feel his skin against her palm.

But then her timer went off on her phone, pulling them apart. And then a timer beeped on his, too.

"We'll continue this after dinner," he said.

She smoothed her hand across his chest. "Definitely."

They got everything ready and served from the stove.

"Sorry it's not fancy," Kane said. "But I don't have a big table or a lot of dishes."

She tilted her head back and smiled at him. "I like that it's not fancy. This is good for me."

"You're good for me," he said, leaning down to brush his lips across hers.

If he kept doing that, she was going to jump him and then she'd miss out on this great dinner. Plus, she was really hungry.

They took their plates and drinks to the table and dug in. The chicken was flavorful and perfectly cooked. The rice was tender and the asparagus turned out awesome.

"This is so good," she said, trying not to speak with her mouth full, but she couldn't help herself. She was hungry and the food was delicious.

"It is. Thanks for helping."

"I didn't do much, but I'm happy to help you cook anytime."

"Hey, if this gets you in my trailer, I'll do this every night."

She took a sip of her wine and shot him a look. "Oh, you're smooth."

His lips curved. "I try."

"When did you learn to cook?"

"On the ranch. First, steaks and potatoes, then sides. My aunt's wife lives there and is an excellent cook, so whenever I wasn't outside working with the horses or at one of the barns, she put me to work in the kitchen. I learned a lot from her. When I got out on my own I experimented with other foods. I started traveling a lot for work, so I got tired of eating out all the time. I liked being able to cook the foods I wanted to eat."

"That makes sense. Plus, you have this nice trailer, which I'm sure helps you feel more at home."

He shrugged. "It's okay. Not like a big sprawling ranch, but as far as on-location living, it gets the job done."

"Don't they put you up at a hotel?"

"They would if I wanted that, but this is easier. I tend to have early calls, and driving back and forth from the hotel to location is a giant pain in the ass. Plus, hotels have a lot of people."

"Ah." She took a drink of her wine. "Which means a greater chance of being recognized."

"Yeah. Not that I mind fans. I don't. But sometimes . . ."

"You just want to be left alone?"

He nodded. "Especially when I'm working. So when they chose this location, with it being nicely remote, I knew the trailer would be ideal."

She looked around. Even though she'd stepped in here before, she noted again how spacious it was. More like an RV and definitely livable. "I've lived in apartments smaller than this."

He laughed. "Me, too. When I first started out in Hollywood? I shared a six-hundred-square-foot apartment with two other people—along with several roaches. And I could still barely afford it."

Mae grimaced at the thought of the lack of space. The bugs would be a deal-breaker for her, but hey, sometimes it was necessary for survival. "That does not sound ideal."

"It wasn't, but we all worked a couple of jobs along with going out on auditions, so it wasn't like we spent a lot of time there. Just to crash and shower, you know?"

She did know. "My mom and I lived in some tight quarters here and there after my dad died. I was too young to get a job, so she was the one responsible for making ends meet."

"I'm sure that was tough."

"It was, but we made do. And I got a job as soon as I turned sixteen, so I could help with rent."

"Not easy when you're trying to juggle school."

She shrugged. "We all do what we have to do, right?"

"That's true. But look at you now. Independent, doing what you love. That's the dream, right?"

"It is. Same for you, right?"

He finished off his wine and laid the empty glass down. "Yeah. Sure."

He didn't seem as enthused about his career as she thought he'd be. But it wasn't her place to ask.

They took the dishes to the sink, washed and dried them along with the pots and pans. Kane put everything away while Mae cleaned the table.

"Feel like a walk?" he asked.

She rubbed her very full stomach. "That sounds good."

They grabbed their jackets and put them on, then stepped outside.

"Can you smell it?" she asked as she led him to her favorite walking path, away from all the trailers and toward the trees.

"Smell what?"

"The rain. It's right there, lingering in the clouds, filling up and just waiting to burst."

He took her hand and held it in his. "Interesting take."

They entered the woodsy area, a path she'd taken countless times before. "You're not buying it?"

"No, that's not it at all. I can smell it, too. I just always go by the animals. They're restless. Some can sense an upcoming storm well before we can. They'll huddle and find shelter under the trees. I think they sense the change in atmospheric pressure. So we watch them for clues to the weather."

"I see. I guess I'm not as sophisticated as animals. I just smell the rain when it's close. But now I'll keep an eye on the horses at the Bellinis' place or at Clay and Alice's ranch."

He laughed. "I can show you what I mean."

She stopped and turned to face him. "How?"

"Thanksgiving is coming up, which means the production will break for the week. I plan to head to the ranch."

The thought of him leaving made her stomach clench. "Oh. Of course you will. You'll want to be with family."

"Right. How about you come with me?"

She was so taken aback she was momentarily speechless. And she was rarely, if ever, without words. Finally, she swallowed. "You want me to go to your ranch?"

"Well, yeah. And that would be with me. I mean, I'd be there, too. Just in case that wasn't clear."

"I think I was clear on that part. Thank you, Kane. I appreciate the invitation."

He cocked his head to the side. "You have other plans."

"No, actually, I have no plans. I mean, of course the Bellinis invite me to their Thanksgiving every year. But otherwise, no."

"Then will you come home with me for Thanksgiving?"

His words were so warm, so inviting. So terrifying with the thought of meeting his family.

She let the words tumble out before she changed her mind. "I'd love to."

He pulled her into his arms, moving her backward until she was pressed against the trunk of a thick tree. She looked up to see the canopy of limbs above her, the sky obliterated, encasing them in a hushed forest. Now all she focused on was the very hot man in front of her.

His lips met hers in a slow, delicious kiss that heated up in a hurry. She lifted on her toes to wrap her hand around the nape of his neck, drawing him closer. And when he pushed himself against her, it was exactly that closeness she needed.

Breathless with desire and anticipation, she palmed his cock, taking in the rough sound of his groan, the way he pushed against her hand while she fought to draw down the zipper of his jeans. He popped open the snaps of her coat, slid his hand inside and teased her nipples. Even through her shirt and bra, she felt the zing of erotic sensation, but oh, what she'd give to be naked out here, to feel the cold air and his warm hand on her skin.

She intended to touch him, but he got to her first, stroking his hand across her sex, finding all the right spots until she saw stars. Not the literal kind, but the ones that made her brain cells go *pow*. She gripped his arms, holding on so she wouldn't collapse as every sweet move of his fingers over her clit drove her closer and closer to orgasm.

Between his mouth and tongue and his ever-so-expert fingers, she was lost, suddenly struck by waves of climax that hit her like a bolt of lightning, making her feel out of control in the best way. She moaned against his lips as she rode it out, feeling the thunder with every beat of her heart.

It was only as she came to her senses that she realized the thunder was real, and the first pelts of rain had finally made it through the canopy of tree limbs. And then the skies opened and the rain came down in a heavy stream.

They ran like hell, Kane taking her hand to guide her out of the woods and back to the trailers. By the time they made it back inside his trailer, they were both soaked. Mae stood there, staring at Kane.

"Well," she said. "Normally I hate getting caught in a storm, but I have to say that was totally worth it."

He laughed, then shrugged out of his coat. "Hell yeah it

was. But we need to get out of these wet clothes. How about a hot shower?"

"Love that idea." She handed him her coat and kicked off her boots, silently bemoaning the suede that might never recover from her wet, muddy run. Still worth it, though.

For a trailer, it had a surprisingly roomy bathroom. Not exactly luxurious, but at least the two of them could stand in there together, though they occasionally bumped butts as they stripped off their clothes, which made both of them laugh. The funny thing was, she wasn't the least bit self-conscious around him. Being around Kane seemed normal. Natural. Which was totally weird, but she wasn't going to question it. He had already turned on the shower and they climbed in.

Between the hot water and Kane's body pressed against hers, her chilled body warmed quickly. She let the spray hit her in the face, then grabbed the bodywash to scrub off her makeup.

"Let me wash your back," Kane said.

She turned around and reveled in the feel of his soapy hands gliding over her skin. When he reached around to cup her breasts, his fingers lingering as he teased and plucked her nipples, she leaned back against him, letting arousal take over.

She pivoted to face him. "My turn." Filling her hands with soap, she stroked her fingers across his shoulders, his chest, down to his rock-hard abs. And lower.

Kane gasped, then groaned. "Oh, yeah. That's good."

She lifted her gaze to his as she wound her hands around his cock, pulling and pushing, making a fist so he could thrust. Her breath caught as she watched the pleasured expressions on his face, the way he reached out to touch her while she touched him. And when he came, she felt such a burst of desire for him it nearly undid her.

Kane pulled her to him and kissed her, a deep, soulful kiss that left her breathless.

The timing was good because the hot water had started to dissipate. They finished rinsing and got out. Kane handed her a towel and she dried her hair and body, then wrapped the towel around her, realizing all her clothes were wet. Okay, this was a dilemma.

Kane left the bathroom and came back with a T-shirt. "This should fit."

The shirt—with the logo of an action movie—was soft and well worn. She slipped it on and it fit like a nightgown. Awesome. She pulled his comb through her hair, then went out into the kitchen to find him dressed only in boxers while he brewed them some coffee that was—she checked—yes, it was, in fact, decaf. Perfect, because the last thing she needed was to stare at the ceiling all night. She had enough thoughts rolling through her head as it was, mostly about the total sex god standing next to her drinking coffee in his underwear.

"Do you have cream?" she asked.

He inclined his head toward the fridge. "Help yourself."

His refrigerator was neat and orderly. She'd bet some assistant did that for him. She grabbed the cream, poured a dollop into her coffee, then headed over to where Kane sat at the small table. She took a seat, pulling one leg up underneath her.

Kane was staring at his phone. "So according to the shooting schedule, we'll break the weekend before Thanksgiving, and resume the Monday after. How does that work for your schedule?"

She sipped the warm coffee, enjoying the robust flavor as she pondered the thought of spending a week alone with him.

Okay, maybe not totally alone, but alone enough. "I'll have weddings to handle the weekend before but I could be ready to go Monday? If that works for you."

"That's perfect. We'll drive because it's only about four hours, give or take, traffic-wise."

Alone in the car? Even better. "I like that."

"And you'll want to pack comfortable clothes. We're not fancy or anything at the ranch. Even on Thanksgiving. So . . . casual?"

She smiled at him over the rim of her coffee cup. "Do I look like I dress fancy all the time?"

"Well, not at the moment."

She snickered. "Hey, I'll have you know this is the latest in sexy lingerie."

He looked her over, his heated gaze raising her temperature a degree or two. "Hey, it's doing it for me."

"Is it, now?" She got up and went over to him, climbing onto his lap and sliding her hands over his chest. "I'm going to need you to be a little more specific."

He grasped her hips and lifted, his cock rubbing against her. "I think my dick being hard as stone should be your first clue."

"We should do something about that."

"Hell yeah we should." He moved his hands under her butt and stood.

She wrapped her legs around him while he walked them to the bedroom. He set her down on the bed, then climbed in, settling himself on top of her. His mouth met hers in a passionate tangle of lips and tongues. And then there were no words, just hands and mouths and bodies touching.

Somehow, they got naked, and his mouth touched her everywhere. Heated, wet kisses and sucks that drove her to the edge of madness. And everywhere she reached for him there was muscle. Hard, flexing muscle against all her soft parts, pressing against her. His push to her pull. A sensual dynamic. She rode that wave of pleasure, lifting against him as he thrust in perfect rhythm, taking her right to the edge, then over.

That he went with her only heightened the moment. She clutched him, drawing him closer, needing his lips on hers, that intimate contact as her climax burst like an exploding star.

Breathless, she stayed like that, with Kane's warm breath against her neck, feeling his body against hers, the two of them entwined, connected.

She could fall asleep like this. Except Kane was a big guy, and just a little heavy.

Fortunately, he recognized that and rolled over, stepping into the bathroom for a minute. When he came out he climbed into bed and pulled her against him.

"Now this is just right," she said, laying her head on his shoulder.

"I guess you need to stay here tonight," he said. "Since your clothes are all wet."

"It's a hardship, but I'll manage."

She could get used to lying here next to him, to hearing his rhythmic breaths as she closed her eyes and drifted off to sleep, listening to the storm outside.

CHAPTER

· · · · · ·

nineteen

KANE WAS SURPRISED that Mae was up before him, which was before dawn since he had an early call. He figured she wanted to sneak back into the house before anyone else got up. Since her clothes were still wet and he didn't have a dryer, he drove her back to the house wearing his T-shirt and a pair of his shorts, her damp clothes wrapped up in a plastic bag. He kissed her in the car, then lingered, watching her walk up the stairs and into the still-dark house. He knew he'd see her later since she was filming scenes with him today.

He drove back to the trailer, got dressed, and headed outside, taking in the cold morning air as he made his way straight to hair and makeup. Someone brought him coffee and a breakfast sandwich and he ate while they prepped him for his first scene. This was when he could read news and emails on his phone and relax before the day got started.

Mae showed up not too much later, dressed a lot differently than she had been when he'd dropped her off. He caught a whiff of her freshly showered scent as she walked by and smiled benignly at him.

"Morning," she said.

"Hey, good morning. Sleep well?"

She blinked. "Yes, I slept great. How about you?"

"I was worn out. I slept like the dead."

He caught the smirk on the makeup artist's face in the mirror, so he knew whatever they were doing wasn't some big secret. Not that he cared, but Mae might.

After hair, makeup and costume, they headed into the barn. It was only half set up because it was just him and Mae today. It was the scene of the night before the wedding, and the decorators got the ambiance down perfectly. Mae looked beautiful in a silver dress that clung to her curves.

She looked down at the dress. "This thing is stunning. I wish I was actually going somewhere in it."

"I'd like to take you somewhere in it."

She smoothed her hand down his suit, making his heart rate kick up like it did every time she touched him. "You look fancy. I could definitely take you out in public."

He laughed. "Good to know."

"Okay, you two." Alexis had walked onto the set. "You ready to nail this scene?"

Mae nodded and Kane smiled at his director. "You got it."

He turned to Mae. "How about a fancy dinner tonight? You open?"

"I'm definitely open."

The way she looked at him made him forget where they were, that there were other actors getting into position for the scene. Time to clear his head and get through this. Then, tonight, he could have Mae to himself.

That thought sustained him as they worked through multiple takes of the barn scene. For some reason Alexis wasn't satisfied, and he knew damn well it wasn't him. And it couldn't be Mae, because her movement and timing had been impeccable, so it must have been the background players. Then again, sometimes Alexis just got into a mood and it was hard to satisfy her. He'd worked with her enough to know you just had to go with it until she was happy with a take.

It took almost until two before they finished that scene. Kane was never happier to take a break.

He walked with Mae back to the costuming trailer.

"What do you have up next?" she asked.

"Just a quick scene where I'm talking on the phone. It shouldn't take long."

"That's good."

"How about you?" he asked. "What does the rest of your day look like?"

"Busy. I have work to catch up on." They walked up the steps of the trailer together, and the costumers immediately separated them so they could remove the clothing. When she came out, he was waiting for her and they exited the trailer together.

"You didn't have to wait," she said.

"How was I going to see you again if I didn't wait for you?"

She laughed, then looked around before rising up to brush a kiss to his lips. "Text me about dinner."

"I'll do that."

She disappeared along the path, and he pivoted to head toward the next scene, which fortunately didn't take long. Apparently whatever mood Alexis had been in earlier had dissipated. When she called cut, the crew dispersed. He went over to Alexis.

"How's everything going?" he asked.

She looked up from the script. "What? Oh, fine."

"You seemed bugged about this morning's scene."

She frowned. "Did I? I thought it went fine."

"Really. You asked for multiple takes, so there was obviously something wrong with it."

"Oh, that. The lighting just wasn't right. And this would be a whole lot easier to film if Everly was here. Then we could get multiple camera angles in on one shot. Not having her here is going to cause delays, and delays cost money, and I've already got producers breathing down my neck."

He watched the way she paced while she talked. There was probably a lot more going on that he wasn't privy to. "I'm sorry. That's a lot of pressure on you."

"Which isn't something you need to be concerned about. It's all going beautifully and we got lucky that Mae and Everly are practically twins—at least from behind. That fact has already saved time and money."

"Everly said she shouldn't be too much longer."

"That's what her agent told me. Let's hope that's true. Once she gets here, we can really get rolling."

"Okay, I'll let you get back to work."

He started to walk away.

"Kane?"

"Yeah?"

Her smile was angelic. "Thanks for checking on me."

He grinned. "Always."

He went back to his trailer, changed into sweats and a T-shirt, got in his car and went to the gym so he could do a hard workout. It felt great to build up a sweat. Taking a morning run, working with the hand weights and doing pushups in his trailer just wasn't cutting it for him. He needed to go through the entire cycle his trainer had set out for him just to keep him in the barest minimum of decent shape, especially when he was filming. Thankfully he wasn't going to be shirtless in this film, which would give him a break, but he still felt a lot better if he could get a full-body workout in.

He was in the middle of a bench press set when a pretty set of green eyes peeked over the bar.

"Um, excuse me, but aren't you Kane August?"

He racked the bar and sat up, taking in some deep breaths as he looked at the young woman, huddled close to her friend. "I am. What's your name?"

"Oh. I'm Karie. And this is my friend Alina. I was wondering, if it's not too much bother, if we could get a selfie with you?"

He was sweaty and disgusting, but if they could handle it, so could he. "Sure."

They clicked a couple of pics, thanked him and were on their way. Fortunately, no one else came up to him, so he could finish his workout. As he did his wind-down on the stationary bike, he scanned the exterior through the floor-to-ceiling windows, watching people come from and go into the various businesses and restaurants. He snapped back when he thought he saw someone with a camera lurking behind one of the pillars of a nearby building. But when he looked again, no one was there.

It was probably just his imagination, sparked by the two women who'd asked for a selfie.

Paranoid much, dude?

So far he'd been lucky here. He knew some people had recognized him, and it was a well-known fact that he was in the area filming, but the production had done an excellent job keeping the paparazzi away from the shoot. No one got on the production site without passing through security.

He got in his car and drove back to his trailer, took a shower, then searched online for a fun place to have dinner tonight. He found a few and texted Mae to ask which one she'd like best.

She replied right away and told him to choose, that all of them were good. He picked one that sounded the best to him and made a reservation, let Mae know what time he'd pick her up, then settled in to answer a few emails. There was one from his agent, who had a few prospective projects lined up for him and wanted him to look over some scripts.

Normally the idea of a new project would excite him, but for some reason he didn't feel that spark and wondered why.

Maybe it was because he'd done the last three films back to back to back, and he needed some downtime. That had to be it. After this film wrapped he'd take a nice, long vacation, decompress, and then he'd be ready to take on a new project. He replied to his agent that they'd talk after the holiday season. That would give him time to decide if that was what he really wanted to do.

By the time he put away his work for the day, it was time to get ready for dinner. His pulse quickened at the thought of seeing Mae again. He changed into dark jeans and a white button-down shirt, slid into his boots, then grabbed a jacket and got into his car to drive over to the main house.

He walked up to the porch and rang the doorbell, surprised when the door was answered by Johnny Bellini. He'd met the Bellinis his first day on set, when Johnny and Maureen had greeted the cast and crew with some homemade pasta and bottles of wine. They'd made everyone feel welcome.

"Kane. It's good to see you again."

"You, too, Johnny."

They shook hands and Johnny invited him inside.

"Mae, she's not ready yet. Come inside, I have basketball on the TV."

"Sounds good, thanks."

He followed Johnny back to the main living room. It felt like home here, warm and comfortable.

"Where's Maureen?" he asked.

"She went to dinner and out shopping with some friends. I get a nice quiet evening by myself to watch my sports and no arguing over the TV shows."

He laughed. "Sounds ideal."

"You want a beer? Some wine?"

Kane shook his head. "I'm good, thanks."

"So," Johnny said, keeping his attention on the game. "You're dating our Mae, huh?"

Uh-oh. "Yeah. She's an amazing woman and I enjoy spending time with her."

"Hmm." Johnny ate a chip.

"You have concerns?"

Johnny leveled a look at him. "She had her heart broken before. Real bad. I don't want that to happen to her again."

Whoa. Okay, that was definitely fatherly protectiveness. And even though Johnny wasn't Mae's dad, he'd obviously taken it upon himself to be her protector. Kane liked that. "I have no intention of hurting her."

Johnny nodded. "Good."

"Hey, did I lose my dinner date to the basketball game?"

He got up and turned around. Mae stood in the doorway dressed in a wow, knock-him-on-his-ass black dress that showed off a lot of her gorgeous legs.

"Wow. You look beautiful."

She graced him with a stunning smile. "Thanks. So do you."

"Kane's right," Johnny said. "You look pretty. Now, go. Have fun."

"Thanks," Kane said. "You have a good night, too."

He walked over to Mae and they headed outside. When he held the car door for her, he inhaled her sweet, lemony scent. "You smell good, too."

She reached for him, swiping her hand across his jaw. "Keep up that sweet talk and we'll never make it to dinner."

"I do know how to order in, ya know."

She laughed. "Get in the car and drive."

He'd already programmed the GPS for the location of the restaurant, so he started driving.

"How did the rest of filming go today?" Mae asked.

"Much easier than the earlier scene. Then I went to the gym and did a hard workout."

"I'll bet that felt good."

"It did. Oh, and I got an email from my agent about upcoming projects."

"Is that right? Anything good?"

"I don't know. I didn't look at any of his suggestions. I told him we'd regroup after the holiday season. I'm . . . busy right now."

She was silent for a few minutes, then said, "Why do I get the feeling there's more to it than just you being . . . busy right now?"

She was right, but since he couldn't put his finger on why he'd hesitated on jumping on potential new projects, he couldn't explain it. Not to Mae. Not to himself, either. Which was why it was the right call to back-burner it for now.

"Honestly? I don't know. I've worked a lot over the past couple of years. I want some time to think about what's next, and I'm not in the mood right now, if that makes sense."

"Fair enough."

He liked that she didn't push him to talk about something when he wasn't ready. He'd dated women before who were only interested in his career, in his celebrity. What was next for him. What exciting projects he had down the line. What famous people he knew. Mae didn't seem the least bit interested in that, but treated his work like his job. She asked him about his day, and if he wanted to talk about it, great. If he didn't, that was fine, too.

It was so . . . normal.

He drove them to Redrock Canyon Grill, a restaurant that sat right on the edge of a nice lake. Even though it was dark, it was a clear night and the moon lit up the water.

"I'll bet sunsets here are amazing in the summer," he said as they made their way inside.

"They're pretty spectacular. Maybe you'll come by sometime if you have free time in the summer and we can eat here, watch the sun go down."

Something about her being so nonchalant about him not being around past the movie shoot made his stomach tighten. "Yeah, maybe I'll do that."

The hostess seated them in a spot next to the windows. Their server showed up right away to take their drink orders.

"Bottle of wine?" he asked.

"You know, I think I'll have an Aperol spritz instead."

He ordered beer and then perused the menu, which looked outstanding, mostly because it had several types of steak.

"What looks good to you?" he asked.

"I'm pondering the chicken or the pork chop. How about you?"

"Either the ribs or the ribeye. Or maybe the filet. They all look good."

She gave him a half smile. "You're such a red meat guy."

Their server brought their drinks, so he had to wait to respond. When he did, he said, "Hey, I like seafood, too. And salad. That has meat in it."

She took a sip of her drink. "Nothing wrong with red meat. I'm a fan. Just not every day."

"It's hard to grow up in Texas, around all the cattle ranches, and not be a red meat guy."

"I suppose that's true. Though I don't know if I could be around those sweet cows every day, knowing they're going to be slaughtered for someone's dinner."

"And yet you eat meat."

"I know. It's an ethical dilemma that I struggle with."

"Agree. There are arguments to both sides." He took a drink of beer, then said, "For example, the potential negative effect on the planet from animal emissions. Ethical treatment of animals. On the other side, potential animal overpopulation and its effect on the ecosystem. Producing an overabundance of vegetables can potentially cause the same environmental problems as meat production."

She blinked. "Wow. You've thought about this."

"I wrote a paper on it in college."

"No kidding. I'd like to read that."

He laughed. "No, really, you wouldn't. It's long and dry and boring."

She lifted her glass, took a sip, her gaze never leaving his. "Do I look bored?"

"You look beautiful." He reached over and slid his knuckles lightly across her cheek. "I want to kiss you."

"Hmm. I'll have to think about all the reasons you should. Or shouldn't. Maybe you could write me a paper about it."

"Funny."

Their server returned to take their food order, and promptly disappeared. He liked servers that didn't linger or make small talk. And he really liked this table in the corner where they had the nice view.

The food was outstanding. It didn't escape his notice that he and Mae never ran out of things to talk about, whether it was something philosophical like the ethics of eating meat or something simple like favorite books or movies. They had even discussed the games they'd played as kids. And with every conversation, he found out new things about her. The more he found out, the more he liked.

After he paid the bill they put on their coats and headed outside. He unlocked the car, but before he opened her door he pushed her against the car, wrapped his arms around her and did what he'd thought about doing during dinner. He kissed her—a long, hot kiss. She slid her hand around his neck, lifting up on her toes to press her body closer.

He heard the familiar click of a camera, then another, then another. Immediately jerking back, he cursed under his breath, spotting the photographers he hadn't even noticed were there when they'd walked out of the restaurant. Hell, for all he knew they'd been inside the restaurant. But now the damage had been done and they'd gotten the shots.

"What's going on?" she asked.

"Paparazzi. Let's go." He tucked her inside the car, angry that he'd let his guard down. He'd been here before, that moment when he was out in public and he was suddenly surrounded by photographers. It was part of his job and he lived with it. But it wasn't part of Mae's life and he felt bad that she was being sucked into it.

He slid into the seat and started the car, getting out of there as fast he could.

"Somehow I get the idea you're pissed off about what just happened," she said. "Isn't this something that happens to you, given your occupation?"

"I didn't see it coming. I should have."

"I didn't see them, either."

"Not your job. It is part of mine. I let my guard down

because they haven't been hovering lately. I should have known better. Now a photo of us kissing will be plastered all over the gossip sites."

"Oh." She shifted in her seat and stared out the windshield. "That is a problem."

He spared her a quick glance. "I'm sorry, Mae. I would have never dragged you into this, exposed you like this—"

"Wait. You're worried about me?"

"Hell yes, I'm worried about you. I'm used to this bullshit. But you—"

"Can take care of myself, thank you."

He dragged a hand through his hair. "Mae, you don't know what kind of ruckus one picture can cause, the amount of negative press."

She laughed. "You sure think highly of yourself."

She didn't get it. She would, though, and she'd blame him. Rightly so. "I'm sorry. All I can say is I'm sorry."

"Look. Am I into this whole celebrity thing? Absolutely not. You're just a person, and having people follow you just to take your picture and invade your personal life is ludicrous. But I knew going in that this was a possibility. I've accepted it. And, like I said, I can take care of myself."

They drove the rest of the way in silence. She was already angry with him, which would only get worse. He figured he might as well support her level of irritation.

He pulled up in front of the house and went around to open her car door. She slid out and turned to face him, placing her palms on his chest.

"Kane, listen. I'm a strong, independent woman who is perfectly capable of making her own decisions."

"I'm aware of that. But, if you'll allow, this isn't something you've been through before and I was trying my best to shield you from the effects of my . . . my . . ."

She arched a brow. "Epic stardom?"

He scratched the side of his nose. "Not the words I'd choose. I just want to prepare you for what's coming."

"I can take it. And I'm sorry if you think I'm some kind of emotional wreck who's going to crumple because a picture of us is going to show up on the gossip sites tomorrow. No one even knows who I am. Unless . . . you think it's because I'm a nobody and your legions of admirers will wonder what the hell you're doing with me."

He frowned. "What? No. I never said that."

"You implied. Good night, Kane."

"Mae, come on."

"Good night."

Before he could argue further, she turned and walked up the porch steps, disappeared inside and turned off the porch light.

Well, hell. That was a pretty definite Go the Fuck Away. So he got into his car and drove back over to the production site. He went inside, stripped out of his clothes, slid into sweats and grabbed a beer from the fridge, plopped down on the sofa and grabbed his phone, scrolling through the gossip sites to see if any pics had hit yet.

Not yet.

But they would, and as angry as Mae was tonight, it was only going to get worse.

CHAPTER

. . . . . .

twenty

IT HAD BEEN two days of nonstop stalking by photographers. The phones were ringing off the hook, everyone was showing up here and Mae wanted nothing more than to go back to her apartment and hide, possibly for the rest of her life. She was appalled by all the attention one ridiculous photo of Kane and her kissing had caused. Now she had to sit in a meeting with the entire Bellini family, and she was certain this wasn't going to be good.

She should have known better than to get involved with a popular actor.

Nothing good ever came from dating men. They were just a catastrophe in the making.

Gathering up her notebook, pen and laptop, she made the slow walk to the meeting, hoping like hell that they weren't going to fire her.

Of course they were all there, staring at her as she made her way to her spot at the table. She decided the best defense would be a good offense. She laid her stuff down on the table and addressed the family.

"I'm so sorry about all of this. I'm going to do whatever I can to fix it."

Erin frowned. "Fix . . . Mae, you do realize this is all good for our business, right?"

Mae didn't understand. "Good for business? How?"

"I know you've been buried in your office the past couple of days," Honor said. "But the phone's been ringing ever since the gossip sites printed those photos of Kane and you."

"Yeah, I know. I'm sorry."

"No, you don't get it," Brenna said. "We've booked wine tastings and vineyard tours for the next several months."

Honor nodded. "And I've scheduled twelve prospective bridal couple tours, plus interest from several more. I know there's a possibility someone wants to come and gawk at Kane August, but some of the more legit media publications also grabbed the story and featured Bellini Weddings in their articles, including that the wedding venue and vineyard will be featured in his upcoming movie. Thanks to you and Kane, we're suddenly extremely popular."

Mae could only gape at them while simultaneously trying to absorb everything they were saying to her.

"So this is a good thing?"

"Yes, my dear," Maureen said, beaming a smile. "It's all good."

She finally exhaled. "Okay, then. Thanks." She finally sat, prepared to go on with the meeting, relieved that nightmare was finally over. She opened her folder to grab her notes.

"So, when are you seeing Kane again?" Honor asked.

Her head shot up. "What?"

"Seeing Kane. You like him, right?"

At the moment she was ambivalent, especially since he'd implied she wouldn't be able to handle the press attention. Though, if she were honest with herself, she hadn't been handling it all that well, so maybe he had been right. Not that she'd admit that to Kane.

"He's okay."

"That photo of the kiss makes me think he's more than okay," Erin said with a knowing smirk.

"Okay, fine. He's a great kisser. Well practiced, I'm sure, from years of movie kissing experience."

"I don't know," Brenna said. "I've seen movie kisses, and I've personally experienced real-life kisses. That didn't seem like a movie kiss to me."

Mae shrugged. "I wouldn't know. They all seem the same to me."

Maureen was giving her that mom look. "Did you two have a fight?"

Mae didn't answer.

"Mae. Did you two have a fight?"

She knew Maureen wouldn't let it go. "We might have had a slight disagreement. He warned me that the paparazzi could be intense and I might not be able to handle it. I took offense."

"Have you spoken to him since that slight disagreement?"

She shook her head.

"I'm sorry," Honor said. "This whole situation must be very hard for you."

She blew out a breath. "Yeah, it has been. I've never known anyone like him. He's nothing like the usual men I date."

"Is that a good or a bad thing?" Brenna asked.

Mae let out a short laugh. "I'm not sure yet."

"Would it help if you talked to him?" Maureen asked.

"Probably. I at least owe him an apology for going off on him like I did. He was right, after all. All he did was try to prepare me for the onslaught, and I got all self-righteous."

"It's hard to admit when we're wrong," Erin said. "Not that I'm ever wrong. It's just what I've heard."

Mae laughed. "Right. I understand."

"I'm sure he'll forgive you," Honor said. "You just have to talk to him."

"I'll do that."

"Okay, then," Maureen said. "How about we start the meeting?"

Grateful for a reprieve, Mae presented her agenda items and they discussed the massive influx of appointments and tours and how those would be handled. She was due for filming two days this week, which meant she was going to have to see Kane whether she wanted to or not.

The thing was, she wanted to. She wanted to clear the air between them, to tell him she was sorry.

After the meeting she went back to her office, stared at her phone, picked it up a few times, even started a text message to Kane, then deleted it. Once. Twice. Three times. Then, disgusted with herself, she shoved her phone in the drawer and focused on work.

She successfully avoided her phone for a few hours until it pinged multiple times, reminding her of its existence. She pulled it out of the drawer and read the messages, all from Kane.

> Hey. I hope you're not still angry. I'm sorry for what I said. Can I see you? Can we talk? I'd really like to see you.

Her heart tumbled at Kane's messages. She clutched her phone to her chest, feeling relieved. Guilty. Happy. Guilty.

She should have texted him right away. She should have been the one to apologize, not him.

She quickly typed a reply: I'd love to see you. She shook her head. No, too mushy. She tried again with: Yes, let's meet. When and where?

That was much better. She sent that one.

He responded right away: I'll pick you up. About seven?

She replied in the affirmative, then sat back in her chair, exhaling a breath of relief.

Okay. Now she could fix things.

KANE FELT A tightening in his gut as he drove his new rental car to the house. A not-all-that-fancy truck this time, because everyone in this state seemed to drive one and he figured maybe he could blend in more.

He planned to lead with that when they spoke. It was important that he let Mae know that he intended to protect her as much as he was able to. The press could be invasive as hell. They thought because you made movies or music or TV shows or were in the public eye in some way, that gave the public the right to know every damn thing about your private life.

They were wrong.

When he was alone, or at a premiere or other event, he played the game, smiled for the press and allowed his picture to be taken. No problem. But out here trying to lead a normal life? They had no business in that life. Which was why he tried to hide out as much as possible.

Now that they'd discovered him on this location shoot? Now that they'd gotten photos of him with Mae? It irked him and made him regret choosing this life.

Sometimes the money just wasn't worth it.

He'd already talked to his agent and his publicist, but

there was only so much spin they could put on a photo of him pressing Mae against the car and kissing the hell out of her.

It was a hot picture, for sure. Video, too. He couldn't craft a scene as smoking as that one by the car. Too bad the press had no business prying into what should have been a private moment.

He could only hope that Mae would forgive him.

She was out the door before he got out of the truck. He hurried around to open the door for her.

"Hi," she said, giving him a smile wide enough that he was encouraged by it.

"Hi yourself. You look amazing."

"Just leggings and a shirt, Kane."

"Yeah, but they're on you."

Her smile got wider. He helped her up into the truck and went around to his side and climbed in.

"New vehicle?"

"Yeah. I had them switch out the rental. Maybe a truck will slow down the photographers."

"Hmm. Maybe."

He'd thought about taking her to a restaurant somewhere in the city, but then he had a different idea, one that would afford them some privacy. He'd asked one of the staffers to book the reservation, prepay and grab the key, so it wasn't even in his name. The hotel wasn't crap and it wasn't super high-end. It was what he'd call above average and not somewhere you'd expect a movie star to stay. He pulled into the side parking lot and slid on his cowboy hat.

"You're taking me to a hotel?"

"I've heard the room service here is really good, and it'll give us some privacy to talk."

She shrugged. "Sounds good."

They went in the side door and down the hall to the room. He'd specifically asked for a fast-entry-and-exit location so he wouldn't run into people who might recognize him. Which meant no lengthy walks down a hallway or taking any elevators. They were four rooms down the hall from the side entry. He made a mental note to tell Paul he'd done an excellent job scouting out the perfect room, at least from a geographical perspective. Now he could only hope the room itself wasn't awful, because at the moment, he didn't think dazzling her with his charm was going to work.

He slid the key card in and pushed the door open, breathing a sigh of relief at a decent living area separated from the bedroom. There was a table and a couple of chairs, a sofa, a bar area with a sink, and it all looked bright and comfortable.

"This is nice," she said, placing her bag on the table and moving fully into the room. She peeked her head into the bedroom and surprised him by lingering there a few seconds before turning around. "Well, then. Let's talk."

"You want something to drink?" he asked, suddenly nervous to engage in what he was sure would be a difficult conversation.

"No, I'm good." She slid onto one side of the sofa, an unsaid invitation for him to sit on the other side, so he did.

"Mae, I'm sorry. I was out of line."

"No, actually, you weren't. You were trying to protect me. I overreacted, and for that, I'm sorry."

This wasn't at all the way he expected this to go. "You didn't overreact. You're perfectly capable of deciding for yourself how much you can handle. I thought I had hidden myself well and I was overconfident. When I heard the click of cameras, I freaked. I was pissed off, and my first thought was to get you the hell out of there before the paps could suss out every detail of your life and spread them across the gossip sites."

She tilted her head to the side. "That hasn't happened. The only thing they said was you have some hot new woman in your life and are you cheating on Everly."

"Yeah, I read that. And, again, there's nothing going on with Everly and me."

"I believe you. And they said I was hot. How could I complain about that?" She gave him a wry smile.

"Well, they were right on that point. But they're intrusive as hell and I'm still pissed about them following you around."

"They aren't following me around anymore. Your production company has increased security and the Bellinis have hired their own. Trust me, no one is getting anywhere on Bellini grounds unless they're getting married, doing a wine or wedding tour, or part of the movie production. And no cameras allowed other than cell phones. Even those aren't allowed during the tours. Plus, Honor is giving the wedding tours and Brenna does the vineyard, so I'm mostly in my office except for already scheduled weddings. Everything's fine, Kane."

He dragged his fingers through his hair. "Okay. And you're right. You do have it all under control."

"Of course I do. And so do you."

That was debatable. "Sure."

She scooted closer to him. "Kane. It's really okay. I'm sure this is something you're used to."

"Yeah. Typically it's just me, or me and other people who are in the business. They know what to expect. It's you I'm worried about."

She laid her hand on his thigh. "You have to stop worrying about me."

"Not possible."

She shifted, drawing one leg up on the sofa so she faced him. "Here's the deal. I'm not going to hide. And I don't think you should, either. I would also like to continue to hang out with you, if that's what you want."

This wasn't going at all like he expected it to. He'd figured he'd have to grovel a little, maybe a lot, because he really liked Mae. He planned to continue to see her, hiding out if they had to. Turned out that wasn't what she wanted at all.

Mae was so damn brave.

"It's definitely what I want."

"Good. Now that that's taken care of, let's check out the room service menu. I'm starving. And since we've got this awesome hotel room for the night, we're going to have a lot of sex."

Wow. He had to be careful or he was going to fall in love with this woman.

CHAPTER

· · · · · ·

twenty-one

M AE WAS FORTUNATE to be given the week of Thanks-giving off, even though they had a couple of bridal tours scheduled on Friday and a wedding scheduled the Saturday after the holiday. But the Bellinis had assured her they had things well in hand, and she hadn't taken any time off since she'd started working for them, so they practically pushed her out the door on Monday morning when Kane came to pick her up, this time in a silver SUV.

He put her suitcase in the back of the car and she climbed in.

"Yet another new vehicle?"

He grinned and slid on his sunglasses. "Gotta stay one step ahead of the paps, ya know. Plus, I thought this one would be more comfortable than the truck for the drive down to the ranch."

She figured it was more about her comfort than hiding from the media, but she wasn't about to complain about the extra legroom.

As they drove off the property, she searched for paparazzi but didn't see anyone lurking at the gates. Which didn't mean they weren't there, just that she hadn't spotted them. Kane was probably a lot better at this than she was, but he hadn't said anything, so she decided to let it go.

"Okay, so in the back within your reach are drinks and snacks, in case you're hungry or thirsty. Or we can stop. I had a couple of cups of coffee before I left, but we can stop if you need something."

"I had coffee as well. And Louise was up early as usual and packed us bacon-and-scrambled-egg burritos with peppers." She dug those out of her tote bag and unwrapped one, handing it to him along with a napkin. "They're best eaten warm."

"Oh, man. This smells so good." He took a huge bite and made a moaning sound. "Tastes even better than it smells."

That made her smile. She had a similar reaction to Louise's cooking. She unwrapped her burrito and ate it, trying not to make the same moaning sounds Kane had made.

Over the next several hours, she discovered that the snack bag had been more than adequately packed as well. There were chips and crackers, fruit, various cheeses, along with teas and juices and sodas. They'd stopped once for a bathroom break and to grab cups with ice, then breezed their way down the turnpike all the way into Texas. It was a beautiful, sunny day and for once the wind was blowing, and the farther south they traveled the warmer it got. She shrugged out of her sweater, leaving her wearing an off-the-shoulder T-shirt. Kane's gaze roamed over her bare shoulders, which made her laugh.

"You should focus on driving," she said.

"How can I when you're doing a striptease in the car?"

"Oh my God. I just took my sweater off."

"Yeah, but you have amazing shoulders and I want to kiss them."

The thought of his mouth on her skin never failed to make her shiver.

"You cold?" he asked. "I could turn on the heat."

"I'm good, thanks." It was nearly eighty degrees outside. Sure, it was November, but weather was unpredictable around these parts, which was why Mae was generally prepared with about three layers of clothes.

She kept watching for the landscape to change. It didn't, since Texas and Oklahoma were mostly the same. Flat, brown this time of year, with mostly bare trees. Not exactly exciting, though they did pass the occasional ranch so she got to check out cattle and horses, even a few sheep here and there.

"Bored?"

She pulled her attention from the window and put it on Kane. "No, not at all. Did you know the farther we get into the wilds of Texas, the more ranches and farms we pass?"

"Yes."

"I keep waiting for you to turn down one of these roads."

As if she'd willed it, he turned on his blinker and made a left turn down a dusty, unpaved road.

"Now you're just messing with me."

He laughed. "I'm really not. This is our road."

She sat up straight and stared through the windshield as Kane came up to an impressive-looking steel gate with the words *Double A Ranch* above it. Kane's phone buzzed. He picked it up, smiled, then replied to the text. The gate miraculously opened, as if the gates of heaven had just parted to welcome them.

"Someone knew we were here?" she asked.

He nodded. "Yup."

They drove through and Mae turned around to watch the gate close behind them.

Impressive.

"There must be cameras I missed."

"Yeah, they're in the trees. It's better to keep things like that hidden. Makes folks feel welcome. Then neighbors and local folk just beep their horn and Grandpa can let them in."

"Whereas other people . . . ?"

"Are given more scrutiny."

She blinked. "I had no idea that ranchers needed that level of security. Then again, I honestly know nothing of ranching."

"We house and train several thoroughbred racehorses," Kane said as he made the turn and pulled in front of what was a surprisingly impressive two-story home. "Some of these horses are worth a lot of money. We take our responsibility to protect these animals very seriously."

"I'm not going to see armed guards patrolling the stalls, am I?"

He laughed. "No, we don't go that far."

It was obvious he wasn't going to elaborate on just how far they did go in protecting the horses.

They got out of the SUV and Mae stretched, very happy to be standing. A woman who looked to be in her midfifties came out of the house and down the steps, throwing her arms around Kane. Slender, wearing jeans and a T-shirt, she had short blond hair and the same blue eyes as Kane's. Wrinkles lined the corners of her eyes, but she was beautiful.

"You don't come around enough," she said, kissing him on the cheek.

"I know. I'm sorry. Aunt Tess, this is my friend Mae Wallace. Mae, this is my dad's sister Tess."

Mae held out her hand. "It's very nice to meet you, Tess."

Tess gave her a very hearty handshake. "It's so nice to

meet you, too, Mae. Come on inside. I made some lemonade and iced tea. We also got whiskey if you're ready for something harder."

Mae watched Tess turn and bound up the stairs in her tight jeans and cowgirl boots.

"Wow, she's something."

Kane grinned. "She's my favorite aunt."

"You have more?"

He nodded as he pulled their bags from the back of the SUV. "My dad is the second oldest of four, and the other three are all girls. Tess was born two years after him and is the only one who stayed to work at the ranch, along with her wife, Donna. If you think Tess is a live wire, just wait until you meet Donna."

"I can't wait."

She heard barking and turned to see two beautiful dogs bounding toward them. One was black and white with fur flying and the other a short-haired solid black.

"That's Shadow and Lucky," he said, bending down to receive the brunt of the attention. The dogs were extremely enthusiastic in their greetings and Kane seemed to love it. After they had been thoroughly petted, they made their way over to Mae, who gave them both copious amounts of love.

"Aren't you two the sweetest things?" Mae asked.

"And spoiled, too, aren't you?"

The dogs' tails whipped back and forth.

"Come on, let's go in," he said.

She walked side by side with him up the wide wooden steps onto what had to be the biggest front porch she'd ever seen. The Bellinis' house had always impressed her, but this place? This place was something. It had all the looks of a modern log cabin, making Mae wonder who had built it.

"My grandparents designed this place about ten years ago

and some fancy contractor built it. My grandparents' first house was a two-bedroom. Imagine my dad and three sisters sharing one bathroom."

She could envision that. "Your poor dad."

He laughed. "Yeah, he tells me the teen years were no picnic, and his sisters were mean to him."

"Your dad's a big whiner," Tess said as they walked into an amazing kitchen that anyone who enjoyed cooking would fall in love with.

"I'm gonna tell him you said that," Kane said, taking a seat at the oversized kitchen island. The dogs had come inside with them, all filled with energy and playfulness until Tess told them to go lie down. Which they did, right near Kane.

Tess shrugged. "Go ahead. I might be younger than him but I can still kick his ass."

The back door opened and a tall, gorgeous brunette came in. "I heard our favorite nephew is here."

Kane stood and wrapped the woman in a huge hug before turning to Mae. "This is my aunt's wife, Donna. Aunt Donna, this is my friend Mae Wallace."

"Hey, Mae, nice to meet you." Donna came over and shook her hand.

"Great to meet you as well."

"You gonna hoard that lemonade or are you pouring?" Donna asked Tess.

"I don't know. You gonna ask nicely?"

"Babe, I'd love some of your awesome lemonade, please."

"That's better." Lemonade was poured and Mae pulled up a seat at the island. The lemonade was tart and sweet and utterly delicious.

"Where's Grandpa?" Kane asked.

"Out working with one of the horses," Donna said. "He

said you and Mae could come join him if you wanted once you get unpacked."

"Your room is ready," Tess said. "You can take your stuff up whenever you want."

Kane nodded. "Okay, thanks. Hey, have you talked to my dad?"

Tess gave him a questioning look. "Not in recent weeks. A couple of months, maybe. Why? Haven't you?"

"No. I mean yeah. We talk. I just thought . . . never mind."

"You thought what?" Now Donna looked concerned. For that matter, so did Mae, but she was going to stay silent.

"Kane," Tess said. "Is something going on?"

"No. Everything's fine."

Tess pulled up a chair on the other side of Kane. "Everything's not fine. I know you. Tell me what's up or I'm calling your dad right now."

Kane had a tell. Mae hadn't known him forever or anything, but when he was frustrated or something was on his mind, he pulled his fingers through his glorious mane of hair.

He did that now, then inhaled and let out a forceful sigh. "He's not talking to me. I mean, he talks to me, but it's all generalities. The weather, how's work going, Mom is fine, that kind of stuff. Our conversations are short like he doesn't want to stay on the phone."

"Maybe he's just busy," Donna suggested.

"He's always busy. This is different. He's different."

Tess leaned across the island and grabbed Kane's hands. "Talk to me."

"I don't know. Something feels off. It's his tone of voice. He's usually upbeat and super busy but always has time to chat, ya know? Lately he either tells me he has to call me back—and he doesn't call back—or the calls are short. And again, it's his tone."

"Tone like what, honey?" Donna asked. "Depressed? Sad?"

"I don't know. Just . . . monotone. Like he isn't present."

Tess straightened. "What are his and your mom's plans this week?"

"I . . . don't know, honestly. We haven't talked about it. I just assumed they're either hanging out at home or taking a trip."

"Okay. Excuse me for a minute." Tess left the room. Donna came over to sit next to him.

"You're worried."

"Yeah, a little. He's not himself."

"Have you asked him if something's wrong?" Mae asked, figuring if he didn't want her in his personal business, he'd say so. But now she was worried, too, and she couldn't stay quiet any longer.

He seemed unfazed by her involvement when he answered her. "More than once or twice. He shrugs it off and says everything's fine. At first I thought I was overreacting, that I was reading something into our conversations that wasn't there. But I don't know, maybe I'm the one that's off."

She squeezed his arm. "When you know someone so well you know their voice, their mannerisms, you know when something is off. Trust your instincts. You're not wrong."

"No, you're not wrong." Tess came into the kitchen and slid her phone on the counter. "Something's off with your dad."

Kane shifted and Mae felt the tension in his arm. "You called him?"

"I did. I told him your grandpa wasn't doing well health-wise and it would be a good idea for him to come here for Thanksgiving."

"You lied?" Donna looked aghast.

Tess just shrugged. "He's coming, so now we can all talk and figure out what's going on with him."

"He's gonna be pissed when he finds out you lied about Grandpa," Kane said.

"When isn't he pissed at me about something or other? He'll get over it. Or I'll get Dad to cough a couple of times while James is here."

Donna rolled her eyes. "You will not. You'll hit James with the truth as soon as he gets here. And shame on you for lying."

Tess looked unaffected by Donna's accusation. "It's not like he'd show up otherwise."

The door opened and a tall, weathered cowboy likely in his late seventies or early eighties walked in, though he still looked muscular and healthy. He removed his hat and put it on the hook before turning his attention on Kane. "Thought for sure I'd see you out by the horses as soon as you drove in."

"Hey, Grandpa." Kane got up and walked over to his grandfather, giving him a big hug. His grandpa returned the tight squeeze.

"Good to see ya, boy."

It warmed Mae to see the affection all the family members had for each other. Even the dogs wound their way around Kane's grandpa.

"Grandpa, this is my friend Mae Wallace. Mae, this is Adam August, my grandfather."

Mae stood and shook his hand. "Very nice to meet you, Mr. August."

"You can call me Adam. Or Grandpa. No one around here calls me Mr. August unless they're tryin' to sell me something."

"Okay."

"Pour me some of that iced tea, Donna."

"Okay, Dad."

"We have a problem to discuss, too," Tess said. "About James."

Adam frowned. "What's going on with James?"

Kane and Tess filled him in on their conversations with Kane's father. In the middle of the conversation they all made their way outside, and, wow, the back porch was a beauty. Huge, with a built-in kitchen, fans overhead and a vista that was not to be believed. Mae saw a winding river a ways out that was certainly within walking distance. She hoped they'd get a chance to see it.

"James and I don't talk all that much," Adam said. "Can't really recall the last conversation we had. I think he called on my birthday, but the call was short."

"Your birthday is in June, Dad," Tess said. "Now it's November."

"Huh. You're right. We used to talk every week. Then it was once a month. I guess I just didn't notice. That's my fault."

"We've been busy here," Donna said. "But that's no excuse. We should have stayed in touch."

"And he could have shown up more often," Tess said. "He hasn't. When was the last time he visited?"

"Not anytime I've been here," Kane said.

Tess raised her hands. "I don't remember the last time."

"Was it for Grandpa's seventieth birthday?"

"He didn't show up for that," Donna said. "Claimed he had a business trip and that your mom wasn't feeling well."

"Well, hell," Tess said. "There is definitely something going on."

"What about your mom, Kane?" Donna asked. "What does she say?"

"As little as my dad. Whatever's going on, it's both of them."

"I guess y'all can get to the bottom of it when your dad gets here," Donna said. "When's he coming?"

"He said he'd be here Wednesday," Tess said. "Oh, and Dad, I got him to come by telling him you weren't doing so well, healthwise."

Adam nodded. "I'll cough a few times."

Tess looked over at Donna. "See? I told you."

Kane shot Mae a shrug. She smiled at him. This family was something. Something she really liked.

They finally took their bags upstairs and Mae had a few minutes to admire all the amazing work that it must have taken to build this home. The structure was incredible. She normally wasn't into the log cabin type of look, but it was such a big, spacious house and they had wisely not put wood everywhere so it didn't feel stifling. Thick wood beams here and there and the occasional paneling were more than enough to give it that woodsy feel. The arched ceiling and floor-to-ceiling windows that showcased the expansive woods and incredible view of the river made her pause at the top of the stairway, gaping at the scenery outside.

"Pretty impressive, isn't it?" Kane asked.

"I don't know how you ever left this place. If I had been raised here, I never would."

"I wasn't raised here, unfortunately. But I came as often as I could. And, trust me, it was hard as hell to leave this ranch. Which is why, when I have a little time off, this is where I come."

"I can see why. It looks beautiful out here."

He started walking down the hall, so she followed. He opened a door to a bedroom that was much larger than she expected, with a huge bed that she also didn't expect. There were French doors that led out to a balcony overlooking that amazing view of the river and beyond. "Wow."

He put the luggage down and walked with her to the door. "Wait till I take you on a tour. You'll fall in love."

"I'm already in love." She turned her head to look at him, seeing the flare of heat in his eyes. "With the ranch, I meant."

A quirk of a smile crossed his lips. "Of course. Come on, let's change and I'll show you the ranch. You brought boots, didn't you?"

"Of course I did. And extremely provocative lingerie—in multiple colors, I might add—that you'll just have to think about the rest of the day."

"Oh, man. Now you're just torturing me."

She laughed, cupped his chin, then rose up to press a soft kiss to his lips. "That's the idea."

Kane was already dressed appropriately but she wasn't, so he left the room. Mae changed into jeans and her boots, along with a gray T-shirt, then braided her hair, reapplied her sunscreen and headed downstairs. Donna was in the kitchen, rolling out dough.

"He's out back waiting for you, honey," Donna said.

"Thanks. What are you making?"

"Biscuits to go with supper. Dad's smoking some ribs to put on the barbecue later. We're having beans and corn on the cob and biscuits. You're not a vegetarian, are you? If you are, I can fix something up for ya."

"No, I like meat just fine, but thank you for asking. And supper sounds amazing. I can't wait."

Donna smiled. "Thanks. Go get your tour, now. Oh, before you head out there, grab a cowboy hat. It might not be summer but you have a beautiful face and you need to protect it from the sun. The spare ones are in the mudroom off to your left."

"Thanks." After picking out a hat, she went out the back door and found Kane sitting at the table, talking on his phone. Or, rather, he was arguing with someone, so she decided to give him privacy. She stepped off the porch and did a slow wander, taking in all she could see, which included multiple horse barns, trails that she was dying to explore and people milling about, all of whom looked extremely busy doing whatever it was they did.

"Sorry about that," Kane said, coming up to walk beside her.

"No problem. Is everything okay?"

"Yeah, yeah. Just a discussion with my agent."

"Sounded more like an argument."

He laughed. "That's how most of our discussions go. He's looking out for my future, so I get why he pushes. But sometimes I push back."

"Ah, I see. It's good to have someone in your corner, though."

"That it is."

He walked her around to the horse barns, which were gorgeous, and she met some amazing, beautiful horses. She could have spent the entire day there, but he finally dragged her away to the arena, where there were several horses and people working. That was where they found Kane's grandfather and aunt.

"Climb on and we'll watch," Kane said, helping her up on the top post of the arena.

It was like a ballet, watching the graceful horses prance around the arena. Adam and Tess were obviously practiced riders who knew exactly how to maneuver the horses, speed them up and get them to quickly turn and then come to an abrupt stop, dust flying up around them like a sudden tornado. Mae was mesmerized at the way horse and rider were in absolute sync.

"This is the way we train the cutting horses."

"For rodeo," she said.

"Yeah."

She'd been to plenty of rodeos. You couldn't live in Oklahoma without having gone to at least one rodeo. She'd been to several. The horses were always her favorite.

"Do you train horses to work here, or for show?"

"We board and train horses here for various people, both those who show and those who rodeo. We also train new riders who want to enter the circuit."

"I'm sure that keeps everyone busy."

"It does." They continued to walk along, coming to another barn.

They went inside and she gasped at these beautiful creatures. Various colorings, but all majestic.

"And then there are the racehorses. They take some special care."

"The ones with the armed guards."

He laughed, but also somewhat uncomfortably scratched the side of his nose, making her wonder if there was, in fact, someone armed watching over these beauties with a rifle.

He finally cleared his throat. "Let's just say no one's going to pull a trailer in here in the dead of night and run off with them."

"Oh, I believe you. And I'm happy remaining ignorant on how they're protected." She reached out to run her hand up and down a filly's forehead. "They're sweet creatures, aren't they?"

"Wild and spirited, for sure. They need someone with a confident hand."

The filly gave an abrupt shift of her head, letting out a loud whinny. "She feels insulted, don't you, baby?"

Kane let out a short laugh, then walked over to the horse, smoothing his hand over her crest. "Yeah, you're fine, aren't you, Annie?"

"Her name's Annie?"

"Her owners named her Run Run Rhianne. Everyone calls her Annie for short."

She couldn't get enough of touching Annie, who seemed to love the attention.

There were more horses, each one more beautiful than the last. Except for Annie, of course. Mae had taken quite a liking to her.

There were so many training arenas and tack rooms and barns and storage areas that it seemed like they walked a mile back to the house. Her throat was dry from the walk and all the dust swirling around in the wind.

They walked inside, immediately assailed by the most incredible smells coming from the kitchen and from the smoker outside. There were pots on the stove, water boiling, and Donna was peeling potatoes. Mae took off her hat and hung it up. She waited to see if Kane would pull off his dusty boots. He didn't, so she didn't, either. Instead, she went over to Donna.

"Smells amazing in here. Can I help you?"

"No. You're a guest and guests don't cook around here. Besides, this is my job and I love my job."

The one thing Mae knew about was not interfering in someone doing work they loved. "Okay. Mind if I get some water?"

"Of course. Help yourself."

"I'll get it," Kane said, walking over to the cabinets to grab two glasses. There was a pitcher in the fridge and he poured water out for both of them, then they took it over to the living area and took a seat.

"Tomorrow we'll saddle up and take a ride," he said. "Then later I'll walk you through the trails."

She laughed. "Trying to make sure I get my exercise while I'm here?"

"We don't have to do any of that if you don't want to."

"I'm teasing. I can't wait to do all of it. I want to see and experience everything. This place is massive and gloriously beautiful. Can we do a sunrise ride tomorrow morning?"

He gave her a wide smile. "Yeah, we can."

She smiled back at him, ready for this adventure. "Great. Let's do it."

CHAPTER

· · · · · ·

twenty-two

Kᴀɴᴇ ʜᴀᴅ ᴛᴏ admit that he thought Mae was mostly joking about the sunrise ride, especially since they'd been up late last night. She'd showcased her lingerie, and one thing had led to another, and then another, followed by another. He barely remembered falling into an exhausted sleep sometime around one. So he figured the idea of getting up before the sun was probably not going to happen. But Mae had left the bed before him, and was already dressed with coffee waiting for him when she woke him up. The coffee was just what he'd needed—that and the beautiful, dark-haired siren leaning over him.

"Let's roll, cowboy," she'd whispered, pressing her lips to his. "Sunrise is coming."

He downed the coffee, brushed his teeth and climbed into his clothes while Mae braided her hair. When they were both ready they were out the door, heading toward the barn where the working horses were housed. The dogs had bounded out the door as well, running amok to parts unknown.

"You need help saddling?" he asked.

"No, thanks, I've got it."

He saddled his horse, Arnold, then watched as she did hers, a mare named Joy.

He watched to make sure she didn't need assistance. He should have known better. Mae was adept, knew every step like she'd done this before and double-checked her work to make sure the saddle was on securely.

"Nice work," he said.

She grinned, put her foot in the stirrup and hoisted herself onto the mare. "Yeah, I did a summer in college working as a hand on a ranch. I learned a lot."

"Yeah? That must have been fun."

"It was hard, but also one of the best times of my life. I met amazing, hardworking people who changed my world-view. Plus, I've always enjoyed learning something new. And that's never a bad thing."

He could well imagine. "I can still remember coming here every summer as a kid. My grandparents would put me to work from sunup until sundown, doing everything from cleaning the chicken coops and horse stalls to grooming the horses. I had to learn how to care for every horse before I ever had the chance to saddle up and ride one."

"That must have been frustrating."

"It was, but, like you said about your experience, I learned a lot. And I never took for granted the importance of caring for the animals and how that had to come first before the fun stuff."

"Like riding."

He looked over at her and smiled. "Yeah. Like riding."

The skies were just starting to lighten when he led them down a riding trail to the east. No trees in this area to obstruct the sunrise view. The horses had taken this path before, so they knew the way without much leading. He knew the way, too, had taken rides every day whenever he came here. Which meant he could focus more on Mae, who seemed comfortable in the saddle, her attention focused exactly on what it should be—her horse and the way in front of her.

The path was wide enough for them to ride side by side, so he pointed out various spots of interest, like a fallen log or a hidden pond, told her about his favorite spot for fishing as a kid.

"I used to go here all the time with my grandpa. He'd tell me stories about when he was a kid."

"That must have been fun. Probably enlightening, too."

"Yeah, it was. Every time I wanted to complain about being worked hard, I remembered the stories he'd told me about his childhood and I shut right up and did what I was told."

She slanted a smile at him. "Smart."

He led them to an overlook just as the sun started to rise, so they stopped and got off the horses, walking them over to some shade trees. Kane took Mae's hand and they hiked up to an outcropping and sat. Kane pulled his water container out and handed it to Mae, who took a sip.

And then the sun lifted over the horizon, sending out orange and yellow streaks like it was reaching its arms out for a wide morning stretch.

Mae was silent for a long time, obviously taking it all in, so he didn't say anything, letting her watch. He liked that she didn't immediately pull out her phone to take pictures. Sometimes you just needed to be in the moment so you could appreciate it more.

"Wow," Mae finally said, looking over at him with a wide smile. "It must be incredible to see that every day. No clutter around, no big buildings blocking your view."

"Yeah, it's pretty sweet. The nice thing about getting up early to do chores or go fishing is you get to watch the sun come up."

"It's good to have some advantage to getting up before the sun."

"Yeah. How about you?"

"What about me?"

"Seen many sunrises?"

She laughed. "A few here and there. Not many as amazing as this one."

He leaned a hand back on the rock. "Wouldn't it be great to live in a place like this someday?"

"A ranch? The thought never occurred to me. What about you?"

"This is where I want to live. I mean, not this ranch. It belongs to the family and I'll always be a part of it. But someday I'd like to have a place to call my own."

"You want space."

"Yeah. A few horses, some dogs, several acres. Just some space to wander."

"Sounds ideal. It would be a nice landing spot for you when you have a break from movies."

He laughed. "I don't intend to make movies forever."

"You're hardly over the hill. I think you've got a lot of years ahead of you."

"Maybe. If that's what I choose to do."

She cocked her head to the side. "You've got something else in mind?"

"Maybe. Acting has been fun, but I'd like to move into producing. Directing, too. Put other people to work and go more behind the scenes. Search out projects, obtain the rights to them and see them through from start to finish. I've always been interested in the process of moviemaking, the way a project comes together."

"I could see you doing something like that. If you produce, would you have to be on set for the entire movie?"

He shook his head. "No. I'd pop in periodically, take meetings with the key personnel, make sure the project stays on budget and on time. But otherwise no. And I could set up my office at home so I'd be free to do whatever I want wherever I want."

"Doesn't it take capital to be able to do that?"

"Yeah, it does. I'd probably start a company with a production partner or two, that way we'd be competitive."

"Why the shift? I mean, you could act well into your later years if you wanted to."

"I know. And I enjoy it, but I want to be able to have free time. I want to have a ranch, some land. I want to have a family and have the time to enjoy them, not go from one movie set to another."

She stared at him for a minute, her expression revealing nothing, then said, "You have thought about this. About your future."

"For a while now. I'm not saying I'm ready to do this tomorrow, but within the next few years or so? Yeah."

"Wow. I'm impressed, Kane. You've got it all together."

He laughed. "I don't know about that, but I'm formulating a plan."

They got up and climbed back on the horses, continuing their trek along the path. As they rode, Kane wondered if he'd revealed too much to Mae about his plans. He hoped he hadn't sounded too full of himself. But just voicing his desires for the future had gotten him so excited that once he'd started he couldn't stop. And Mae had asked questions. She'd seemed interested, so he'd just gone on and on about it. But maybe it hadn't been so bad. She hadn't rolled her eyes or told him it wasn't something he should consider.

And why was he so worried what Mae thought?

Because you care what she thinks.

Yeah, he did.

They made their way back to the barn, unsaddled the horses and brushed them down while the horses enjoyed some feed and water. After they put the saddles away in the tack room, they walked out.

"You've been pretty quiet since we watched the sunrise," she said.

"I was thinking that I'd vomited out my thoughts for the future and maybe I overwhelmed you."

She stopped and turned to him. "Your thoughts about the future were fascinating to me, Kane. Don't ever be afraid to tell me what's on your mind."

Okay, that was settled.

"Thanks. Sometimes I think I get ahead of myself."

"Sounds to me like you have a solid plan. I don't know if you've written it down somewhere in some official long-term business plan yet, but even if it's only in your head right now, you know where you're going. That's huge."

He slung his arm around her shoulder as they walked to the house, then stopped before they walked up the back steps. He pulled her close and kissed her, long and slow. "Thanks."

"I'm always here for you." She laid her palm on his chest and he felt that warmth all the way to his heart.

MAE WATCHED KANE as they sat at the table and ate one hell of a hearty breakfast with his grandpa, Tess and Donna.

He'd poured his heart out to her at the rock this morning, telling her his plans for the future.

He had mentioned wanting a family, a home, a new career. He just hadn't asked her to be part of all of it.

Aren't you jumping the gun just a little, Mae? Have you asked him to be part of your *future?*

Okay, fine. Point taken. Maybe she'd gotten excited listening to his ideas, and she had pictured herself in that scenario with him. The ranch, the land, the horses and dogs and future sunrises. And marriage and kids.

Silly idea, really. She liked where she was right now and had no plans to upend her life for anyone ever again. And marriage? Really? When had that gotten back on the table for her?

"Are you going to stare at those biscuits all day, honey, or are you going to eat them?"

She looked up to see Tess smiling at her from across the table.

"Oh. Sorry. Lost in thought. Did you want me to pass the plate?"

"I wouldn't say no to another biscuit."

Mae held up the plate and it got passed around. She listened to everyone talk about their plans for the day, though they weren't as animated at the breakfast table as they were over dinner last night. Mostly because everyone was busy drinking coffee and filling their stomachs with biscuits, gravy, eggs and bacon and sliced cantaloupe. She normally ate a small bowl of oatmeal or the occasional granola and yogurt in the morning, so she considered this a feast. She also knew they worked every calorie off during the course of a day on the ranch. Whether she would was another matter, but it didn't stop her from filling her plate.

After breakfast, everyone hustled out the door. Mae started cleaning the table.

"Uh-uh," Donna said. "That's my job. You go have some fun with Kane."

"Are you sure? I hate to leave you with this mess."

"This mess is what I love, so go on, get out."

"Okay."

She put on her hat and headed outside. Kane was waiting for her. They walked down the steps and toward the barns.

"What's on tap for today?" she asked, trying her best to keep up with his long strides.

"I thought we might start with some stall cleaning."

"Sounds good."

He laughed. "You wouldn't mind cleaning stalls?"

"Why would I? They need to be done, don't they?"

"Yeah, but it's a shit job. Literally."

"That's okay. It'll be fun if we do it together."

"I was kidding about the stall cleaning. How would you feel about giving some of the horses a bath and a good grooming?"

"I'd love that."

"Let's go, then."

The day had dawned sunny and warm with just a touch of a breeze, which would keep it from being too hot. Not that it would be all that hot in November, but then again, Mae had known of heat waves at Christmas, so anything could happen. She just knew it was a good day for grooming horses, and she couldn't think of anything she wanted to do more than getting her hands on these beauties.

They had a bathing area that was enclosed and warm, perfect for keeping the horses clean in the colder months. It took a minimum of an hour to bathe each horse, so they were at it the majority of the day, breaking only to grab a quick sandwich for lunch. This was harder than any hot yoga class Mae had ever taken, but she had to admit it was a lot more fun. The horses enjoyed being handled, and she loved every minute of grooming them, especially after they were dried and she could brush and comb their beautiful manes.

Of course she'd had to be the one to bathe and groom her favorite horse, Annie, in fact couldn't wait to spend time with her. She'd talked to Annie in a low, sweet voice, and the horse spoke back to her in soft snuffles against her head.

"You think anyone would notice if I stuck Annie in my luggage when we left?"

Kane's lips curved in a wry smile. "Worth it to see you try."

"Oh, you mean those hidden armed guards might take me out?"

Kane threw a blank look her way. "I have no idea what you're talking about."

"Uh-huh. I know they're here somewhere, skulking about, making sure I don't slip off with her in the dead of night."

He snorted out a laugh. "Right. But just to be on the safe side, I wouldn't."

"Trust me, I value my life."

"I value your life, too."

Once she was certain Annie was good and dry and utterly shiny, she walked her back to her stall, which had been miraculously cleaned during her absence and now sported fresh, clean bedding. Just as they arrived, Annie's trainer showed up and took over, so she smoothed her hand over Annie's nose and left the barn.

She went back to the bathing area and she and Kane put all the supplies away and hosed everything down, tossing all the items to be laundered in the nearby basket.

"I don't know about you but I'm starving," he said.

She pulled her phone out of the back pocket of her jeans, surprised to see that it was already dinnertime. "I can't believe the whole day is gone."

They started toward the house. "You worked hard."

"I'm sure I'll feel it tomorrow."

"You know, I'll be happy to work out any kinks in your muscles with a full-body massage later."

She leaned against him. "I'll hold you to that."

They went inside and washed up for dinner, which consisted of pork chops, mashed potatoes, applesauce, green beans and salad. After today's workout she was so ready for food. Surprising even herself, she gobbled up everything on her plate with not one bit of remorse. If she'd been by herself she might have even licked the plate.

"You were hungry," Kane said.

"Yeah, I was. Plus, the food is excellent. Thank you, Donna."

Donna beamed a smile.

"You want seconds?" Kane asked.

"No, I'm good."

"She's leaving room for the peach cobbler I made for dessert," Donna said.

Mae gave Donna a look. "You didn't."

"Oh, but I did." Donna grinned.

"I might be in love with you."

"Don't make me fight you, girl," Tess said, squinting. "I might be older, but I can still kick butt."

Mae laughed. "I believe you. I'll be sure to maintain my distance, then."

Donna sat back and took a sip of her iced tea. "Oh, I don't know. Been a while since I had two women fighting over me. I'm kind of enjoying this."

Tess rolled her eyes and Kane smirked.

Kane's grandpa cleared his throat. "Yeah, well, while you're enjoying the attention, why don't you serve up that peach cobbler."

Donna arched a brow. "Patience, old man. And while I'm getting dessert ready you can all clear the table."

It was obvious who was in charge of the kitchen, because everyone got up and took their dishes into the kitchen, then put leftovers away while Donna served up the cobbler, along with oh, sweet lord, vanilla ice cream.

Mae got her scoops of both and sat at the table, resisting the urge to shove her entire face into the cobbler and ice cream. Instead, she took small, petite bites, enjoying the delicious melty peach and vanilla flavor on her tongue. She couldn't resist the moan that escaped her throat.

Kane leaned over and whispered in her ear. "Fan of cobbler, huh?"

She nodded. "And ice cream. I really like ice cream."

"Hmm." He straightened, then gave her a hot smile. "Noted."

She wanted to inquire about that smile he'd given her, but the table was filled with people. Instead, she looked over at Donna and said, "This cobbler is amazing. And the ice cream? Oh my God."

Donna grinned. "Thanks. I'm kind of a fan of ice cream myself. I even make it in the winter, though Grandpa and I are the only ones who like it. Tess is more of a hot chocolate girl."

"Yeah, ice cream is a summer thing only for me," Tess said.

"Not summer now," Kane said. "And you're having ice cream."

Tess shrugged, licking ice cream off her spoon. "It was warm today."

"Hey, it's always a good time for anything Donna makes for dessert," Grandpa said. "Marrying Donna was the best thing Tess ever did."

"Damn straight," Tess said.

After dessert, they cleared the plates and put away the cobbler and ice cream. Once again, Donna kicked them out of the kitchen. Everyone else moved into the living room with their drinks. Mae pulled up a spot on the sofa and Kane snuggled in right next to her, his hand on her leg. She liked that he didn't seem concerned about showing affection in front of his family. In fact, when Donna came back in, she took a spot on the other sofa next to Tess, rubbing her neck as they all carried on conversations.

"When is James coming in?" Donna asked.

"Tomorrow afternoon," Tess said.

Kane's hand gripped her leg tighter. Mae put her hand over his, and when he looked at her, she gave him an encouraging smile.

He was worried about his dad. Or maybe worried about talking to him about what was going on. She couldn't blame him.

After a short while everyone headed to bed. Once upstairs, Mae took off her boots and wriggled her toes, stretching her calves, then lay back on the bed, utterly exhausted from the day's work.

Kane climbed on the bed and loomed above her. "I promised you a massage."

She reached up and swept her fingers over his jaw, loving the feel of a day's growth of beard on his face. "So you did."

"Let's get you undressed." He popped open the button of her jeans, then drew the zipper down, drawing them down her legs. He pulled her socks off and she sat up, removing her top and bra, then rolled over onto her stomach.

Kane took a few minutes to undress, then climbed onto the bed, straddling her, his fingers lightly sliding upward along her spine, making goose bumps pop up.

"Time to relax, Mae," he said, his voice low and sensual as he moved his hands slowly over her back, then added some pressure.

She moaned. "I like the way you touch me."

He swept his hands across her shoulders, bringing them down on all her pressure points, teasing the sides of her breasts before moving back in to press on the muscles of her lower back.

She moaned again, and when Kane adjusted his position she felt him rock against her butt with his hard cock.

Obviously she wasn't the only one enjoying the back rub. Her needs moved away from the massage to desire. She lifted against him, and this time he groaned.

"I'm trying to focus here, Mae."

She pushed off him and he rose enough for her to roll over. She raised one arm over her head and gazed up at him. "I've got something for you to focus on."

And then she arched again, rubbing herself against him.

"Okay. Enough with the massage." He pulled off her underwear, and before she could say anything, his mouth was on her sex.

And this time, her moans were for something entirely different. She spiraled in a hurry, feeling that hot, delicious sensation coiling around her as he pleasured her with his lips and tongue.

He took her there, right where she needed to be, and then over, making her shudder and shake with the force of her orgasm. And he held her there, kissing her gently while she came down and caught her breath, still feeling the aftereffects of that utter bliss.

His hands skimmed across her belly and upward, teasing her breasts. He followed up with his tongue flicking across her nipples. She grabbed his head to hold him there so she could continue to experience these mind-blowing sensations.

He lifted his head, gave her that intense, hot smile of his that never failed to make her insides quiver.

"Come up here," she whispered.

He did, taking her mouth in a searing kiss. She wrapped her legs around him, needing him closer. Inside her.

He felt it, too, because he pulled away only long enough to put on a condom, and then he was back, sliding inside her. She gasped as they entwined themselves around each other, as if they couldn't get close enough.

"More," she moaned against his lips, gasping as he thrust harder, giving her exactly what she asked for.

Sweat pooled along her spine as he ground against her, taking her right to the edge, and then plummeting over.

As she climaxed, Kane's dark, wild gaze met hers. He gripped her ass cheeks and drove deeply into her, shuddering with his own orgasm. She'd never felt anything so intense, like a wild storm whirling around inside her. She held tight to Kane, needing him as a lifeline to help her weather this maelstrom of sensations.

She didn't know how long they stayed like that, or when he left her and then came back to pull her against him. She only knew she fell asleep with his body pressed against hers and his arms wrapped around her.

And she'd never felt more content.

CHAPTER
. . . . . .
twenty-three

KANE WOKE UP in the dark, knew it was well before dawn even without checking his phone. He got dressed and went downstairs to make coffee. Lucky and Shadow slept downstairs, so they came over to him for morning pets. He gave them some love, then let them outside.

Grandpa was always the first one up and he wasn't down here yet, so it was too early to wake Mae. He sipped his coffee, pacing the kitchen and living room, his head filled with thoughts about seeing his dad today.

He didn't know what was up with his father, but something definitely was. Maybe it was just stress, or he was busy with work, like everyone suggested. He hoped it was something simple like that, but he knew his dad, and he got the idea it was something a lot more.

Mom hadn't been forthcoming any more than his dad had been. In fact, she'd been even less so, giving him her happy-sounding voice and telling him everything was fine and he was worrying for nothing. But there was something off with her as well.

He hoped they were both coming. It was Thanksgiving, after all, and he hadn't seen his parents for—well, for a while. He realized they were entitled to have their own lives. Hell, he wasn't a kid anymore, and it wasn't like he needed them to take care of him. He had that handled.

Mostly.

But still, it would be nice to see them once in a while, even if they didn't take an interest in his career.

He sighed and stared down at his coffee cup.

"Shit, you scared the hell out of me, boy." His grandfather flipped the light on in the kitchen and glared at him. "Thought someone had broken in."

"Sorry, no. Just me."

Grandpa let the dogs in and fed them breakfast. He fixed a cup of coffee and took a seat across from Kane at the kitchen table. "Trouble sleeping?"

Kane shrugged. "Just got up early."

"Tell me what's got you worried."

He knew his grandpa would keep digging until he talked. "Just worried about seeing Dad today and wondering what's going on with him. But it's probably nothing."

"Maybe." Grandpa took a swig of coffee, then continued. "Maybe it is somethin'. Won't know until we see him and get a feel for what's up. You might wanna be prepared for him not wanting to talk about it, if there is somethin' going on."

"Yeah, I get that. It'll be good just to see him."

"It will. Been too long."

Donna came in, followed by Tess, then Mae came downstairs, and suddenly the kitchen bustled with activity and conversation about anything and everything except Kane's dad. He pushed thoughts of his father to the side and ate his breakfast, then headed outside to work.

Work would get him through, keep the anxious thoughts at bay.

Mae was working inside with Donna today. Donna had actually asked for help, which was highly unusual. Mae had told Kane she was delighted to do some cooking prep in advance of Thanksgiving, so he'd do his thing outside.

He fed horses, saddled them, cleaned stalls and worked up a hell of a sweat. Time flew, and before he realized, it was past lunchtime.

Which meant it was time for a sandwich. He went to the house, up the steps, and heard laughing. He smiled listening to Mae's lilting laughter.

Obviously they were all having fun. He liked how perfectly Mae fit into his life on the ranch, and how easily his family had accepted her. That had a lot to do with who she was.

He opened the door, hoping to join in on the good times, then stopped dead in his tracks when he saw his father sitting at the table, surrounded by Donna, Mae and Tess. Surprisingly, his father was the one laughing the loudest, swiping a tear from his eye as he kept laughing.

Mae looked up and grinned. "Kane. I was wondering if you were going to come in for lunch."

His dad looked over at him and gave Kane a smile. "Hey, son." He got up and came around the table to embrace Kane in a hug. "It's so good to see you."

Kane returned the hug. "Hi, Dad. How are you?"

"Couldn't be better. How about you?"

"Doing well." He looked around. "Mom come with you?"

"Oh, well, no." His dad shifted from one foot to the other, a clear-cut signal that he was uncomfortable with the conversation. "She's . . . uh, spending Thanksgiving with your aunt

Serena. They haven't caught up in a while so she really wanted to see her. They were going to go antiquing over the holiday weekend."

Now that sounded more normal—or at least normal for lately. "Uh-huh."

"Your dad's been telling us about some of his travel experiences," Mae said. "Some of them are very amusing."

"Really." His dad hadn't told him anything at all about his travel experiences lately, mainly because their phone calls never lasted more than five minutes.

"Sit," Donna said. "I'll fix you something to eat."

Kane grabbed a chair at the table and sat, his dad sitting next to him.

And then his grandfather walked in and his dad stood right up.

"James," his grandpa said to his father.

"Hey, Dad." They hugged and then Grandpa sat at the head of the table. Tess gave him a look and Grandpa let out a couple decent coughs.

"You feeling okay, Dad?" James asked.

"Oh, yeah. Fine. Just a little tired these days." He gave another cough for effect.

Kane tried not to roll his eyes. His grandfather was the picture of health, could outwork him on the best of days and would likely outlive him.

Kane's dad looked concerned. "That cough doesn't sound good. Have you seen a doctor?"

"I have. He said it's just the dust or something. And I'm old."

"You should think about slowing down."

Grandpa laughed. "I'll slow down when I'm dead, kid. How are you?"

"I'm good. Work's kicking my butt, so you know, the usual. But I'm up for a promotion, so it's worth the effort."

"Uh-huh."

Donna laid plates in front of them. Absently, Kane picked up one half of the sandwich and devoured it, then the pickle, digging his fork into the salad without even looking, his attention focused on his dad.

Physically, his father looked okay. He'd lost some weight, but he didn't look unhealthy, so that part was good. But there was a hollowness to his eyes that Kane couldn't figure out. Sadness? Unhappiness? Stress? What did any of that look like? He didn't know, and for all he did know he could be totally off base. Maybe Dad was just overworked and tired and needed some rest. A few days on the ranch might help.

They'd talk. Everything would be okay. And then he could stop worrying about his dad and everything would go back to normal.

THE LONGER THEY sat at the table and talked, Mae saw the way Kane's shoulders dropped, saw the tension leave his body.

His father had said all the right things about how he was fine, how great things were. The problem was, Mae didn't quite believe him.

Sure, she didn't know him, like at all. But there was something about his eyes, the way they shifted down every time he said something positive, that made her think he wasn't being truthful.

After they cleared the table, Kane's dad and grandpa went outside for a walk, Donna cleaned up the kitchen and Tess headed outside to go back to work.

"You going to work outside?" Mae asked Kane.

He nodded. "Want to come with me?"

"Sure." It would give her a chance to have a conversation with Kane.

They walked outside toward one of the barns. They saddled two of the horses and climbed on, heading out on one of the paths on a slow pace to exercise these beauties.

When Kane pulled up alongside her, she asked, "So, how's your dad?"

"He's good. I think. I need to sit down with him and talk, figure out what's been going on. But he seems okay."

"Kane, I . . . I mean, I don't know him, but he seems . . . unhappy."

Kane slanted a frown as he looked her way. "Why would you say that? You don't know him."

"I know. I don't know how to explain it, other than I can see it in his eyes."

"Nah. You don't know what you're talking about. I know him, okay? You don't. Trust me when I say he's fine."

She didn't want to argue with him about his dad. Maybe she was wrong and those shadows she'd seen on his face hadn't been real. After all, Kane was right. He did know his father better than she did. So she'd wait it out and see. He'd talk to his dad. Then he'd talk to her and let her know.

Hopefully, everything would be all right.

And if it wasn't, she'd be there for Kane in whatever way he needed her.

CHAPTER

· · · · · ·

twenty-four

KANE LOVED THANKSGIVING. Everything about it, from the morning breakfast casserole to the smell of the turkey roasting in the oven, which drove him crazy for hours on end.

He'd gotten up early. So had everyone else, because on Thanksgiving everyone pitched in.

They invited everyone who worked on the ranch over for Thanksgiving dinner—at least everyone who was staying—so it was a big to-do. Kane and his dad and grandpa brought extra tables in from the storage barn, cleaned them off and put fresh linens on while Mae and Tess helped Donna with the cooking.

Whatever anyone needed, they did it. Kane chopped onions and celery, Dad peeled regular and sweet potatoes and Grandpa set the tables.

And throughout all the prep, the smell of turkey filled the house, making his stomach rumble.

Kane noticed that his dad had stepped out back and hadn't come back inside, so he went outside to see if he was okay.

He heard him talking around the side of the house. He started around the corner, then stopped.

"I told you I was going to the ranch for Thanksgiving, Helena," Dad said. "I even invited you to come along and you said no. Did you know Kane's here?"

He was talking to Mom. Kane paused, listening for the next thing his father would say.

"It's not my fault you don't listen. It's not my fault we don't talk anymore or that you're completely unreasonable about everything. If we could just meet somewhere, have one conversation without fighting—"

Mom was obviously saying something, because Dad had stopped talking. Kane felt like a rock had dropped into his stomach.

They had never fought. Ever. And Mom and Dad weren't talking to each other? Was that the gist of the conversation? What the hell was going on?

"You can still fly out here. Kane would love to see you." He waited a beat, then said, "No, of course I haven't told him anything. Don't you think we should do that together?"

Tell him what? His legs felt weak. He backed up and took a seat at the table on the porch, having heard enough. It was a while until his dad rounded the corner, his eyes widening when he caught sight of Kane.

"How long have you been out here?"

"Long enough to overhear you talking to Mom. So what's really going on, Dad?"

His father sighed, raked his fingers through his still-thick, dark hair. He pulled up a chair next to Kane. "I didn't want to tell you like this. I wanted your mom and me to be together. The problem is, she's avoiding the conversation."

"What conversation? Just tell me."

"Your mom and I have split up."

Kane frowned. "What do you mean, you've split up? Like, separated?"

"It started out that way. We tried counseling, but then it became clear there's no salvaging our marriage. Our lives have moved in opposite directions. We want different things. I'm sorry, Kane. Your mom and I are divorcing."

For a minute he lost the ability to use his voice as he tried to soak in what his dad had just told him. "A divorce? But you two have always been so happy."

"Not for years, actually."

"What? I had no idea."

"Of course you didn't, because we didn't want you to know."

Kane leaned back in the chair. "And that's why I haven't seen much of the two of you. Avoiding my premieres, not visiting the ranch here. All so I wouldn't catch on to your struggles. But why? I'm hardly a kid anymore, Dad."

He shrugged. "We both feel like we failed you. We set up an example of a perfect marriage, and now this."

"Do you think I care about you two having a perfect marriage? I care about you. About Mom."

"Yeah, I know. I'm sorry."

"So what happened?"

"I don't know. I focused a lot of time and my energy on work. I chased promotions like they were the newest drug. One right after the other, working hours of overtime, traveling all the time, and I was never home. Your mom begged me to quit that job and I kept telling her the reward would be worth it at the end. But she got tired of waiting for something that hadn't happened. She got tired of waiting for me and she . . . developed other interests outside of our marriage."

Dread filled him. "Mom had an affair?"

Dad frowned. "Oh, no, nothing like that. Not that I'm aware of, anyway. She's got all these activities and new friends that keep her busy and happy. She has a knitting group, a book club, she goes to the gym every day with a couple of her friends and she has something called a happy hour club. And I guess I woke up one day and realized that all I had was work and your mom. I had no friends, no social life whatsoever. And I no longer had your mom because she went out and found another life—without me."

Kane wanted to feel sympathetic toward his dad, but he couldn't. "Dad."

"Yeah, I know. I brought all this on myself by chasing that rainbow of 'someday,' only to discover that the one wonderful thing I had was right in front of me the whole time. And now she wants a divorce so she can continue to live this awesome life she's carved out for herself. Without me. And I have no one to blame but myself. I let her slip through my fingers, Kane."

Kane's mom was the most wonderful person he'd ever known. Giving and unselfish. He knew it had taken a lot for her to make this decision. If Dad had truly ignored her all these years, then he couldn't blame her for choosing to move on with her life. Still, it couldn't have been easy for her to decide to end a thirty-five-year marriage. But damn, he was angry as hell at her for avoiding him just as much as Dad had. They were treating him like a kid and he didn't appreciate it at all.

"I want to talk to Mom."

His dad opened his hands wide. "You should. I'm going to go inside and tell everyone else what's going on."

"Good idea."

After his dad went inside, Kane took a minute to catch his breath. Of all the things he'd expected to hear from his father, a divorce hadn't been one of them.

With a heavy sigh, he grabbed a spot at the table and pulled out his phone, about to call his mom when Mae stepped out. She had two glasses of iced tea. She put those down on the table and took a seat next to him.

"Are you okay?" she asked.

"Not really."

"Your dad's in there talking to the family. I figured I should step out. It seemed personal."

"It is. He and my mom are getting a divorce."

"Oh no. I'm so sorry, Kane." She laid her hand over his. "That must have been devastating news."

"Yeah, it was."

"Is there anything I can do for you?"

He looked down at his phone, then up at her. "I was about to call my mom. I've heard his side. I need to hear hers."

"I'll leave you alone." She started to get up, but he held her hand.

"No. Stay."

"Okay."

He punched in his mom's number and it rang a few times before she answered.

"Kane."

"Hi, Mom."

"You talked to your dad."

"Yeah. He told me everything."

"I'm sorry, honey. We should have told you sooner. I guess we were waiting for the right time."

He leaned forward. "I don't think there's a right time to find out your parents are ending their marriage."

"I guess not. Still, I wish I could have been there with you."

"Then why aren't you?"

"It's . . . complicated. Your dad and I aren't in the best place right now. Me being there? On the ranch, surrounded by his family? That doesn't feel right to me."

"And you think that the family is going to treat you any differently just because you and Dad aren't going to be married anymore? Don't you know them at all?"

She went silent for a minute before she answered. "Okay, you're probably right. But I'm with your aunt, and I need my family's support right now."

"What about me, Mom? I'm your family. Don't you think I need support?"

"This isn't your marriage we're talking about, Kane. This isn't your life. You don't understand. Your dad and I are taking huge steps to split apart everything we've known most of our lives, both physically and emotionally. I need . . . I need some space. I hope you can understand that."

Kane had been wrong about so much, including his mother. "Yeah. Yeah, sure. You take your space. I'll talk to you later."

"Kane, I—"

He hung up before she could say anything else. He knew he'd been short with her, but while his mom and dad had worked through this for months—maybe years—this was all brand new to him. And, to be honest, he was pissed off at both of them right now. Probably an immature reaction, but that was where he was at the moment.

Mae rubbed his back, a balm to his tortured soul.

"I'm sorry," she said, her voice low and soothing.

"Yeah. Me, too. I didn't expect this. For her to be so fucking heartless and only think about herself and her own needs."

"She's probably in pain and isn't thinking clearly. No doubt they both are."

He slanted a look at her.

"I know. I'm not making excuses for her, I just think I understand her motivations. Right now both she and your dad are wrapped up in their own pain and feelings with no room for anyone else's. They probably think you're too busy to notice or care what's going on in their lives."

"They're wrong. And if they'd bothered to talk to me about what was going on, they'd know that."

She squeezed his hand. "Of course they're wrong. And once they're past this and can breathe again, they'll both realize it."

"Yeah, well, I'm not going to dwell on it. If they don't care, I don't, either." He stood. "Let's go back inside and help out with Thanksgiving prep, okay?"

He started moving but she stopped him, wrapping her arms around him. He wanted to push her away, to stay aloof, surrounded only by his hurt and self-pity, but Mae was warm and, God, he needed to feel wanted right now. He pulled her closer and breathed in her sweet scent, holding her like that for a few minutes.

Right now, she was his balance in a world that had been turned upside down.

And he was damn glad she was part of his world.

CHAPTER

· · · · · ·

twenty-five

MAE COULD TELL that the family was doing their best to keep both Kane and James occupied during today's Thanksgiving festivities. But Mae was focused solely on Kane and his well-being.

They'd all sat and talked with James about the divorce. Mae had excused herself and gone upstairs. It didn't feel right to be a part of such a personal family discussion, so she'd busied herself with checking email and tidying up her and Kane's clothes, and then she'd walked out onto the balcony and enjoyed the beautiful day while she read a book.

After a couple of hours Kane had come upstairs.

"You didn't have to hide up here," he said, bending over to press a kiss to the side of her neck.

She reached up to sweep her hand across his jaw. "You needed time with your family. Alone."

"Thanks for that. Now I need you, so come downstairs?"

"Sure."

He brightened up considerably at dinner, and she was happy that he had his family around to help lighten the blow he'd suffered today. With the whole ranch crew there, there was no room for personal stuff, which was ideal. It was a real party, and it kept Kane occupied. He ate well, he laughed at Tess's jokes and after they'd stuffed themselves with some incredible food, they all played poker and drank.

She was also happy to see that he hadn't had too much to drink. It would have been understandable if Kane had wanted to drown his sorrows in alcohol. Instead, he'd kept it to a few beers and then switched to coffee, which he'd had along with two different types of pie.

He seemed okay, but he wasn't quite himself. He was quiet. Answered questions and engaged in conversation, but she thought she knew him well enough by now that she knew his moods. And this one was still tense. Not that she could blame him. He'd had a hell of a shock today—one you just didn't get over right away. So he might seem fine on the surface, but underneath there was a powder keg of emotion just waiting to explode.

James, on the other hand, appeared to be blissfully relieved to have it all out in the open, and maybe that helped to ease some of the tension between Kane and his dad. She wished that Kane's mom had come, but Mae wasn't in control of that. She wasn't in control of anything, frankly.

And wasn't that frustrating as hell? She was a helper, which was why she loved the business she was in. Helping people get married, making their dreams come true, was what she lived for. She was good at solving problems, alleviating crises, and calming anxieties. When there was a bride in meltdown? Mae had it all under control. Whatever the problem was, she could fix it.

But this? Kane's family falling apart? She did not have this under control. She couldn't fix this.

Some things couldn't be resolved. The best she could do was to be here for Kane and offer comfort.

Everything started to wind down around ten. Those who lived on the ranch took off. Early for most nights, but everyone had been up at dawn this morning, and would be at it again tomorrow, so they all headed to bed.

Kane shut the bedroom door and heaved a sigh.

Mae went into the bathroom, grateful to have a nice soaking tub in there. She turned it on and let the water run.

"Taking a bath?" he asked.

"I thought I might." She leaned against the doorway. "Care to join me?"

His lips curved. "Tempting. Think we can both fit?"

"Oh, we'll fit."

She undressed. So did Kane. He got into the tub while she wound her hair up in a bun. She turned from the mirror to see him holding out his hand for her. She climbed in, settling her back against his chest. The water was steamy, and sliding her legs along his felt intimate, and even hotter than the water surrounding them.

She loved this deep tub that allowed the water to rise around them, covering her. Not that she was cold or anything. Not with Kane's hot body behind her. She laid her head back and just . . . rested.

FOR THE FIRST time today, Kane relaxed. Having Mae's body against his probably had a lot to do with his current state. Today had been a shitshow of emotions, and all he wanted right now was a little peace.

Mae seemed to instinctively know exactly what he needed—some warmth and comfort. They stayed like this for a while, neither of them saying anything or even moving. It felt peaceful, serene, to just be with each other without feeling the need to talk.

God, the last thing he wanted was to engage in conversation. He was talked out and his mind needed to rest.

She sighed. A deep inhale followed by a long sigh. He wondered if she was getting uncomfortable.

He swept his hand over her, his fingers resting on her rib cage below her breasts. "You okay?"

"Mmm-hmm."

He smiled. Yeah, he was good, too. Really good, in fact. The hot water and Mae's warm body were really doing it for him. The only thing he needed right now was—her.

Just the thought of her, the feel of her, the way her body had started to shift against his—made him harden. When she turned around and straddled him, his breathing quickened and all he could think about was sinking inside her and losing all sense of time and place, being only with Mae.

He swept his hand around the nape of her neck and brought her lips to his, kissing her with a depth of passion that swamped him. He broke out in a sweat. Then again, Mae always heated him up. And now, with her body undulating against his cock and his need for her at an all-time high, he was desperately feeling the heat.

"Let's get up," he said.

"Mmm, good idea."

He stood with her, intending to get out of the tub. But she had other ideas. She got up on her knees and took his cock in her wet hands, looking up at him as she encircled her fingers around it and began to stroke it slowly.

For a few seconds he forgot to breathe, mesmerized by the movements of her hands, the way she pleasured him slowly, easily.

And then she took him in her mouth, her sweet lips closing over the head of his cock.

He could have gone off right then, but the sight of her, the feel of her hot mouth taking him in, was so damn good he wanted it to go on forever.

Her mouth and her hands did magical things, making him tighten and thrust and wish for release while at the same time mentally begging to hang on, because it was a slice of heaven on earth and he couldn't get enough.

But he felt the waves and there was nothing he could do to stop it.

"Mae," he said, her name coming out breathless and husky. "Mae."

That was all he could manage, because she gave him more, deeper, and he lost it, coming as he groaned and held on to the wall for support while his legs shook from the force of his orgasm.

Sweat trickled down the sides of his face and he still held on to the wall when Mae stood and reached for him. He grabbed on to her, kissed her deeply, then they stepped out of the tub.

He let the water out, then turned on the shower for a cool rinse. She stepped in with him, rinsing quickly as she shivered.

"That's cold."

"You made me sweat."

She dashed out of the shower and grabbed a towel, drying off quickly and disappearing into the bedroom. He dried off and followed her, meeting her at the bed where she lay, beautifully naked and spread out.

He took a sip of water and then lay down beside her.

"I'm not sure I've got any strength left."

"That's okay." She climbed on top of him. "You just lie there. I'll do all the work."

He swept his hand over her back. "I was just kidding about having no strength. I can do this all night long."

"Oh, I know." She gently scraped her nails along his chest. "Let's see how long."

He gave her a half smile. "Think I'll cave before you, huh?"

As she rocked against his quickly hardening cock, he let out a groan.

"Oh, I think you will." She leaned down and brushed her lips across his, whispering against his mouth. "Let's get started."

CHAPTER

······

twenty-six

KANE HAD GONE off with his grandpa and his dad to pick up some lumber to build something or another. Mae had only been half listening because it had been early and she wasn't at her best until her second cup of coffee.

They had finished eating before she'd come downstairs, and were out the door in a hurry, so she'd eaten with Tess and Donna. Tess didn't have anything pressing to deal with this morning, so it was nice to spend time with both of them.

"How did Kane seem last night?" Tess asked.

Mae felt the immediate blush all over as she recalled their hours-long sex session. She didn't actually recall which one of them had passed out first. It might have been a simultaneous thing. All she knew was that she was deliciously sore and very satiated.

"He seemed fine, though we didn't talk about it."

Donna nodded. "I think he might need some time to process it all. When my parents told me they were going to get divorced, it took me a week or so for it to actually sink in. I was numb."

She'd make a note not to push him to talk about his feelings. Donna was right. It probably would take him a minute to regroup and ponder his feelings about the whole thing.

If it were her that it had happened to, she'd feel the same way. He'd thought his parents' marriage was solid, only to discover that it was falling apart and he hadn't even known. She couldn't imagine the shock he'd gone through. Which meant she was going to have to give him all the space he needed.

"It's good he has you here," Tess said. "I think you keep him from getting in his head about this."

"You think so?"

Donna nodded. "We do."

It was quite the compliment. "Well, thank you. But really, it's been helpful for him to be here with all of you. He's told me how much family means to him. I'm glad he was here when he found out."

"He means everything to us, too." Donna took the last bite of her scone and took a sip of coffee. "He belongs to us as much as he belongs to James."

Tess nodded. "Sometimes more so. Or at least that's how Donna and I always saw it."

Donna reached over and took Tess's hand, squeezed it. "When he'd come here for summers, his parents weren't always with him. So we'd teach him everything we thought he should learn."

"That's true," Tess said. "Like respect for the outdoors, how to treat animals."

"And how to respect women," Donna added.

"Definitely that. And Dad taught him all about the horses and the land. Things he didn't learn in the city."

"Invaluable lessons, all of them," Mae said. "You helped raise a fine man."

Tess gave her a confident smile. "We think so."

It was clear how much Tess and Donna loved Kane. It showed in how he treated her, too. She'd dated quite a few men. Some awesome. Some not so much. She ranked Kane high up there on the list of honorable men.

After Tess headed outside to work, Mae helped Donna clean up the kitchen despite her protests, then went outside to see what she could do to help. She cleaned the horse stalls alongside Lana, one of the staff whose dad also worked at the ranch as a trainer. Lana attended college and worked part-time on the ranch whenever she was on break.

"I've been comin' here since I was six years old," Lana said as they hauled in fresh straw for the stalls. "It gives me a chance to hang out with my dad, and be near the horses."

"You love the animals."

"I do. I'm going to veterinary school."

"Oh. How exciting for you. That's hard work."

"It is. But it'll be worth it in the end."

"Yeah, it will."

After she finished cleaning stalls, Lana went off to do something else, which meant Mae was left with nothing to do. She went to the stalls to visit her favorite horse, Annie, surprised to see that she wasn't in there, so she wandered outside to see if she could find her.

She asked around and someone told her Annie was working out at the racetrack. Since she hadn't been there yet, she had to ask for directions. It was left of the arenas, and when she found it she gasped at how big it was. She supposed it had to be good-sized for the horses to be able to stretch out and run. Adam was at the track along with a couple other people, including the jockey who currently sat atop Annie, taking her on a walk around the track. Mae didn't know that Adam and Kane had returned from their errands, and she had searched the area for Kane as she'd headed this way but hadn't seen him. Figuring he was busy elsewhere, she walked near the track, stopping by Adam but not saying a word. She was entranced by Annie's utter beauty as the jockey took the horse through her paces.

And when he urged her into a trot, and then a full run, Mae held her breath. She was like dark lightning, as if her feet weren't even touching the ground. She flew around the track, as graceful and beautiful as anything Mae had ever seen. The jockey finally slowed and edged her into a walk, cooling her down.

"She's so beautiful," Mae said.

"That she is," Adam said. "She's a perfect horse. Just about ready for her first race."

Mae looked over at Adam. "She hasn't raced yet?"

"Not yet. But she will. And she'll be a winner."

"You can tell?"

"We've run enough racehorses through here that I can tell a winner from one who can compete but will never be a champion. Annie will be a champion."

For some reason, that made her so happy.

"What are you doing out here?" Adam asked.

"Just . . . wandering. Is there something you need me to do?"

He shook his head. "You're not here to work. Enjoying yourself?"

"Yes. You have an amazing ranch. Thank you for letting me come here."

He studied her, his face all craggy lines and years of wisdom. "My grandson's lucky to have you in his life."

Momentarily shocked, she didn't know what to say. But then she found her voice. "Thank you. I feel pretty lucky being part of his life, too."

"Because of his movies?"

She laughed. "Honestly? I think that's the least interesting thing about Kane."

Adam tilted his head back and laughed, then turned and headed back toward the main arenas, so she walked with him. "That's what we all think. I always wanted him to be a rancher, but the kid followed his own path."

"A lot of us do. I mean, don't get me wrong, I've watched a couple of his movies. He's a very good actor and he can embody a role very well. But I don't think that defines everything he is as a person. He has so much more to offer."

"No wonder he likes you. I'll bet you challenge him, too."

Her lips curved. "I try my best."

They reached one of the arenas and stopped. Adam laid his hand on her arm. "You keep doing that. My Elizabeth, she kept me on my toes every day of her life. I miss that."

"I'm sorry for your loss."

"Me, too. But I got good memories of Ellie and me, and those will last me until we're together again."

"That's a sweet perspective, Adam."

"It's what keeps me going every day."

"What keeps you going every day?"

Mae looked over to see that Kane had asked that question. She hadn't even heard him come up to them.

"Coffee and the occasional whiskey before bed, kid," Adam said. "Where you been?"

He motioned with his head toward a spot off to the north. "I took the tractor and cleared some brush on that spot you wanted to build at. Got it mostly cleared, but wanted to talk to you about digging a trench."

"Okay. I'll be along in a bit. I want to see how this training is going first."

"Sure."

Kane walked away without asking Mae to come with him. She wondered if he was upset with her, so she followed, nearly jogging to keep up with his long-legged stride.

"Hey," she said, but he was still about six steps ahead of her. "Kane."

But still, he kept walking, which was starting to irritate her.

"Kane. Stop. Dammit, stop." She ran and grabbed his arm, squeezing it. "I said stop."

He frowned. "What?"

"What do you mean, what? I've been running this whole time to keep up with you, calling your name, asking you to stop. And you ask me *what*? What the hell is going on with you?"

"Nothing. I'm . . . busy."

"No. You're angry. At your parents. Not at me, remember?"

He blew out a breath. "Yeah. Sorry. I woke up in a pissed-off mood thinking about my parents and I didn't mean to take it out on you." He stepped closer and smoothed his hands up and down her arms. "I really am sorry. I need to take out my irritation on chores. And maybe I need some space."

She thought he needed to talk it out, but that wasn't how he felt right now, so she'd abide by his feelings. "Of course. Come find me later?"

"Yeah, I will." He gave her a quick kiss and walked off, leaving her standing there all alone.

Okay, so he was in a mood, and now she was, too.

She wandered back toward the main barns and found Shadow and Lucky sleeping in the shade of one. The dogs woke up when they sensed her approach, their tails wagging as they ran up to her.

"Hi, pups." She crouched down to pet the dogs, laughing when they both licked her face. "Aww, thank you."

"Careful. You keep letting them do that and they'll follow you home when you leave."

Mae looked up and smiled at Tess. "I don't think I'd mind."

"Where's Kane?"

Mae stood. "He's off doing something to work off his anger. He's in a mood and wants to be alone."

"Ah. That's typical. He always was a brooder. As a kid, when he got pissed off he'd climb into the tree house and lift the ladder so none of us could get up there."

"So you tormented him?"

Tess shrugged as she lifted up a bucket and made her way to the barn, so Mae followed. "Us? No. But him? He was a little shit. Hiding twigs and mud in our beds, emptying our shampoo and replacing it with dish soap, wiping his goobery fingers on us. Little-boy stuff. He thought he was funny. My sisters and I? Not so much."

Mae wrinkled her nose. "Why are boys so gross?"

"Probably because he knew it would bother us. I have to admit that we gave it back to him tenfold. It's tough when you're outnumbered by women. We did the same thing to his dad when we were all kids. James backed down, but Kane? He threw it right back at us. I tried to be on his side but he was a brat and made it hard."

Mae grinned. "I don't have siblings so I have no idea what that dynamic is like. But the people I work with—my friends—are three sisters. I've borne witness to several of their battles, so I can well imagine the difficulties. Sometimes it is the people you love—especially family—who get under your skin the most."

Tess was gathering supplies and paused, looking at Mae. "You speak from experience, not just observation."

She shrugged. "Maybe."

"Family can be rough sometimes. I commiserate."

Mae appreciated that Tess didn't ask probing questions. First, she didn't want to bring up her complicated relationship with her mother. Second, Kane was going through enough, as, she was certain, was the whole family. The last thing Mae wanted to do was pile on with her own family history.

So she'd let Kane have his space, and they'd talk later.

If he wanted to. If not . . .

She didn't know what she'd do. She cared about him. Maybe too much. And that scared her. She'd gone into this with him wanting to keep things light and easy between them.

Nothing felt light or easy right now. It felt deep and complicated. Sometimes warm and exciting. At other times frustrating as hell.

She didn't know how to feel about that.

Scared. That was how she felt. Scared. Because every day her feelings for Kane grew exponentially.

The thought of falling in love again made her stomach hurt. The possibility of being hurt again made her heart twist inside her chest.

How could she have let this happen?

CHAPTER

······

twenty-seven

IT WAS THEIR last day here. Kane's last full day on the ranch, and his last opportunity to talk to his dad, to make peace.

The only problem was, he wasn't feeling peaceful. He was angry—at both his father and his mother—and he didn't know what to do with all these feelings. And the more he thought about how they had shut him out of what had been going on, the more pissed off he got.

He didn't need the intimate details, or all the details. But they could have told him they were having problems, that they were in counseling. That they had separated. Some kind of preparation instead of finding out abruptly that they had ended their marriage. And the only reason he'd found that out had been by accident, because he'd overheard.

Plus, his mother refused to even talk to him about it, let alone come and see him.

Tension coiled around him like a hungry snake, squeezing him so tightly he could barely breathe. He was going to have to find a way out of this vise of anger, and soon, because in a few days he'd be due back on set, and he needed to be ready to roll.

Right now he was anything but ready. All he wanted to do was punch something. Repeatedly.

The door opened and his grandpa and father walked in, both of them laughing, which only increased Kane's ire to the nth degree. His dad looked happy. Relaxed, even, and all Kane saw was red.

"Morning, Kane," his dad said. "Your grandpa and I took an early morning ride to oversee some of the fences. I forgot how good it felt to get out there and breathe in that cool morning air sitting on the back of a horse."

"Yeah, well, maybe you can take some time off from your precious job and remember where you came from." Kane took a sip of his coffee. It tasted as bitter as the words that had spilled from his mouth.

"Watch it, boy," his grandpa said.

"Sorry," Kane muttered.

Dad grabbed a cup and pulled up a chair at the table. "No, Dad, that's okay. Kane's right. I haven't been here in a while. I've ignored a lot while focusing on work. My family. My marriage. It's cost me and I'm fully aware of that now." He looked over at Kane. "I can see how that's hurt you. My not being there for you. I'm sorry. I'll do better in the future."

He wanted to blurt out that it was too late, but he kept that thought to himself. "Sure. Thanks."

Mae was suspiciously absent during breakfast. He'd been so in his own head when he'd gotten up, he hadn't even checked on her. Was she sick?

He headed upstairs, surprised to see she wasn't there. He went back downstairs.

"Donna. Have you seen Mae?"

Donna shot him a look. "What's the matter, honey? Can't keep track of your woman?"

"Donna."

"She and Tess were up in the dark. One of the horses is sick and Tess was tending to it. They'd been talking about the horse last night and Mae said she'd help out, so Tess woke her."

He hadn't even woken up when Tess had come to get Mae. Probably the whiskey he'd had last night. Setting his jaw, he put on his hat and went outside in search of Mae and Tess, found them in one of the barns. They were talking in soothing voices to Montgomery, one of the geldings. The vet was there, too.

"He should clear up in about twenty-four hours," the vet said. "No food until tomorrow."

"You got it, Doc," Tess said. "Thanks for coming over."

The doc nodded to Kane on his way out.

"What's going on?" Kane asked.

"Colic," Mae said. "Tess was worried about him last night, and we walked him for a bit, but he wasn't improving, so she called the doc out."

"Fortunately, he doesn't need surgery," Mae said. "Doc did a nasogastric tube and that seemed to help. Montgomery has been given some meds, and he should recover completely."

"Good. I'm glad. I didn't even know you were gone."

"I tried to be quiet so I didn't wake you." She walked over to him and hugged him. "Good morning."

Even spending all that time with the horse in the barn, she still smelled good. He wanted to bury himself in her sweet scent and forget about everything that upset him.

And yet he wanted to hold on to his anger, so he backed

away from her. "Glad that Montgomery's gonna be okay. You should go have some breakfast."

He walked off, feeling shitty for pushing her away but not knowing what to do with this anger boiling up inside him. So it was probably best he keep his distance from Mae until he figured it out.

He spent the day keeping himself busy, digging that trench for the new building, clearing more brush along the north side, and anything else that brought out a good sweat and kept his mind focused on anything but his parents.

It was getting dark by the time he put up the tractor. He drove it into the barn because it looked like it could rain tonight. He was surprised to see Tess in there when he climbed off.

"Run out of things to do to avoid the rest of us, or are you planning to bed down in here tonight?"

He took off his work gloves and climbed off the tractor. "Don't know what you're talking about."

"You know damn well what I'm talking about." She grabbed his arm when he tried to brush past her. "You're so pissed off about your mom and dad's divorce that you're taking it out on your whole family, and on Mae. You know she's in love with you, don't you?"

That surprised him. He and Mae had never discussed their feelings. Not deep feelings. And how the hell could Tess know that? "I—no, she isn't. Did she tell you?"

"No. But I can tell."

"Right. And I'm not pissed off. I'm trying to help out before we have to leave."

"We do just fine when you're not here."

He lifted his chin. "So do my parents, apparently."

"You do know that their divorce doesn't have anything to do with you, Kane. But you're making it all about you. Stop it, before it eats you up and makes you bitter. Holding all that anger inside could cost you everything—and everyone—you love."

He was about to argue with her that it wasn't at all what he was doing, but she'd turned and had already left the barn, leaving him feeling empty and hollow, her words ringing in his ears as loud as his heart was pounding.

Dammit. He pulled off his gloves and threw them across the barn, irritated with Tess for calling him out, pissed off at his parents for ruining his vacation at the place he loved the most and wishing he could wind back time so he could remain oblivious—and happy.

Which meant Tess was right. He needed to pull his head out of his ass and just get over it. Nothing he did was going to change the fact that his parents were splitting up, and this childish tantrum only hurt the people he cared the most about.

He went up to the house, realizing that everyone had gone up to bed. Shadow and Lucky came over to greet him, so he bent down to pet them.

"You're both so loyal," he whispered, burying his face against theirs. "You know what unconditional love is all about, don't you?"

"You didn't have dinner."

Mae's soft voice caught his attention. He looked up to see her standing at the top of the stairs, regarding him warily. He hated seeing that look of discomfort on her face.

"Yeah, I kind of got caught up doing stuff." He stood and walked over to her, mesmerized by the soft fall of her hair over her shoulders and the sweet scent of her freshly show-ered skin. "I'm kind of hungry now."

"Donna wrapped up a plate for you," she said, stepping off the landing. "Can I warm it up for you?"

Her question was testing his mood. She was waiting for him to snap at her again. He swept his knuckles gently across her cheek. "That'd be great. Thanks."

She warmed the plate while he washed up. He really wished he could shower the layers of dust and dirt off his body, but that would have to wait. Since he'd missed both lunch and dinner, he was starving.

She laid the plate in front of him. Slices of beef, with potatoes and vegetables and a side salad, along with bread and butter. While he dove in, she poured him a glass of water and took a seat across from him at the table.

At first he concentrated on the food, unable to even make basic conversation until his appetite had been appeased. All the while, Mae was seemingly content to watch him eat.

There was a lot he wanted to say to her, but God, he needed to be clean before he did that. After he finished eating he took his plate to the sink, rinsed it and loaded it into the dishwasher.

"I need to clean up," he said.

She nodded. "Okay. I'll be up in a minute." She turned away from him and toward the dogs, who were eager for her attention.

He went up to their room, stripped off his dusty, dirty clothes and headed straight into the shower, lingering long enough under the hot water to scrub away the filth and his three-day bad mood. Once he felt like a human being again, he got out, dried off and went into the bedroom.

Mae was standing at the French doors, her long legs peeking out of her satin shorts. She wore a tank top and she looked stunning, like always. Tess's words echoed in his mind.

Holding all that anger inside could cost you everything— and everyone—you love.

He wasn't that guy. He refused to be that guy. What he

needed was a little normal in his life. A little happiness. He could have that with Mae, provided she wasn't going to turn tail and run away as soon as they got back to Oklahoma. And he wouldn't blame her if she did.

"It's raining," she said, her voice low and soft.

He made his way over to her and looked out the French doors. Rain fell softly, a light patter against the windows. Kane took a deep breath and let it out, hoping the rain would wash away the last of his anguish. He wished he could wrap his arms around Mae. The touch of her skin always made him feel good, but it didn't seem as if he had the right at the moment.

"I'm sorry," he said. "I've been awful the past couple of days and I've taken a lot of it out on you."

To his surprise, she smoothed her hand over his back. "You're hurting. Anyone who lo—who cares about you understands that."

He shuddered out a breath, her touch a balm to his tortured senses.

Her fingers entwined with his. "Come on. Let's get in bed."

They climbed into bed, Mae facing him.

"Close your eyes," she said. "Relax. Clear your mind of all the things you can't change. I'm here with you. You need to sleep."

Her cool fingers massaged his face, melting away all the tension, the worries, the anger, until all he felt was peace.

He drifted off.

CHAPTER

. . . . . .

twenty-eight

OKAY, WE WANT to hear everything."

"And what Erin means by everything," Brenna said, "is every detail of every day."

Honor nodded. "Spare nothing. Even if you think it's boring. Because it's not boring."

Mae blinked, not sure what to say. Mainly because she planned to say nothing. Nothing of value, anyway. Because so much had happened between her and Kane, and mostly between Kane and his family. And those secrets were not hers to reveal.

"We had a good time. The ranch is phenomenal. And huge. I got to spend a lot of time with the horses. And his family is incredible and fun and funny and it's like I found a new family there."

"Aww," Honor said. "That's really sweet."

Brenna poured a refill of coffee from the carafe. "But about you and Kane. Did you two have serious alone time?"

"We had some, yes . . . but honestly, we were nonstop

busy during the day, cleaning stalls and working with the horses. Then we spent time with the family over dinner and in the evenings. So by bedtime, we were tired."

"What?" Erin asked. "So you're telling me there was no hot sex?"

"I'm not saying that at all."

Brenna leaned back in her chair. "Yeah, you're mostly not saying anything at all."

"Tell me, Brenna," Mae said. "Did we ask you to spill the intimate sex details of your honeymoon with Finn?"

Brenna's eyes widened, her mouth opening and closing before she answered. "Well . . . I . . . that's different."

Mae poured herself a cup of coffee, added cream, then asked, "In what way is it different?"

"She does have a point, Bren," Honor said. "We might be a little pushy because we're all married now and living vicariously through Mae's sexy single life."

Mae sputtered out a laugh. "Oh, right. Like I ever gave you details before."

"Fine," Erin said. "It's just that he's so hot. And a movie star."

"Honestly, he's just a really nice, normal guy," Mae said. "So let's leave it at that, okay?"

Brenna huffed out a sigh. "Fine. Boring, but fine."

"Okay, enough of all this," Maureen said. "I'm sure you're all intrigued with Mae's relationship with Kane August, but can we get back to work now?"

Mae was relieved that her sex life was no longer the topic of discussion, and they got down to the business of their meeting. Mae was more than happy to immerse herself in wine and wedding biz again. She had to admit that she missed this part of her life. Having a week off had been fun but also fraught

THE BACKUP BRIDE PROPOSAL

with complicated family dynamics that had badly messed with Kane's head. When he'd dropped her off last night, he'd seemed tired. She couldn't imagine the emotional toll that finding out about his parents' divorce had taken on him. He needed some time to unwind and get back into the swing of work, while also coming to terms with everything that had gone down in Texas. He had a right to have whatever moods he wanted to, but she needed to take a step back.

She had no idea how long that would take.

"Filming resumes today, Mae," Maureen said. "Do you have scenes to do with Kane?"

She checked her phone and her filming days, then shook her head. "No. Nothing today."

Fortunately.

"Hmm. I'd like to see how things are moving along. Can you go over there and check?"

She'd planned to give Kane some space, but she could probably pop in and speak to Alexis, get a feel for the production and schedule, then hightail it out of there without him even knowing she'd been there.

"I'll definitely do that."

"While you're there," Honor said, "please remind them that we have a fairly sizable wedding this Saturday, so we'd like to make sure there's no filming that day and that the production crew doesn't interfere with the guests."

"Of course. I'll mention it to them."

She made notes about the wedding schedule and then went about her business for the day. After confirming flowers and caterers for Saturday's wedding, she answered a few emails, then went outside. She had a tour scheduled at ten, and fortunately the couple showed up right on time, which was great as far as her schedule for the day. The couple fell in love with the venue—and who wouldn't—so they went over their requested dates for the wedding. They scheduled for a year and a few months away, put down a deposit and were happily on their way after taking a few pictures.

So far, today was going extremely well. She looked at her schedule, realizing she had about thirty minutes free, so she wandered over to the movie set. She saw Kane filming a scene with two of the other actors, so she avoided that area and headed into the production office. Alexis was on set with Kane, so she met with the scheduling coordinator, Veronica, and talked to her about this weekend's wedding.

Veronica scrolled through her laptop. "We have nothing on for this weekend, filming-wise, so we're clear there. But it's my understanding our schedule and yours were gone over and approved before filming began."

"They were. My boss just wanted to confirm that your team was aware of this weekend's wedding."

Veronica lifted her head and gave her an empty stare. "We're aware."

Though she wasn't completely satisfied, she supposed it was the best she could hope for. "Okay, then. Thanks."

"Is there something else?"

She realized she had been standing there saying nothing, no doubt wasting Veronica's time. "No. Sorry. Thanks for your help."

How embarrassing. She'd been hoping she could go back to Maureen with something a little more concrete or positive other than "We're aware of the contract terms," but there wasn't much she could do about it. She left the trailer, intending to work her way back to the house.

"Mae, what are you doing here?"

She grimaced at the sound of Kane's voice. Pivoting, she offered up a smile. And, oh, did he look delicious in dark jeans and a dark blue button-down shirt. Part of her wanted to step into his arms and feel the strong warmth of his body surrounding her. The other part of her wanted to flee.

"Oh, hi. I had some business to discuss with the production company on behalf of the Bellinis. I'm sure you're busy with work and so am I. I'm just going to head back."

"Wait. Wait. Why the hurry? And why didn't you stop by to say hello?" He stepped up to her and picked up her hand. "Are you okay?"

"I'm fine. Just busy. Mondays are very hectic days. I'm sure you have a lot to do as well."

He shrugged. "I'm in between scenes right now so we've broken for lunch. How about you? Feel like grabbing something to eat?"

Actually, she was hungry. But she wanted to put some distance between them so he could have the opportunity to heal and reflect. And maybe so she could avoid her feelings for him. "I . . . can't right now. Sorry."

"Okay. Talk to you later?"

"Yes. Sure. Gotta go." She pulled her hand away and left, feeling miserable about leaving him standing there. He'd looked so disappointed it made her heart hurt.

And what was she doing, anyway? Who was she to decide how he should best get over his parents' divorce? Was leaving him alone the best option? Hadn't she told herself she was going to be there for him? Fleeing was not the way to be there for a man she claimed to care so much about.

But he'd been so angry, and the last thing she wanted was to put herself in the position of bearing the brunt of his anger. She'd already had one disastrous relationship and didn't intend to have another.

So while she wanted to be there for Kane, self-preservation had to take over.

She stood at the entrance to the wooded area, staring back at where Kane was, her heart aching for him.

But this time she intended to use her head to protect her heart. She turned away and headed toward the house.

KANE FINISHED FILMING for the day and went to his trailer, kicked off his boots and went to the mini fridge to grab a beer. He settled on the sofa and scrolled through his phone, catching up on his texts and emails. His agent was still on him about the next project, but he wasn't in the right frame of mind to even begin to think about it.

There was a call from his dad, who had left a voice mail. Yeah, he definitely wasn't going to listen to that. Not at all surprising that his mom hadn't bothered to call or text since she was all about her own feelings and no one else's.

Move forward, not back.

Yeah, yeah. He took several swallows of his beer and scrolled through his texts, hoping he'd see one from Mae. But there was nothing, and he couldn't push away the disappointment at that realization.

Something had been off with her when he'd seen her this afternoon. It was like she couldn't get away from him fast enough.

He scrubbed his hand over his face. No, that couldn't be right. Things were good between them. Or, at least he thought they had been. Was he misremembering dropping her off last night? They'd talked, right? He'd kissed her and told her they'd talk today. He'd been tired, sure, but he'd apologized for his shitty behavior and he thought they'd moved past everything bad that happened between them in Texas.

Move forward, not back.

His head hurt. He needed something to hydrate him, and

probably some aspirin. Not beer. He emptied the can in the sink and tossed it, popped some meds and pulled water out of the fridge, guzzling it down while walking the length of the trailer and back. Maybe that would help.

The problem was, twenty minutes later he still felt shitty. He couldn't stay holed up in this trailer so he changed into sweats and a T-shirt, laced up his tennis shoes and went for a run, starting off slow and then increasing his pace, getting his heart rate up to a good click. He ran the path all the way to the Bellini house, intending to turn around and head back, but a truck pulled up in the drive and Johnny Bellini got out. Kane slowed his pace so he could say hello.

"Kane, how are you doing?"

"I'm fine, Johnny. How are you?"

"Just finished up helping out a friend with their horses. And I'm ready for dinner. Did you eat yet? It's pasta night here."

"Oh, well, thanks, but I'm sweaty after my run."

"So, you wash up, then you come eat with us, yes?"

Not wanting to be rude, he smiled. "Of course. Yes. Thank you."

Johnny led the way into the house. Maureen met them in the hall, kissing Johnny on the cheek, then looked over at Kane. "Oh, Kane, I'm so glad to see you. Are you staying for dinner?"

"I was invited by Johnny."

She gave him a sweet smile. "Wonderful."

"I was running and I need a place to wash up."

"Right this way." She led him to a half bath off the hall. "There's washcloths and towels in the cabinet."

"Thanks." He made his way into the bathroom, found a washcloth and used it to wipe the sweat from his face and body. Feeling a little more refreshed, he walked out and heard talking, so he followed the sound, realizing it was coming from the dining room, where all the good smells were.

Johnny and Maureen were there, along with Erin and her husband, Jason, and their baby, JJ.

"Kane will be joining us for dinner tonight," Maureen said.

Jason grinned, stood and walked over to Kane, shaking his hand. "Hey, man. Good to see you again."

"You, too. How's it going?"

"Busy as always. How's the movie star thing?"

Kane shrugged. "Keeps me out of trouble."

"Hi, Kane," Erin said, offering up a knowing smile as she fed crackers to the baby, who grabbed them from his high chair.

"I can smell the meatballs from upstairs. I can't wait—" Mae stopped when she caught sight of him. "Kane, what are you doing here?"

"Uh, Johnny saw me outside when I was running and invited me to dinner." He offered up an apologetic half smile.

"Oh. Well, isn't that nice?"

She'd changed from when he saw her earlier. Now she was in leggings and a sweatshirt, her hair pulled back in a loose bun. He wanted to hug her, kiss her, breathe her in, but he kept his distance because he distinctly got the "back off" vibes from her. He didn't know why, but this wasn't the place or time to question her.

Instead, he sat next to Johnny, who talked to him about the ranch and the horses, something he was always keen to chat about. He ate an amazing spaghetti and meatballs dinner, along with salad and freshly baked bread.

"This is excellent," he said.

"Louise is quite the cook," Maureen said. "She keeps us all well fed."

"You're very lucky."

"Oh, don't tell me that your catering services on set are starving you to death," Erin said.

"Not at all. The food's good. But there's a lot to be said for a home-cooked meal."

"I can't imagine being away from home while you're on location," Jason said. "I'm sure it's hard."

"It can be. But I've seen some amazing places, so I can't complain."

Maureen and Johnny both asked him about some of the places he'd been, so he spent the rest of the meal telling them about his favorite location shoots. He'd noticed during dinner that Mae had been uncharacteristically quiet. She'd answer questions if she was asked, but she was normally so engaging that her being so introverted wasn't like her at all.

Maybe she'd just had a bad day. Then again, maybe it was him being here that set her off. She hadn't wanted to have lunch with him today. In fact, she'd been in a hurry to get away from him. Before he left tonight he intended to find out what was going on.

Except that after dinner Johnny had taken him out back to show him his horses. Jason had come with him, the reason he and Erin had stayed for dinner. One of the horses had a hoof infection that Jason had been tending to, and Jason had showed up after hours to check on the horse, a mare named Rosemary.

"She's a beauty," Kane said as Jason gave the mare her meds.

"She's bella, sì." Johnny swept his hand over her back. "Such a sweet girl."

"She'll be fine in about a week," Jason said. "But you know you can call me anytime if something comes up."

Johnny nodded. "I will. Grazie."

"I'm . . . gonna head back inside to talk to Mae."

Johnny and Jason barely acknowledged him with nods since they were deep in conversation about one of the other horses, so he made his way to the house.

He came in the back door, making his way into the dining room. Mae sat at the table with Erin, the two of them in animated conversation about something. Erin said something and Mae shook her head furiously.

"Nothing gets resolved until you talk," Erin said.

Mae shushed her when he walked into the room. "Hey."

Erin stood. "Is Jason finished out there?"

"I think so."

"I'm gonna go tell him I'm ready to go. We need to put JJ to bed."

"Okay," Mae said. She got up. "I should—"

"Mae, wait," Kane said. "Can we talk?"

"I guess."

"How about we take a walk?"

"Sure. Let me say goodbye to Erin, and then I need to grab a jacket."

She went out back for a minute, came back and grabbed her jacket by the door. They walked outside. It was a cool, clear night, but no wind. Stars were out, and if this were a date, it would be a great night for it.

But it wasn't.

"How are you doing?" she asked as they walked down the path through the woods.

"I'm good. I got a lot of rest last night. That helped."

"I'm happy to hear that."

He stopped and turned to face her. "Tell me what's upsetting you."

"Nothing is upsetting me. I'm just . . . giving you space."

"I don't want space from you, Mae. I want to be with you.

I want to spend time with you. Tell me how I fucked up so I can make it better."

"You didn't—"

"Mae. Tell me."

He could tell from the consternation on her face that she had a million thoughts running through her head and he was about to get hit with all of them. He welcomed them because he needed to know why she was upset.

"Okay, fine. You got a raw deal with your parents, and I sympathize, I really do. But instead of sharing your pain with me, you shut me out and got into your own head. And then you yelled at me. I don't like being yelled at. I mean, sure, you apologized and all, but how can I be sure that you won't fly off into an angry mood the next time—I don't know, you have a shitty day of filming?"

He started to laugh, because that just wasn't who he was. Then again, he hadn't really shown her who he was the past few days, had he?

"I'm sorry, Mae. You're right. I did get into my head. My parents' marriage blew up and I didn't know anything about it. That's life-changing news. It's not 'Hey, I had a bad day of work' kind of shit. And you're right that I should have shared with you, but I didn't know how to handle all these negative feelings I was having. It was kind of a first for me, ya know?"

"Okay. I can understand that."

They had made their way to the production area. He led her toward his trailer and paused, asking without words if she was interested in stepping in. She nodded, so they went inside.

"Something to drink?" he asked.

"Just water for me."

He grabbed waters for both of them and they sat on the

sofa. He got close to her, because he wanted to make sure she understood what he was saying.

"It's obvious I hurt you, and I'm really sorry about that. My feelings were confusing to me. If I'm honest, they still are. I'm constantly pissed off and I don't know why and I'm not the kind of person who holds anger inside, so I just don't know what to do with it. If you feel like I keep taking it out on you—I am so sorry about that."

She took his hand. "I appreciate the apology. And to clarify, you're not taking it out on me. It was my feelings about the situation that I needed to work through, which you're helping me with. I wanted to help you and . . . I don't know, I guess there was no way I could ease your pain. That's hard for me."

He shrugged. "Some problems can't be solved."

"Also hard for me to acknowledge."

He smiled. "I can't tell you how much you being here for me has helped. Even if the situation hasn't changed—can't be changed. It helps knowing you're here to talk through it."

Now Mae smiled, and his whole world brightened. "The fact you're talking to me about how you feel is helpful. Closing yourself off only makes that anger fester."

"You sound like you know what you're talking about."

"Oh, believe me, I do. When I found out about Isaac's cheating, and right before our wedding? I can't even explain the level of anger I felt. I mean, I-wanted-to-kill-him levels of anger. And I had nowhere to go with that rage, because obviously I couldn't actually murder him."

"Too bad."

She let out a laugh. "Yeah. I held all that anger inside— for a while, but all it did was make me lash out at everyone else. The smallest thing would set me off. It wasn't long before I realized I was alienating myself from everyone who cared about me. And I was mimicking Isaac's personality of blowing up about every little thing, which was one of the things that irritated me the most about him."

No wonder she was so upset with him. "So, what helped you?"

"First off, talking about my feelings, which wasn't always the easiest thing for me to do, because I had always prided myself on being able to handle things on my own. Until I couldn't anymore, and I realized I didn't have to. I had friends who were willing to sit, listen and commiserate with my pain. And a few suggested therapy so I could talk to someone who wasn't directly involved in my situation. It was the best advice I'd ever been given."

"I've never tried therapy. Not sure that's really going to be for me."

She squeezed his hand. "Maybe it's not, but if you don't mind a little unsolicited advice?"

He nodded. "Of course."

"Your world has turned upside down in an instant. Your parents' loving, stable marriage—or at least that's what you thought it was—has disintegrated, and you're upset about it. Rightly so. And you have all these feelings about it. I am here for you to talk about those feelings anytime you want to because I care about you. But having someone to walk you through your feelings, to channel that anger so it doesn't eat you up inside, might be worth your time."

"Maybe."

"And if you find out it isn't worth it, then you've lost nothing but a few hours, right?"

"Yeah."

"Even better, you can do therapy online. I can recommend an excellent therapist here locally, and she also takes online appointments. She is very discreet. Or, you can have your agent or PR people or whoever your Hollywood people are recommend someone."

He had to admit that having someone outside the business to talk to might be a good idea. "I'll book an appointment with someone. I appreciate it. I think you're right that I need someone on the outside of all this to talk to."

"I hope it helps."

"I hope so, too. And thank you for understanding. I'm sorry again for being such a jerk."

"The fact that you realized it gives me hope for you." She gave him a lopsided grin.

He laughed, instant relief washing over him.

"Do you want to hang out for a while and watch a movie?"

She shrugged. "As long as it's not one of yours."

"Oh, you think you're funny, huh?"

"I'm hilarious and you know it."

He laughed, shook his head and grabbed the remote. She grabbed the blanket off the back of the sofa, kicked off her boots and draped her legs over his while he started the movie.

Now things felt a little more normal, and a lot more right with his world.

Things were always right with his world when Mae was in it.

CHAPTER

······

twenty-nine

MAE COULDN'T BELIEVE there were only a few weeks until Christmas. Since she was currently staying at the Bellinis', she hadn't bothered digging out the decorations at her apartment, but she'd really enjoyed helping the Bellinis decorate their house.

They went all out with two Christmas trees, seasonal décor all over the house, and lights on the house, the barn and all across the property. The outside lights were all white because of winter weddings, and since they celebrated weddings of all faiths, the white lights would suffice no matter what type of wedding they celebrated. Besides, since the nights were getting colder, most of the weddings were inside the barn and could be lighted according to the couple's wants and customs.

Once decorating was done, baking started. Louise rarely gave up control over her kitchen, but since she left at night, Mae enjoyed making breads and cakes and cookies whenever she had the chance. She had spent last night elbows-deep in flour and sugar and decorating.

She wasn't filming today, but Kane had been busy with back-to-back scenes with his film brother and best friend the past couple of days, so she hadn't seen him and, frankly, she'd missed him. They'd talked, but they hadn't really been together since he'd also been filming some night scenes. She figured if she brought some of the stuff she'd baked, maybe she could see Kane for a few minutes.

After packaging up some cookies and bread she'd made the night before, she put on her sweater and walked over to the production area.

The weather continued to be ideal. Sunny and in the low seventies, and today there was no wind, making it a perfect day. She figured the production company was probably pretty happy about the ideal conditions for filming, too. In some places, late November and December were awful, but here, it could stay nice all the way into January.

She made her way through the path. Security knew her well by now and let her in, and she headed toward where filming was occurring, surprised to see a woman and a man in the middle of a scene that had been set up at a small gazebo they had erected in a clearing in the woods. It always surprised her how quickly the crew could put together something phenomenal and beautiful, making it look like it had always been there. She stood quietly while the actors completed the scene, an emotional one with declarations of love that ended in a very passionate kiss. When Alexis called cut, there was a flurry of activity as if that romantic scene hadn't even happened.

Moviemaking was weird.

"Hey."

She flipped around to see Kane standing there. "Hey, yourself. I was watching the scene they were just filming."

"Oh, yeah. My best friend and my ex-girlfriend."

"Oh. Complicated."

"Very. I slip in next, though it's kind of filmed out of order since in the movie he comes in after I leave. He's actually in love with her, only she doesn't realize it yet because she thinks she's still in love with me. Which she isn't. Kind of a subplot."

"Got it. That should be fun in the movie."

"I hope so. What are you doing here?"

She picked up the bag she'd brought. "I baked."

His brows lifted. "Ohhh. I can't wait to see what you brought. Can you hang out while I do this scene?"

She thought about what she had going on and realized she didn't have any meetings, so she nodded. "Yes, I have some time."

After putting the snacks on the table for everyone to enjoy, she made her way back to the scene in the woods. Kane was standing inside the gazebo, a prop phone in his hand. He looked amazing in dark jeans and a striped button-down shirt. He had started pacing, and Alexis called action. He was talking on the phone with someone, and the actress stood just outside the gazebo. Kane noticed her and told whoever he was talking to that he'd call them back.

"I'm sorry, Blake. I didn't know you were on the phone."

"It's okay, Sarah. What's up?"

The actress—or her character, Sarah—walked fully into the gazebo, stopping in front of Kane. "I thought we could have a minute to talk—alone. See if we can recapture that magic we had."

Kane laid his hands on Sarah's shoulders. "Sarah. I think what you're looking for from me is an apology, something you didn't get when we broke up all those years ago."

She laid her hand on his chest and moved in to him. Close to him. "No, what I want from you is what we both want. What we both need, Blake. A reconciliation."

He took her hand and wrapped both of his around it. "What about Jeff?"

She frowned and backed up a step, turning away from him. "Jeff? I don't have feelings for Jeff."

"Don't you? You're so afraid of getting hurt again that you're throwing yourself at a guy you don't even care about—that would be me, by the way. Come on, Sarah. Jeff loves you."

She turned to face him again, her eyes wide. "He . . . loves me?"

Even from this distance, Mae could see the tears welling in Sarah's eyes. Wow. She was good.

"Hell yeah he does."

This was spoken by the actor who'd been with Sarah in the last scene as he walked into the gazebo.

Kane smiled at Jeff. "I don't think I'm needed here anymore. I'll let you two talk."

Kane walked out of the gazebo, leaving Sarah and Jeff looking at each other.

"And . . . cut," Alexis said. "Great work, everyone."

And just like that, Kane and the other two actors laughed and high-fived.

Whew. That had been a tight scene. Kane grabbed a bottle of water from the table, along with two of the cookies she had made.

"Wow," she said. "There was some emotion in that scene."

"Yeah," he said, taking a bite of a cookie. "Alexis digs that stuff. I'm glad we hit it in one take."

She shook her head. "Well, you—and your actor friends—are very good at it."

He had started walking away from the area, so she followed. "Thanks. I need to change out of wardrobe and into something that looks a lot like what I'm wearing now." He tossed the other cookie in his mouth and mumbled something that sounded like "I'll be right back," so she waited while he climbed into the costuming chamber.

He came out about five minutes later dressed pretty much the same—except this time the jeans were relaxed and he was wearing a T-shirt and scuffed boots.

"You look a lot more comfortable," she said.

"Feel that way, too. I know it's still early, but how much more work do you have today?"

"Just paperwork. Calendar stuff and notes. Why?"

"I thought we might go somewhere. I don't have any more scenes today. Feel like getting out of here?"

She shrugged, figuring she could catch up on work later tonight. "Sure." She'd worn leggings and tennis shoes along with a long-sleeved shirt and she had her sweater, so she was probably appropriately dressed for . . . wherever.

They went to his car and he took off, taking them onto the expressway and heading toward the city. When he pulled off at the sign for the zoo, she smiled.

"Like the zoo?"

"I love zoos. I try to visit them at every city I'm in." At the stoplight, he turned to her. "How about you? Do you like them? If you don't we don't have to go."

"I love them. Let's do it."

KANE WAS SO relieved that Mae seemed to enjoy the zoo as much as he did. He supposed he should have suggested it to her instead of just driving here and hoping for the best. But he wanted to surprise her with a fun day out.

"My therapist suggested I get out and do some fun things instead of hanging out in my trailer stewing in my anger juices."

She wrinkled her nose. "Anger juices? That sounds gross."

"Yeah, like my mood lately. And he's right, so I figured I'd do something that makes me happy."

She looked over at him and smiled. "I'm glad you decided to seek therapy."

"It's been helpful, though it's early. But you were right that it's good to have someone to talk to that doesn't know me personally. I can really dive in and lay it all out there without judgment or personal bias."

"Therapy is super helpful. I recommend it for everyone."

They arrived at the zoo and started at the snakes. He'd told Mae she could choose where they went. They could take the elephant train, or go see the giraffes, but no, she wanted to see the snakes.

He loved this woman. Uh, he loved the things she loved, anyway.

No, you love her, jackass. You should think about telling her that.

That was the last thing he wanted to do. Love didn't last—that much was clear after seeing what had happened with his parents. But he and Mae were getting along great right now. Wasn't it best to keep things the way they were without fucking it all up with love and forever and bullshit like that?

Just have a good time, and when it was over, it was over.

Great pep talk, self.

"Look at this boa," Mae said, grabbing his hand to bring him over to one of the more colorful snakes from the Amazon.

"Pretty cool." He was not a snake fan, but Mae seemed to love them, so they wandered and she gushed over all of them.

"Did you have pet snakes as a kid?" he asked.

"Me? Oh, God no. My mom would have freaked. But I dated a guy in high school who was into snakes. He had quite a few, and he took very good care of them. He taught me a lot and let me handle them. They're amazing creatures, but you need to respect them."

"So they don't bite you. Or eat you."

She laughed. "Right."

After the snakes they went to the elephants. He'd always enjoyed the elephants. "Did you know that elephants feel things? Emotions, like sadness and happiness and love?"

"I didn't know that," she said. "But they're such majestic, beautiful creatures, and their eyes tell a story, so I'm not at all surprised."

"I did a movie in Africa and got the opportunity to travel into the Serengeti, see the animals in their natural habitat without disturbing them. It was incredible. Herd upon herd of elephants living freely, along with rhinos, lions and an abundance of other creatures."

"That sounds amazing. It must have been an incredible trip."

"It was. We . . . you should go there sometime." His first impulse had been to talk about taking a trip together. What stopped him? The fear that there was an expiration date to their relationship? That if he'd asked she'd have said no?

He wanted her in his life.

Maybe you should start by asking her.

That voice in his head was really pissing him off.

They spent another hour or so there, visiting the monkeys, bears, lions and tigers. It was great to wander, and no one seemed to recognize him, likely because the animals were much more interesting than he was. Fortunately, the paparazzi hadn't been on his ass lately. He was either getting better at dodging them or maybe they were all on holiday break. Either way, he enjoyed a nice leisurely couple of hours at the zoo with Mae, until they both decided they were thirsty and hungry, so they headed out.

They drove for a while out of town until they found a Mexican restaurant that had a parking lot filled with cars. Kane always knew that was how you could tell a place had excellent food, so they stopped there.

Not much to look at on the inside, with small tables and a couple of booths, but the smells coming from the kitchen made Kane's stomach grumble. The whole place was bustling. They were seated at an empty table in the corner and a server came right over. He ordered a beer and Mae wanted iced tea. Chips and salsa along with queso appeared right away.

"This is so good," Mae said, talking while sliding another salsa-filled chip into her mouth. "I'm so hungry."

He popped a chip into his mouth, the salsa like a tangy appetizer whetting his appetite for something more substantial. A lot like the woman who sat across from him, always stimulating his hunger for more.

Drinks were brought and the first thing Kane did was guzzle down half the glass of water.

"You were really good in your scene today with . . . I only know her character's name, Sarah."

"Right. That's Hannah. She's pretty great. Always shows up prepared and she's easy to play off of."

"Which makes your job easier, right?"

"Exactly." He scooped up some queso on his chip and slid it into his mouth. "David is good, too. He and Hannah have awesome chemistry. I'm sure you saw it in their scene."

"I did. I don't know how you all do that—the faking of the love thing."

He laughed. "It's called acting. You just replace yourself with the character. It's that character's feelings and emotions, not yours. If we make it look real, then we've done a good job. If we do a good job, we get booked for other jobs. That's how we become successful."

"I see. It's just that easy, huh?"

"No, it's not easy at all."

"Because you can be good—just like a lot of actors can be good. But there are only so many parts out there, right? Which means unless you're the top one percent who's constantly in demand, it's always a fight to get the good roles."

Mae had nailed it. Which was pretty impressive for someone who wasn't on the inside of the business. "Pretty much."

"So are you?" she asked.

"Am I what?"

"In the top one percent."

Kane took a long swallow of his beer. "Not even close. I do okay. I work fairly steadily. But I figure I'm average."

"Huh." She leaned back and studied him, and when their server returned they put in their order. "I've always considered your work above average."

His lips curved. "You're not talking about my acting, are you?"

"Not at all."

"So you think I'm a hack."

"I didn't say that." She leaned forward to take a sip of tea and scoop some queso onto a chip. "However, now that I know you're not a true movie star, I'm rethinking our entire relationship. If you're a nobody, how will I become vicariously famous?"

He snorted out a laugh. "I had no idea that was one of your goals."

"It wasn't. But I am a stand-in bride, you know. I have my own reputation to consider, even though no one will see my face."

"Yeah, but they'll see your butt, and I speak from experience when I say you have one very fine ass, Ms. Wallace."

She batted her lashes and tilted her head. "Why, thank you."

The server brought their food and they dug in. Kane's enchiladas were excellent—loaded with beef and cheese, and the rice and beans were outstanding. Mae shared a bite of her chimichanga and the chicken was tender and flavorful.

"Good food," he said after he'd completely obliterated everything on his plate. And some of Mae's as well.

"It was. I'll definitely have to come back here. But now my stomach is full and I need a nap."

"Want me to rent a hotel room so you can sleep off our dinner?"

She gave him a wry smile. "Nice try, but since I blew off most of the day, I have to go to work."

Too bad, because he wanted to get her alone. But he also respected her work, so he drove them back to the Bellini property, pulling up in front of the main house.

"Thanks for the great day," she said as she unbuckled her seat belt. "And for the awesome food. I'm only sorry that I found out this late in our relationship what a loser you are."

"Oh. You're funny." He got out and came around to her side of the car and pulled her out, pinning her between the car and his body. "Given enough alone time with you, I can show you just how much of a winner I am."

"Does that mean sex? And what exactly do you win at? Coming first?"

He rolled his eyes. "I always make you come first and you know it."

"Hmm. My memory is a little fuzzy. I might need reminding."

He pressed up against her, showing her how quickly she

could get him hard. Her breathing quickened and she reached between them to rub her palm against his erection.

"Your place," she whispered. "And hurry up."

"Yeah." He put her back in the car and tried not to run to his side. He drove them around the property, parking in the closest spot. They got out and he took her hand, trying not to drag her to his trailer. But, dammit, he was in a hurry.

He held the door for her and she walked in, Kane right behind her, closing and locking the door. He turned her to face him, his hands in her hair, his mouth on hers, taking in the taste of her, the feel of her body moving against him.

She whimpered against him, dropping her purse, shrugging out of her sweater at the same time she toed out of her tennis shoes. He pulled off his jacket and started unbuttoning his shirt while he walked them toward the bedroom.

By the time they got there he had his shirt off and his jeans unzipped. Mae sat on the bed and wriggled out of her pants, teasing him by drawing the straps of her bra down each arm, then turning around for him to undo the clasp. He was dropping his jeans at the same time he undid the clasp of her bra.

In the next few seconds they were both naked and on the bed. He reached over and grabbed a condom, tossing it nearby so he could focus on Mae, sliding his hand over her breast, taking a nipple into his mouth, feeling her lift upward to give him more.

"No foreplay," she said, raising her legs. "I'm ready for you to be inside me."

Since he was more than ready, he grabbed the condom package and tore it open, put it on, then rolled to his side, grabbing one of Mae's legs to rest it over his hip. And then he slid inside her.

"This what you wanted?" he asked, moving in, then out.

"You are what I want. Just like this." She swept her hand over his chest, then held on to his shoulder while she moved against him.

Then there were no words as they both gave and took from each other, their lips and tongues meeting in a frenzy of passion. Their movements increased as they chased that pleasure that led to an explosion in record time. That they came together surprised the hell out of him as he held on to Mae while she trembled against him. He had to admit it had left him shaky, too.

He'd never shared a passion as intense as he had with Mae. And he knew why, though he pushed those feelings deep down. Right now he just wanted to feel the aftereffects of really awesome sex.

They lay like that for a while, until Mae pushed at his chest. "I need to go. I have work to do."

"Okay."

They got up and cleaned up in the bathroom, then got dressed. Kane drove her back to the house and walked her to the front door. He pulled her close and gave her a lingering kiss that made him want to hold on to her much, much longer. But they finally pulled apart and he saw the heat, the emotion in her eyes, reflecting what he felt.

"See you tomorrow," she said.

He smiled. "Yeah, you will."

He walked down the steps to his car, turned to see her standing at the door watching him, then got in and drove away, unable to lose the smile on his face.

You love her.

"No, I don't."

Yeah, you do. Better pull your head out of your ass and figure out your shit, dude.

Inner voice was right about that.

CHAPTER
······
thirty

MAE ABSENTLY STIRRED her coffee, the drone of voices in the room like bees buzzing around her. Her thoughts lingered on yesterday, on the intimate way she and Kane had connected. It had been furious and passionate, the two of them as one.

Which seemed hokey as hell, but there it was. She knew him like she'd never known another man.

She loved him.

"Okay, Mae," Erin said. "What's going on?"

She snapped out of her daze and looked over at Erin. "Excuse me?"

"We've been talking and talking and you haven't said a single word," Honor said.

"Yeah," Brenna said. "You've just sat there with a goofy grin on your face. What's up with you?"

"Oh, uh . . . nothing. I stayed up late working so I'm a little tired, that's all."

"Uh-huh." Erin gave her a once-over. "We've all had that 'little tired' look before, honey. It's called great sex."

Brenna snickered. "Still going hot and heavy with the actor, huh?"

"I think it might be more than that," Honor said.

She blinked. "I don't know what you're talking about."

"You know we're family," Honor said. "You can confide in us."

"Oh, well. It's just . . ." She didn't know why she was trying to hide her feelings. They were right—they were her family. "I'm in love with him."

They all stared at her.

"Is that a good thing or a bad thing?" Brenna asked.

"Honestly? I don't know."

"Has he said anything about how he feels?" Honor asked.

"Not a word. He's gone through a lot of emotional stuff lately, so I don't think this is the right time to tell him how I feel."

Erin frowned. "What do you mean? What emotional stuff?"

"It's not for me to say. I just know that talking to him about relationship things right now wouldn't be good for him—or for me. We're getting along fine and I'd like to keep it that way."

Honor reached over and grasped her hand. "You know best, honey. Just know that we're here for you any time you want to talk."

"Thanks. And I'm good right now. Really."

Erin grinned. "Then that's all we need to know."

"Great," Brenna said. "Then we can get on with the meeting."

An hour and an excellent breakfast later, Mae had taken her notes to her office and sat at her desk. She was due on set at ten thirty to film a scene with Kane, so she updated her calendar, sent out a couple of confirmation emails to vendors regarding upcoming weddings, then headed over to the production office, trying to tamp down her excitement about seeing Kane.

She checked in at the production office. The guy in charge there frowned. "Uh, they crossed you off the schedule today."

And then she frowned. "Really? I was supposed to film with Kane. Can you point me in the direction of where he is?"

He checked the schedule, then told her where Kane was supposed to be, so she headed that way.

Surely there was some misunderstanding. Then again, she might have gotten the dates wrong, though that was unlikely. She was always good at managing her calendar and making sure it was always right.

As she came up on the scene that was being filmed, she slowed her steps, having learned that any extraneous sounds could ruin the scene. She moved as close as she could until she saw Kane and some actress, the two of them having a serious conversation. The actress had her back turned to Mae so she didn't know who it was.

"I don't know what you're talking about, Blake."

"Don't you? You've moved on with your life, Caroline. Seems to me you've forgotten all about what we had."

"Oh. I've forgotten? Who left who? Who moved all the way to London without a word? Because that wasn't me. And now you're here asking me that question?"

"I'm here because I'm Keith's best friend. No other reason."

"Right," the actress said. "Because you couldn't be here for me. You never have been before. Why start now?"

She started to walk away but Kane grabbed her wrist. "That's not true and you know it."

"And, cut," Alexis said. The actress threw her arms around Kane, who lifted her up and swung her around.

Then recognition hit. That was Everly Sloane, the actress Mae had been standing in for.

The woman was the same height and build as Mae, with the same dark hair. From the back she and Mae could almost be twins. No wonder they had asked her to be a backup for Everly.

They were obviously busy and had a lot of scenes to catch up on, so Mae turned to leave.

"Mae!"

She stopped, pivoted and put on a smile as Kane—along with Everly—made his way toward her.

"Sorry to disturb the filming. They didn't tell me I wasn't needed."

"It's okay. And I'm sorry about that. Everly flew in yesterday and surprised all of us by showing up on set this morning. Everly Sloane, this is Mae Wallace. Mae has been working as your stand-in for some scenes while we were waiting on you."

Everly smiled brightly and shook Mae's hand. "Thanks so much for doing that, Mae. I put the whole production in a bind while I finished up my last movie. I'm so glad they could count on you to help out."

"Me, too. And it was fun. I'm not in the movie business so it was kind of a blast. I'm very happy you're here, though, so I can get back to my other job."

"Mae works for the wedding business here," Kane said.

"Oh, wow," Everly said. "You've really been doubling up. I'm sorry we took up so much of your time on my account."

"It's fine. It wasn't a lot."

"Well, I still feel like I owe you." She paused, then said, "Oh, we should have dinner. We'll even let Kane come along."

Mae didn't know what to say, so she looked at Kane, who grinned.

"Sounds great," he said. "Mae?"

She shrugged. "Sure. Thanks."

"Awesome. Let me get your number and I'll text you about a time."

They exchanged numbers, and then Mae excused herself to head back to work.

Okay, that was weird. Everly was super friendly. Was that genuine? She had no idea. She supposed she'd find out tonight.

In the meantime, she had work to do.

KANE HAD A great day of filming. It was awesome having Everly there. They had always worked well together, and she was always prepared, just like him, so they knocked out four scenes in perfect takes, which made Alexis super happy, especially since they were behind schedule due to Everly's late arrival.

The first thing she had done was apologize to the cast and crew for her delayed arrival and promised she'd work fast and make up the time. After she and Kane had worked their scenes, she did a couple more scenes with other actors.

The one thing Kane had always known about Everly was that she worked hard. They'd be caught up in no time.

Everly had texted both him and Mae after she finished filming to say she was ready to eat if they were, so Kane told her they could meet and pick up Mae. Mae texted back to let them know she was ready anytime.

"I am so hungry," Everly said, climbing into the front seat of his car. He hadn't had a chance to tell Everly about his relationship with Mae, and asking her to sit in the back seat seemed rude, so he let it go, figuring Mae wouldn't care.

He pulled up in front of the main house.

"Wow, this place is beautiful," Everly said.

"Yeah, it's very cool. We'll film some scenes in the barn and over at the arbor where they perform weddings."

"I can't wait."

Mae came out and didn't even pause when she saw Everly sitting in the front seat. She smiled, waved, then got into the back seat.

"I hope everyone is as hungry as I am," Everly said.

"I'm always hungry," Mae said.

Everly laughed. "You and I are going to be best friends."

"What are you in the mood to eat, Everly?" Mae asked.

"Oh, I don't know. I like everything. And nothing fancy. Low profile suits me best."

"Perfect. How about burgers and beer in a very nondescript location?"

"That sounds ideal."

Mae directed Kane to a place called the Garage, where there were all kinds of burgers, including vegetarian. They ordered their beers and burgers and grabbed a table. There were TVs placed all around, and even better—sports. Kane could eat here every day. Hopefully the food was good.

"I can't believe you never brought me here before," he said to Mae.

She shrugged. "We've eaten lots of places. I was getting around to it."

"You two have gone out a lot?" Everly asked as she took a sip of her beer.

He could tell Mae was going to defer to Kane, who nodded. "Yeah, she's been putting up with me."

Everly laughed. "He's a hardship. I know. But he needs friends, so you're a real sport."

"Mmm." Mae nodded, taking a drink of beer. "He did look like a lonely kid in a corner. I took pity on him."

"Hey, now," Kane said. "I can go sit at another table."

"But then you'd miss out on the company of two beautiful women," Everly said. "And you wouldn't want to do that, would you?"

He shrugged. "I guess not."

Mae laughed, then engaged in conversation with Everly about her films and where she traveled. Kane sat back, sipped his beer and focused on the sports update on the TV until their burgers arrived. He took a bite of the juicy burger, then shoved fries in his mouth, nodding.

"Oh, yeah," he said. "These are good burgers."

"Right?" Mae asked. "Kind of perfect."

"This veggie burger is tasty," Everly said. "And the spicy sweet potato fries are to die for. Good choice, Mae."

"I'm so glad you like it."

After she finished her burger, Everly wiped her hands with the napkin, then took a long swallow of beer. "So, Mae, tell me about yourself. Have you always been in the wedding business?"

"Not always. I got involved with the Bellinis a couple of years ago. Before that I was in marketing and management for a bridal dress company."

"Ooh. That sounds fun."

"It was. But the owner and I had different ideas on how to promote the company and we clashed—often. When Honor Bellini asked me to come on board and help them manage their wedding business, I jumped at the opportunity. The three sisters along with their parents have a beautiful wedding and winery operation, and I knew my style and theirs would mesh."

"Isn't it awesome to know where you fit?"

"It is. How did you decide to get into acting?"

"Oh, well, I fell into it, actually. I did plays in school and I was pretty good at it, and since we lived in L.A. I was scouted by an agent who signed me. I ended up on some teen show—that's where Kane and I met, actually."

Mae looked over at Kane. "You and Everly have known each other since you were teens?"

"Yup. We go way back."

"We do. Our paths seem to have crossed a lot, both in television and film. I think it was the chemistry thing, which is why we often end up doing movies together. It's been fun, hasn't it, Kane?"

He gave Everly a smile. "Sure has."

Kane watched a range of emotions cross Mae's face, and hoped she understood that there was absolutely nothing going on between Everly and him. He'd explain it to her when they had some alone time.

After dinner they headed back to the Bellini property.

"Could you drop me off at the house?" Mae asked. "I have tons of paperwork to prep for tomorrow. We have some couples coming in to tour the wedding venue."

"How fun," Everly said as Kane pulled up to the house. She turned around to look at Mae. "It was great to spend some time with you, Mae. We'll definitely have to do it again."

Mae laid her hand on Everly's. "It was so fun. I can't wait to see you again. Thanks, Kane. I'll see you both later."

"Wait," Kane said. "I'll walk you to the door."

She shrugged and got out.

Kane walked her up. "Are you sure you can't come by the trailer tonight?"

"No, I really do have a lot to do."

He stopped at the door, wanting to kiss her, but she took a step back, a clear signal that she wasn't comfortable with that with Everly watching them, so he shoved his hands in his pockets.

"Talk to you tomorrow?" he asked.

She gave a quick nod. "Absolutely. Night, Kane."

"Good night, Mae."

He waited for her to go inside, then walked down the steps and got back into the car, feeling wholly unsatisfied with how that had gone down.

"So," Everly said as Kane turned around and drove toward their trailers. "You and Mae, huh?"

He shot her a look. "How did you know?"

She laughed. "You were antsy and I could tell you wanted to touch her or kiss her and I can tell when I'm a third wheel, dude. Why didn't you just say something? It would have been a lot more comfortable for all of us."

"I don't know. I didn't want Mae to feel weird. I didn't want you to feel weird."

"Well, now we all feel weird, jackass."

He sighed. "Sorry."

She punched his arm. "You better talk to your woman and fix things."

"I will."

They got out of the car and he walked her to her trailer. She pulled him into a tight hug. "Love you."

"I love you, too."

"I'm going to go to my trailer, call Ethan and then face-plant on my bed. We have five thirty makeup tomorrow."

He grimaced. "Yeah, yeah. Good night."

As soon as he got back to his trailer, he took out his phone and called Mae. She didn't answer, which made him frown, so he sent a text.

Are you busy? I tried calling you.

He waited, watching his phone for a reply, then got tired of waiting, so he opened his game console to play some games. About thirty minutes later his phone pinged. He grabbed it to see Mae had replied.

Sorry. Was taking a bath and reading a book.
What's up?

At the moment, he was thinking about her naked in the tub, bubbles up to her neck while she relaxed and read. But that wasn't supposed to be his focus, so he typed a reply.

Sorry about tonight. Everly knows about us.

She replied with a ?

He wasn't going to do this with a text, so he FaceTimed her. She answered right away this time.

"Hey," she said, looking beautiful with her hair in a bun, sitting on her bed wearing a tank top.

"Hey. Everly said I made tonight weird when it didn't have to be because I didn't tell her about us. I was trying to be sensitive."

"Because . . ."

He dragged his fingers through his hair. "I don't know. I didn't want you to feel weird. I didn't want her to feel weird."

"So instead you made us all feel weird."

"That's exactly what she said."

Mae smiled. "I knew I liked her. Look, it's fine. I understand why. She's your friend and you wanted her to be comfortable with us. Next time, just make her feel comfortable—like your friend. Because I really like her, Kane."

"I like her, too. She's been like a sister to me ever since we first met as teens. And, trust me, that's all we are to each other."

"I believe you."

Now that he'd gotten things straightened out with Mae, he felt the fatigue overwhelm him. "I've got to be in makeup at five thirty tomorrow."

"Ugh. Go to bed."

"Yeah, I will. I'll see you sometime tomorrow, okay?"

"It's Friday and we have a wedding, so I'll be busy most of the day—and night. And we have two weddings on Saturday."

"Hey, we'll figure something out."

"Yeah, we will."

"Don't work too hard, Kane."

"You, either."

They clicked off. Kane turned his game off and went into the bedroom. By the time he climbed into bed he was more than ready to sleep.

He couldn't wait to see Mae again. Hopefully sooner rather than later.

CHAPTER
· · · · · ·
thirty-one

IT HAD BEEN a long weekend. The wedding on Friday went off without any complications, and fortunately it had ended by eleven, which meant they had all the guests out and were done cleaning up by midnight.

Weddings always hyped Mae up and it was hard to come down from that. She wished she could have hung out with Kane, but he'd texted her earlier in the day and told her they were filming all through the day on Saturday, and she figured he'd gone to bed already. So she'd done the same thing, though it had taken her a while to go to sleep. They had two weddings on Saturday so she'd been busy the entire day and night without a break, and she hadn't seen Kane at all. She'd barely had time to eat. By the time the evening wedding had finished she'd been so exhausted she'd gone right to bed.

On Sunday, she slept in. When she woke there was a text message from Kane saying he was catching up on filming with Everly and he'd be tied up the entire day.

Well, damn. They had planned to spend Sunday together,

but now that wasn't going to happen. But, whatever. She spent the day cleaning her room—which, technically wasn't really hers. In fact, now that she wasn't filming anymore, she could move back to her apartment. She'd deal with that later, though. Instead, she did all her laundry and made some notes for the meeting tomorrow. The family was coming over for dinner, so she took a shower and put on leggings and a sweater, heading downstairs when she heard voices.

Brenna and Finn had come in at the same time as Honor and Owen.

"Hey, everyone," she said. "How's it going?"

"I don't know about you," Brenna said as she poured herself a glass of wine. "But this weekend was intense and I'm exhausted."

"Me, too," Honor said. "I slept hard last night."

"Same," Mae said.

Erin and Jason came in, and Maureen ran over to take JJ from them and disappeared into the living room.

"Hi to you, too, Mom," Erin said, shaking her head. "It's like I don't even exist anymore since I had JJ."

"Yeah, you really don't," Jason said, earning a jab in his middle from Erin.

Mae smiled at how much Maureen was enjoying being a grandma.

Erin took a seat at the dining room table and started scrolling through her phone, obviously deciding to ignore her family.

"Hey, I saw that the dress you liked was on sale," Honor said to Mae as they made their way to the table.

"Oh. The red one?"

"Yes. The one you said you wanted to get for Christmas."

"Send me a link?"

"I will."

"Whoa," Erin said, looking over her. "Mae. Did you see this?"

"See what?" Hopefully another sale. She did love to shop.

"There's a story on the gossip sites about Kane."

She gave Erin a wry smile. "I'm pretty sure there's always a story on the gossip sites about Kane."

"No. This one is about him and his co-star. With pictures."

"Yeah, Everly finally showed up. They've been filming all weekend. The paparazzi probably got pics of the two of them doing a scene together."

"From the looks of it, that's not all they've been doing. I'll send you the link."

Her phone pinged with the link, so Mae clicked on it. Frowning, she studied the pic. It definitely wasn't taken on the property, but rather somewhere in the city. She wished she could figure out where but it was outside some restaurant. And Kane—was it Kane? It had to be him, though it was a view of the back of his head. But same height, same dark hair, dark jeans, and he had Everly in his arms, kissing her.

Her stomach knotted.

"I'm sure he can explain this," Brenna said. "Don't worry about it."

She laid her phone down and put on a smile. "I'm not worried. Not at all."

She was worried plenty, but there wasn't anything she could do about it until she talked to Kane.

KANE HAD JUST finished a scene with Everly. It had gone well. They were catching up in a hurry and this was one of the many times he was damn happy she was his co-star. She grabbed her phone off a nearby table and started scrolling, stopping suddenly and grabbing his arm. "Oh no. This is not good."

"What's wrong?"

She handed her phone to him. The first thing he saw was a picture. It was from a distance, but it was clearly Everly, kissing some guy in front of a restaurant. But the headline was what really caught his attention. **Everly Sloane Hot and Heavy on Location with Kane August.** He looked up at her. "Oh, shit."

"Yes. I'm so sorry." She pulled him around the corner so they were alone. "Ethan flew in yesterday and we met in the city, snuck out for a late dinner. He grabbed me and kissed me and I guess there were paps around that I didn't see. I had no idea. And now this."

Mae was going to freak out. "Yeah."

"The last thing I want is for my relationship with Ethan to get out. You know how the tabloids are. They'll ruin things between us before we have a chance to get on a solid footing."

"So what do you want me to do?"

"Let it play out. Rumors die down and we'll deny them. I just can't have anyone knowing about this."

He cocked his head to the side. "Everly. What am I supposed to tell Mae?"

Her eyes widened. "I completely didn't think . . . Oh, Kane. I'm sorry."

"Yeah, me, too." He dragged his fingers through his hair, trying to figure out what he was going to stay to her.

"Tell her . . . tell her it was nothing. Please, Kane. Just for a while."

"You're asking me to lie to her."

She paced back and forth around him. "I know, I know. I hate this as much as you do. But I really like him, Kane. This might be love. When was the last time I really cared about someone? Really trusted someone? He's good for me and I need someone good in my life."

Well, hell. Everly had been burned badly in the past. And Ethan was a good guy. They deserved a chance. "Okay. We'll hope this is a one-off and it'll die down. But you and I need to keep our distance so this rumor evaporates. On set, during scenes, and that's it. After that we go our separate ways so if cameras are lurking, they get nothing."

She gave a quick nod. "Got it. Promise. Thank you."

She moved in to hug him, but he took a step back. "I mean it, Everly. I have something—someone—important to lose, and I can't risk it."

"I understand."

He walked away, figuring that if this was on the tabloid sites, Mae had probably already seen it, which meant he was going to have to talk to her. He pulled out his phone to see if she had texted. She hadn't, so he pressed the button on her number to call her.

She didn't answer.

Shit.

He sent her a text: If you saw the gossip sites, it's not true. Let's talk.

All he could do now was hope that she believed him.

CHAPTER

· · · · · ·

thirty-two

"HE SENT YOU a text?" Brenna asked. "What did it say?"

Mae swept one hand to the side, trying to act nonchalant when she was anything but. "He sent a lot of texts, all basically saying the same thing. That it wasn't what it looked like. He doesn't have anything going on with Everly. That we need to talk."

"Do you believe him?" Erin asked.

"No. I've been down this road before. Cheaters lie."

"Oh, honey," Honor said. "Do you really think Kane is the same as your ex?"

"I don't know. But the one hard lesson I learned with Isaac is that where there's smoke, generally there's a big ole fire. I won't be made a fool of again. It's best to just end things before someone gets hurt."

Brenna gave her a sympathetic look. "You're already hurt. You love him."

She casually lifted one shoulder, trying to show that she

didn't care. "Yeah. Well, I've been here before. I got through it. I'll do it again."

"No." Honor got up and pulled Mae from her chair.

"What are you doing?"

"It's not me who's going to do anything. But you are. You're going to go talk to him. If this is truly over, then you need to get the truth from him face-to-face, not this whole text messaging thing."

"I don't see the point."

"The point is that sometimes feelings get lost in text messages, and you two have things to say to each other. Talk to him, Mae. In person. Then you'll know for sure if it's really over or not."

She did not want to do that. She looked over at Erin and Brenna, hoping they would see her side of the situation.

Erin shrugged. "I have to agree with Honor on this. If this ends you should do it face-to-face."

Brenna nodded. "I'm with them. Don't run when you can face it. And if he is a cheating asshole, you'll get the satisfaction of punching his face before you walk out on him."

She held her hands up. "Fine. I'll go see him. But if I crumple into the fetal position after, I'm counting on all of you to put me back together."

"We'll be here with margaritas and nachos," Honor said.

"Or pizza and beer," Erin said.

"Pfft." Brenna shook her head. "It'll be wine and brie."

Mae offered up a sigh. "Maybe all the above."

They took care of Monday morning business and everyone dispersed to their offices. Mae was going to dig into the calls she had to make, but she had promised the girls, so she pulled out her phone and sent a text to Kane.

I want to talk to you. Can we meet tonight?

She laid the phone down, figuring he was filming and it would take him a while to answer. She was surprised when she got a reply almost right away.

I'd like that. What time?

She replied with: Seven. I'll meet you at your trailer.
He came back with: Can't wait to see you.

Her heart did a little leap, which only irritated her, so she shoved her phone to the side and concentrated on work. After a full day of calls, tours and meetings, she realized it was after six and the entire day had zoomed by. She went upstairs and brushed her hair and her teeth, though she had no idea why. It wasn't like Kane was going to get anywhere close enough to her to even notice her breath, and he sure as hell wasn't going to be kissing her.

She changed from her flats into boots because it was cold outside at night, then went back in the bathroom to brush her hair—again—before coming out to look in the mirror again.

"Ugh. This is ridiculous." She went downstairs and grabbed her coat and walked outside, following the path she knew so well toward the production area. Security was like family now, smiling and waving her through as she made her way toward Kane's trailer. She knocked on the door and he answered right away.

"Hey," he said, moving out of the way so she could come inside.

She walked in, feeling more uncomfortable than she ever had around him.

This had been a mistake. If she had just avoided all his calls and texts, he'd eventually have gotten the hint that it was over between them. But seeing him made her ache all over. And knowing what she knew about him made the hurt all the more powerful.

"I didn't kiss Everly. I have never kissed Everly outside of a film scene. You have to believe me."

She cocked her head to the side. "Then what was that picture?"

"I . . . can't explain it. But it wasn't what it looked like."

Rolling her eyes, she said, "It's exactly what it looked like. You and Everly embracing. Kissing."

He blew out a heavy breath. "No, it's not."

"Then if it isn't that, tell me what it is."

"I can't."

And this was exactly what she'd expected from him. Lies. "This argument isn't going anywhere, Kane. You don't even have a legitimate explanation other than 'I can't.' At least be decent enough to tell me that you and Everly have a thing, and now that she's here, whatever you and I had going on is over."

"But that's not what's happening here. Everly and I are not a thing. We've never been a thing. She . . ."

Mae waited for him to finish his sentence, for him to give her anything in terms of a reasonable explanation that she could grab on to so she could believe in him.

But he only stood there, fumbling for words that wouldn't come.

"I'm out of here." She turned and walked away, hoping like hell that he would stop her, that the truth would spill out, even if it wasn't the truth she wanted to hear.

All she heard was painful, heartbreaking silence.

CHAPTER
......
thirty-three

CUT. FOR THE third time." Kane winced at the frustration in Alexis's voice. "Okay, everyone, we'll break for lunch and try this again after."

Before Alexis could lay into him about his shitty performance, he walked off the set and headed for his trailer.

"Kane. Kane, wait."

He heard Everly calling him, but he didn't want to talk to her. To anyone. He just wanted to be alone.

"I'm not going to let you walk away from me," Everly said, following him up the steps and into his trailer before he could shut and lock the door.

"Leave me alone, Everly."

"Not until you tell me what's going on. I've never seen you blow a scene over and over again like you did today."

He went to the fridge and grabbed a bottle of water, opened it and took several long swallows. "I don't want to talk about it."

Everly plopped down on his sofa. "Well, you're going to because I'm not leaving until we talk."

The last thing he wanted to do was make Everly feel responsible for his breakup with Mae. "It's nothing. I'm just in a mood."

"I'll say. What's wrong?"

"Nothing I want to talk about." He tipped the bottle to his lips, taking several more gulps, wishing it were beer, wishing he could drown out the pain swirling through his body like a plague.

"You know I'm your friend, right? That you can trust me with anything. That I'll always keep your secrets like you've always kept mine."

"Yeah."

She patted the sofa cushion next to her. "Come, sit down and talk to me."

He shook his head. "I've already hurt one woman I care about. I won't hurt another."

She frowned, then her eyes widened. "Mae. You and Mae? This is about the photo in the tabloids, isn't it?"

He didn't answer.

"She thinks it really was you and me, doesn't she? You didn't tell her?"

He gave her a straight look. "I don't betray my friends."

"Oh, Kane, I'm so sorry I put you in that position. This is such an awful situation." Everly pondered. "You told her it wasn't you, didn't you?"

"No. I just said it wasn't what it looked like."

"That's not the same thing."

He shrugged. "It's not my story to tell and you know that."

Everly inhaled and let out a deep sigh before standing up. "What a mess. I'm sorry. I'll fix this."

"How are you going to fix it?"

"I don't know, but I'll think of something."

She started to walk out.

"Everly."

"Yeah?"

"Don't do anything you'll regret. It's bad enough one of us is hurt. Don't hurt yourself trying to make things right for me, okay?"

She smiled at him. "I won't. Just get your head together so we can get that scene knocked out today, okay?"

"You got it."

She walked out and left him alone with his thoughts.

Everly wouldn't be able to fix this, because what he'd done was irreparable. Mae didn't trust him anymore, and that was everything to her. It was everything to him, too, only he'd realized it too late.

And now he'd lost her.

CHAPTER

······

thirty-four

Mae had spent the past couple of days moving back into her apartment. She'd like to say she was happy having her own space back, but she honestly missed living with the Bellinis. Having missed out on a strong family unit as a kid, she'd reveled in waking up every morning to the cheery sound of Maureen's and Johnny's voices, and Louise fixing her breakfast every day.

This morning she rolled out of bed and shoved bread in the toaster, wondering why she hadn't taken the Bellinis up on their offer of staying at the house longer. No doubt because she wanted to be alone with her heartbreak. And why not make herself even more miserable by moving back to her not-so-glamorous apartment?

She made herself a cup of coffee, grabbed her toast and went into the living room to sit, sip and read the morning news.

A text message immediately popped up from Honor: Omg read the gossip sites right now!

Before she could do that, another text popped up, this time from Brenna: Wake up and read the gossip!

And then another from Erin: Are you awake? Read the gossip sites as soon as you get this text!

Okay, then. Lots of exclamation points, so it must be important. She scrolled over to one of the more prominent sites to see a big headline.

Everly Sloane and Ethan Rogers spotted at an Oklahoma restaurant!

She frowned. Wait. What? She scrolled through the article that said "sources" informed them that the two actors had been seeing each other exclusively for a couple of months now, and that the picture previously posted of Everly and Kane had actually been Everly and Ethan out on a clandestine date.

He had told her he'd never kissed Everly outside of acting.

Kane hadn't been lying. He'd been protecting Everly.

She was more confused than ever. Relieved that he hadn't cheated on her, but why hadn't he just told her about Everly's relationship with Ethan? That didn't make sense. Didn't he trust her not to share that information? Because she never would have done that.

So while she appreciated that he didn't cheat on her, he still didn't trust her. Which meant they still weren't meant to be together.

It was still over between them.

And her heart still hurt.

AFTER THE NEWS broke about Everly and Ethan on all the gossip sites, Kane figured he'd hear from Mae.

He didn't. Not that day, and not the day after. Sure, she might be a little upset that he hadn't just told her, but he'd explain that when he saw her. But she hadn't contacted him, and by the third day he'd started to worry.

He texted her, asking if they could meet.

She didn't reply to his text so he called. She didn't answer.

He went by the house one night after he finished filming. Maureen answered, smiling at him but informing him that Mae had moved back to her apartment. He asked if she would tell him where that was but Maureen politely declined, telling him that if Mae wanted him to know where she lived, then she'd tell him.

Well, hell.

In a couple of days the production would break for the Christmas holidays. He wasn't about to leave without working out his relationship with Mae. Which meant he needed to talk to her. And he couldn't do that where she lived because he had no idea where that was.

Everly had scenes with one of the other actors this morning, so he made his way to the house, hoping like hell Mae was working.

It was shaping up to be a really nice day. The sun was out and it was already warm outside. If he weren't in his head he would have enjoyed the walk over, but as it was, all he could do was think about what he was going to say to Mae—if she let him talk to her.

When he got to the house he rang the bell and waited. The door opened and Johnny Bellini smiled at him.

"Oh, Kane August. Come on inside."

"Thank you. I was wondering if Mae was available."

"They're all in the dining room talking before the meeting. Would you like coffee?"

"Oh, no, sir, I'm fine, but thank you."

He followed Johnny down the hall and into the dining room. Everyone was in there—Mae, Erin, Brenna, Honor and Maureen. It looked like they were having a meeting, because the table was filled with laptops and papers.

"Look who showed up," Johnny said, beaming a smile.

There was a chorus of hellos, but he noticed that Mae refused to look at him.

"Kane," Maureen said. "What brings you here today? How's filming going?"

"It's going great, thanks," he said. "I'd like to talk to Mae for a few minutes if she's free."

"I am not," Mae said. "As you can see, we're in a meeting."

"Oh, I think we can spare you, Mae," Erin said.

Mae shot Erin a glare. "I have important agenda items."

"They'll hold," Brenna said.

"Yes, we'll table them until tomorrow," Honor said.

With a disgusted sigh, Mae got up. "Fine. But I'll be back before the meeting ends. This won't take long."

Relieved she hadn't shut him out completely, he followed her to the front door. She grabbed her jacket and they stepped outside.

"Want to walk or sit on the bench here?" he asked.

"I don't intend for this conversation to last long, so here is fine."

Okay, so this was going to be a hard sell. He accepted that.

"I didn't tell you about Everly's relationship with Ethan because it wasn't my story to tell. I had promised her I wouldn't tell anyone about it."

"I appreciate that. I also appreciate what a good friend you are for keeping Everly's confidence. But when faced with the situation where I thought it was you kissing Everly, did it ever occur to you to set the record straight instead of letting me believe that you cheated on me? You could have just said it was some other guy, and not you."

"I could have, yeah, but then it would have made Everly vulnerable. It was a hard place to be, Mae. I was asked not to tell anyone about her relationship with Ethan. When someone asks me to keep a secret, that's what I do. And I know that hurt you, but I was hoping when I told you that I didn't kiss Everly, you'd believe me."

"I can appreciate that, but it hurt that you didn't trust me enough to think I wouldn't immediately go tell everyone about Everly. I can keep secrets, too, Kane."

He shifted to face her. "I don't have a lot of close relationships. Everly is one of them. When someone tells you something in confidence, you don't betray that confidence. Not to anyone. If you told me something in confidence, even if not betraying that confidence would hurt someone else, I wouldn't betray you. Not for anything. And I know it hurt you and, God, I'm sorry about that. But I just felt it wasn't my story to tell. Was I wrong? Probably. I mean, yeah, I was. And I'm so sorry that I hurt you. You are the last person I'd want to hurt. I'm in love with you, Mae. I've bungled everything and I don't exactly know what to do to fix things between us."

Mae's heart pounded so hard against her chest she could barely hear herself think. Listening to Kane's words as he poured his heart out was the most honest truth she had ever heard. She knew he'd been in a tough position between her and his close friend. It wasn't just a bunch of flowery talk, but real, honest, brutal talk. Had he screwed up? Absolutely. Was there a perfect fix? No. But wasn't that what love and relationships were all about?

Love. He'd told her he loved her. Had she even heard that right or was that what she wanted to hear?

She finally took a seat on the bench, and Kane sat next to her.

"Trust has been a big issue for me," she said. "And when you don't have faith in me enough to trust me with your secrets, it hurts me."

He took in a deep breath. "You're right. No one and nothing should come between us. I'm sorry. It won't happen again."

She believed him. She didn't know why. Wait, she did know why. Because she loved him, because when he said something to her he meant it. Because he was loyal and true to his friends, and that would translate to her. She had to have faith and make that leap with him. It would be hard, but she had to do it. If she wanted to love again, she had to do it. And maybe that was the big thing she'd been looking for all this time, the one thing that would make her put the past away for good.

"You love me?" she asked.

"Hell yeah. Heart and soul."

She should have been elated, so why did her heart squeeze so painfully? "Love hurts. How come it hurts so much?"

He took her hand. "Because real love can be painful sometimes. I know this because my heart hurts being without you. Because I love you so much it feels like someone has reached inside my chest and squeezed my heart, trying to break it. Because the thought of losing you is an unbearable thought that I refuse to even contemplate. I need you, Mae. I need you to be the sun in my mornings, the balm to my pain, the reasonable to my unreasonableness and the answer to all my questions. I don't feel whole anymore unless you're with me."

She laid her hand on top of his. "I love you, too, Kane. When I said love hurts, I meant that it hurts to be without you. I don't ever have the expectation that you have to be perfect. In fact, it would bother me greatly if you chased an idea of perfect, because I surely am not. So don't try. Just be you. And just love me."

"I do love you." He pulled her against him and kissed her, a searing kiss that made her feel whole again. She didn't know how long the kiss lasted, but enough that she felt warmed through and through.

When he pulled back, he swept his thumb over her bottom lip. "We're breaking for the holidays in a couple of days. Can you take some time off?"

"I think I can arrange that. What did you have in mind?"

"I was thinking the Maldives. Just you and me and a lot of sun and sand and sex and making plans for the future."

The future. She couldn't even imagine a future with Kane. It was fraught with lifestyle and geographical impossibilities. She also couldn't imagine a future without him in it, so she looked forward to working out the details. Because that was what you did when you loved someone.

Her lips lifted. "Well, I don't know. That kind of trip sounds like a hardship, but I'd suffer through it for you."

"See? You're always thinking of me."

She curved her fingers around his neck to pull him closer. "It's the sacrifice I make for love."

He swept his hand around her neck and kissed her, and she knew that no matter what plans they made, it would work out.

EPILOGUE

· · · · · ·

ONE YEAR LATER

T͟HIS͟ W͟AS͟ M͟AE'S͟ first official movie premiere. She was happy it was going to be in Oklahoma. And, okay, it wasn't the official premiere. That would be in Los Angeles next week. This was the early premiere for a select few, but to her? It was more than fancy enough.

"You look gorgeous, and stop fussing." Brenna smoothed her hand down the back of Mae's dress, a black off-the-shoulder full-length gown that made her feel incredible.

"I'm not fussing." She turned and looked at Brenna, her hair falling in burnished red waves over her shoulder. "You look stunning. That copper color is amazing with your skin and your hair."

Brenna laid her hand over the slight bump of her belly. "It's too bad I haven't hit the looking-pregnant part yet, so now I just look like I had too many burritos for lunch."

Erin laughed as she moved in to hug her sister. "I know exactly how that feels. But you look gorgeous."

So did Erin, in a silver gown and dangling silver earrings.

"Hey, we're all beautiful and our men will be falling at our feet tonight," Honor said, wearing a shocking red gown that clung to her curves.

"So true," Mae said. "And isn't that what really counts?"

"It's all that counts," Maureen said, looking particularly stunning herself in a green gown as lush as her home country of Ireland.

They had gotten ready at the hotel near the movie theater so they'd have plenty of time and space, plus have some time for socialization before they faced the cameras. It wouldn't be as hectic as the L.A. premiere, but Mae had decided to look on tonight as practice.

Once ready, they headed out to the main part of the suite where the men were congregating—and drinking.

Mae couldn't help but take in a breath at the sight of Kane. The man could wear a tux quite well. Then again, he took her breath away in dusty jeans and a cowboy hat, too. Fortunately, she got to see a lot more of him in dusty jeans these days, and that sure made her happy.

They'd bought several hundred acres of land not that far from the Bellini property, and the big house they'd designed together was already under construction. It was close to the vineyard so she could still do the job she loved, and close enough to the airport for Kane to fly in whenever he wanted—which, happily, was often. The plan was for him to set up his production office there in a separate building, while also raising a wide variety of animals. Mae couldn't wait to move in. She drove to the construction site a couple of times a week to check progress, and it should be completed by spring.

In the meantime, they lived in a lovely rental house that was much better suited for the two of them than her small condo had been.

Kane turned to look at her and smiled, leaving the group

of men to walk toward her. The way he looked at her never failed to make her heart do that happy leap. It probably always would.

He picked up her hand and kissed the back of it. "You are the most beautiful woman I've ever seen."

She couldn't help the little shiver of delight that skittered down her spine. "Why, thank you. You look rather dashing yourself. I might take you home with me tonight."

"Well. Aren't I the lucky one."

"You two should get married," Jason said as he walked by, winking at them.

"Yeah, when are you going to ask her to marry you?" Erin asked.

Mae pulled her gaze from Kane and grinned at Erin. "Oh, he asks me at least once a week."

"She's making me wait," Kane said. "It's torture."

Honor shook her head. "What in the world are you waiting for?"

Mae laid her hand on Kane's chest. "I'm going to marry him. I'm just making him work for it."

Kane laughed, then leaned in and whispered in her ear. "Don't make me wait too long. We need to get started on those two sets of twins, ya know."

Heat flowed through her and she looked up at him. "Then, yes."

"Yeah?" he asked. "Really?"

"Yes."

His eyes grew darker. "Can you find us a spot on the Bellini Weddings calendar? Sometime really soon?"

"Oh, I think I can carve out a spot fairly quickly. For you."

He leaned down and brushed his lips across hers, and she wanted nothing more at that moment than to be alone with him.

But then the door opened and one of the assistants walked in. "They're ready for us."

She looked up at Kane. "Let's go do this."

He smiled down at her. "And they lived happily ever after."

Yes, they would.

ACKNOWLEDGMENTS

· · · · · ·

To my former Berkley editor, Kate Seaver. Without you, this series wouldn't have existed. Thanks for the dinner and brainstorming session where Boots and Bouquets came to life. And thanks for the sixteen years of working together. It was a blast.

To my editor, Leis Pederson, thank you for your keen insights on how to make a book better. I appreciate you so much.

KEEP READING FOR AN
EXCERPT FROM JACI BURTON'S

HOUSEBROKE

CHAPTER

· · · · · ·

one

HAZEL BRISTOW LINED up all her babies, preparing them for their early evening walk. Today she waited until almost dark because even though it was late summer in Orlando, it was still muggy, and just chasing after these hellions all day inside was a sweat-inducing activity, let alone taking them on a long walk.

Of course as soon as she dragged the harnesses and leashes out, there were excited tail wags and butt wiggles. Even from Gordon the pug, who at twelve years old couldn't make it more than two blocks but gave it his best effort. Which was why she always brought the stroller along.

She got all five dogs hooked up and prepped the stroller, and they were out the door, Lilith the Chihuahua leading the way, even though she was the smallest of the pack. But Penelope the golden retriever was too busy sniffing every blade of grass in the front yard, and Freddie the dachshund had to pee on every bush they passed, and they hadn't even gotten off the property before Boo the pit mix parked his butt at the end of the driveway, refusing to go any farther.

"What's wrong, Boo?"

He looked up at her with his sad eyes, pulling on the leash to head back toward the house. She frowned and studied him, trying to figure out what the issue was. Then it hit her.

"Oh, right." She looped the leashes around the stroller, knowing they wouldn't go anywhere without her. "I'll be back in a sec, kids."

She dashed inside and found Boo's stuffed bear by the front door. She grabbed it and hurried back outside to find all five dogs waiting ever so patiently for her, though Lilith looked like she was ready to bolt any second and take the rest of them on the walk by herself.

"I'm so sorry for the delay, Lilith. We can go now."

She handed Boo his bear. He gently took it in his mouth, and now they were ready to roll.

The dogs always started out at a brisk pace, especially Boo, who was the youngest and full of energy. Which suited her just fine, too. Even with the heat, she enjoyed walking.

She loved this neighborhood with its nice homes and amazing trees in every yard. It had always felt friendly and homey to her. She was so grateful to her friend Ginger for letting her crash here, even though the house was currently for sale. And empty. But it was a roof over her and the dogs' heads, and she'd find something else soon. She'd promised her friend it would only be a short stay, and she'd keep the place superclean, which she had. And since Ginger and Greg had already moved out, Hazel felt like she was providing a service by keeping an eye on the place.

Plus, Hazel didn't have a lot of stuff, so it was easy enough to pack up and vacate whenever Ginger alerted her that the real estate agent was coming by to do a showing. Fortunately— or maybe unfortunately for Ginger—there hadn't been any activity for the past few weeks. Which had worked out well for Hazel, though she knew she was going to have to find another place to live soon. But right now? It was awesome, and she liked to imagine she and the dogs actually lived in the house.

As was typical, Gordon's tongue started hanging out after about fifteen minutes, so she scooped him up and placed him in the stroller, where he promptly turned in a circle, curled up and went to sleep. The rest of the dogs kept up the pace, though after thirty minutes she could tell they were hot and ready to head for home. So was she.

They made their way back to the house, and she unhooked the dogs from their harnesses. Everyone ran for their water bowls to hydrate while Hazel put everything away, then she went to the fridge for the pitcher of water, pouring herself a glass. She drank the entire thing, breathing out a relieved sigh when she finished it. She washed and dried the glass and put it away just in case someone wanted to come look at the house. She never left dirty dishes or anything lying out, because just packing up the dogs and their things made it enough of a rush to leave.

Not that she had much.

She changed into her swimsuit, then opened the back door, and all the dogs ran outside.

The best thing about this house was the pool. It was screened in to keep the bugs out, an important thing in Florida, so she could swim any time of the day or night. It was also great therapy for Gordon, whose arthritis had gotten bad in the past year.

She grabbed his swim harness and put it on him, smiling as his tail swept back and forth.

"You ready for a little dip, baby?" she asked as she walked over to the steps and waded into the pool.

Gordon followed her to the side of the pool. She reached

for him, and his short legs were already pumping before she set him in the water. She walked around the shallow end, letting him swim while she held on to the harness for support.

"You like the water, don't you, Gordon?"

Gordon didn't answer, of course, but she could tell from his goofy pug smile that he loved it. Because when Gordon didn't love something, he let you know with lots of grunts and whines.

So did Boo, who jumped into the deep end and swam around for a while before making his way to the steps. He got out, shook the water off, and lay down under one of the shade trees.

"You've got to have some Labrador in you, Boo. You just love your swims."

Boo rolled over on his back, stuck his feet up in the air and went to sleep, ignoring her praise.

Typical. She continued to enjoy the cool water, though at times she wished she could swim laps. Sometimes she did, late at night, after the dogs were all asleep. She'd come out here and slice through the water, remembering the times she'd have a late night swim in her own pool, at her own house, enjoying that quiet. Before her marriage went to hell and she lost everything.

Well, there was no point in reliving the past, was there? That part of her life was over. There was only now, and now was pretty great.

Temporarily great, anyway. This wasn't her home.

Not wanting to overtire Gordon, Hazel kept track of the time. Gordon would spend all day in the water if he could.

The other dogs would swim on occasion, but not every day, preferring the copious amounts of shade over in the grassy area of the yard. And it was getting late, so she scooped Gordon into her arms, unzipped him from his harness, and placed him on the ground, letting him shake off the water. Of course he'd dry in no time, so she grabbed a towel and dried herself off, put on her T-shirt, and headed into the house to get dinner ready for the dogs.

They all followed, knowing the routine.

She stood at the kitchen peninsula, prepping their food, the dogs sitting and waiting patiently nearby. All bets were off once she set the bowls down and told them to eat. Then it was slurping and crunching and Hazel should probably think about making her own dinner.

Except she needed to make a plan. She had the foster dogs, and the agencies she worked with paid for their medical care and provided a stipend for their food, which was great. But as far as income? She had mostly . . . Okay, she had nothing. And that wasn't going to put a roof over her head and gas in the car.

She took odd jobs here and there to pay the bills, but long term it wasn't ideal. And she was dipping into her meager savings more than she wanted to.

She sat on the fold-up chair and watched the dogs eat, realizing she was going to have to come up with something more permanent and soon. Living day-to-day and sometimes hour to hour just wasn't cutting it.

For her or for her dogs.

LINCOLN KENNEDY PULLED into the driveway of his next project, a nice four-bedroom in a prime location in Orlando. He turned the engine off in his truck and wished it was still daylight so he could take a look at the outside of the house, but that would have to wait until morning.

What a shit day. Shit month, actually. He gripped the

steering wheel, wishing he'd had time to take a long vacation to somewhere tropical and shake off the dregs of his breakup with Stefanie.

It had all boiled down to the money. His money. Once Stefanie had found out how much he had, she'd changed. He thought the two of them had a chance at something, but she'd turned out to be no different than any other woman he'd ever had a relationship with. He'd been judged by his wallet, and once a woman found out his was fat, she saw him differently. Wanted things from him. Planned a future based on his income.

So he'd ended it, just like he'd ended all his other relationships.

Whatever. Girlfriends were too much trouble. And he needed to get to work.

He grabbed his bag and the keys that the Realtor had overnighted to him and walked to the front door, then slipped the keys in the lock, noting the lockbox was still on the door. He made a mental note to contact the agent in the morning so it could be removed.

As he opened the door, he yawned. The flight from San Francisco to Orlando had been long and exhausting, but such was the nature of his business. Not that he was complaining, since he loved the travel, and he was excited to start this new project. At least this would give him something to get jazzed about.

He dropped his bag at the front door, then paused, certain he'd heard a noise. He waited a few beats, listening for anything else that didn't seem right. When he didn't hear another sound, he headed straight to the kitchen.

From the photos he'd seen of the place, he knew that was where he'd need to do the most work, so he might as well take a look.

He was about to hit the light switch when he caught movement out of the corner of his eye. Something was headed toward him, and he caught whatever it was in mid swing, his heart pumping triple time as he figured he was about to get blasted on the head by a tire iron or something equally skull smashing. In what felt like hours but in reality was probably only a few seconds, he had the offending weapon in one hand and the intruder wrapped around him in the other.

"Hey, hold on there," he said, realizing whoever was trying to kill him was a lot smaller than him. And lighter, since he'd grabbed their arm and their weapon, which was a . . .

Cast-iron skillet?

He held the squirming burglar against his chest and leaned back to fumble around the wall for the light switch. He hit the switch with his elbow, which bathed the kitchen with light.

Okay, this was unexpected. He quickly let go of the intruder, and they made a hasty retreat to the other side of the room.

Linc had figured maybe a teen, or a small man. But never in a million years did he figure he'd come face-to-face with a gorgeous woman dressed only in a T-shirt and underwear, along with several glaring sets of eyes directed at him. He quickly counted—

Five dogs. And they hadn't even barked.

"What the hell's going on here?" he asked. "What are you doing in here?"

She tugged the T-shirt over her flowered cotton panties. "I think I should be the one asking the questions here, since you just broke in."

He shook his head. "No, I own this place."

"You do not. I'm friends with the owner."

"You mean the former owner. I closed on this house three days ago."

She frowned. "Prove it."

He frowned. "You prove it. Who's the owner of this place?" He wasn't about to give her a lead.

"Ginger and Greg—"

"Powell," he finished for her.

Her eyes widened. "They sold the house?"

"Yeah."

She lifted her chin, a defiant look on her face. "I don't believe you."

Now that his heart rate had come down to a more manageable level, he could think a little more clearly. And since whoever this woman was seemed to know the former owners, she was likely scared, too. Which was so not his problem, since she was the one squatting in his house. "You should call her. Now."

She grabbed her phone off the corner of the peninsula while she eyed him warily. She pressed a button and waited.

"Ginger. It's Hazel. I'm at your house and some guy just came in and said he bought the place."

She listened, still staring at him.

"It's okay. I just didn't know. I would have left if I'd known."

She listened some more.

"I'm fine, honestly. Nothing happened other than both of us scaring the hell out of each other."

Then she laughed, and it was such an amazing sound. Light and easy.

He didn't care how she sounded. Why would he care? His first objective needed to be getting her the hell out of there.

"Yeah, I don't think either of us would want to see pics of what just happened. But we're both okay. No harm, no foul."

Linc motioned to her. "Mind if I have the phone for a second?"

She hesitated. "Uh, Ginger? He wants to talk to you."

She listened, then gave him the phone. He put it on speaker and laid it on the counter. "Hey, Ginger, how's it going?"

"Linc. I am so embarrassed. For some reason I had it down that you weren't coming in until next month. And then with our move and everything going on, I totally spaced and forgot to tell Hazel that the house had sold. This is all my fault. I'm so sorry to both of you for this."

Linc looked over at the woman, who still had her arms wrapped around herself but seemed a lot less terrified than she had a few minutes ago.

"Hey, it's okay. We both survived the scare. Is Greg there?"

"Oh, he's here, trying not to laugh."

"I wasn't laughing," Greg said. "Glad you didn't get arrested, bud."

He saw Hazel cock her head to the side. "Greg and I know each other," he told her.

"Oh. Okay."

"I'm so sorry, Hazel," Ginger said.

"Me, too," Greg said. "But it's still Ginger's fault."

"Hey, you could have called Hazel, too," Ginger said.

"I could have. My bad."

"It's all good," Hazel said. "Love you guys."

"I'll call you after this project, Greg," Linc said, "and we'll get together for a round."

"You got it," Greg said.

Hazel clicked off. "Okay, apparently you're legit. Ginger didn't tell me. She told me she'd let me know when they accepted an offer so I could clear out before the new owner arrived. I guess that's you."

"And I guess you're not a burglar."

She slanted a look at him. "Do I look like a burglar?"

He gave her the once-over, from her wildly tousled dark hair to her tanned bare legs. "Not any burglar I could ever imagine."

"Do you mind if I put some pants on before we continue this conversation?"

Actually, he did mind. She had amazing legs. "Sure, go ahead. And while you're at it, you can pack up whatever things you have so you can leave."

Her eyes widened. "Oh, right. Sure. I can do that. Sorry."

The look on her face was one of utter dejection. Linc would not feel sorry for her. She wasn't his responsibility, and he had things to do to this house that did not include a woman and five dogs.

"Come on, babies," she said, and just like that, her dog entourage followed behind, but he could swear that little beige Chihuahua gave him a dirty look before leaving the room.

Finally, Linc had a chance to exhale. And put the skillet on the stove.

The woman—Hazel—was talking upstairs. He should follow and make sure she didn't do any damage. And while she might be friends with Ginger and Greg, she wasn't his friend. In fact, he didn't know her at all. He'd known of squatters who kicked in drywall or did any number of things to screw up property before running off. He had his investment to protect, so he quietly made his way up the steps, stopping in the hallway when he heard the sound of her voice just inside the bedroom.

"It's okay, babies," she said, her voice low and trembling. "We'll figure something out. We always do, don't we?"

He peeked his head inside the door to see a blow-up mattress and an oversized backpack. Was that all she had? She'd put on a pair of shorts and wound her long, dark hair into a bun on top of her head.

"I promise I'll take care of you. You won't be homeless. We won't be homeless. I'll make this work. Somehow." The pit bull came over and laid his head on her thigh, and Hazel dropped her head to her chest and her body shook.

Dammit. She was crying. Linc turned away and made his way back downstairs.

This—she—was not his problem. He didn't even know her.

Hazel came downstairs a short time later, her eyes swollen and red rimmed, but she had a smile on her face. The dogs all followed her, then sat at her feet like little statues.

Weird little fuckers.

All she had were the remnants of that mattress and a couple of bags. Was that all she owned?

"I'm really sorry about nearly crushing your skull with the skillet. We'll get out of your way now. I have a chair outside—oh, and my skillet. I'll just put these in the car and be on my way."

She headed toward the front door, the dogs following. It was the most pitiful entourage Linc had ever seen.

Fuck.

"Wait," he said.

She stopped and turned to look at him.

"It's late and you obviously don't have anywhere to go. You can stay in the guesthouse for a day or two until you figure something out."

Her eyes lit up like bright round diamonds. "Really? Oh my God, thank you so much. I'm Hazel Bristow, by the way." She held out her hand, so he did the same.

"Lincoln Kennedy."

She gave him a look. "That's very . . . historical."

"I go by Linc. And my mother's a history teacher. She named all of us after historical figures."

"All of you. So you have siblings."

"Two brothers."

"I see. So you're moving in?"

"Sort of. I mean, not really. I'm renovating this place."

She frowned. "Why? What's wrong with it? It's a great house."

"It needs some updating before I sell it."

"Oh." She chewed on her lower lip for a beat. "So you're one of those people."

The way she said that told him she wasn't a fan of his livelihood. "You mean people who invest in homes, fix them up and make them better, then sell them and improve the neighborhood?"

He didn't miss her derisive snort. "Yeah. House flippers. You come in, do some cheap modifications so you can make a quick profit, then turn around and sell and then you're off to the next house."

"Well, when you say it like that it does sound bad. But that's not what I do."

"Uh-huh. Sure."

"And what do you do, Hazel?"

Her gaze shifted down to her dogs. "I foster dogs."

"Is that what those are?"

"Yes. Sort of. Mostly."

That was vague. "And you're staying in an empty house because . . . ?"

"It's complicated. Say, are you hungry? I'm hungry. I was going to fix myself some dinner. Would you like something to eat?"

She was avoiding the question, but he was hungry. "Sure."

"Awesome."

She seemed relieved not to answer the question about what she was doing staying at the house, but Linc supposed the answer to that question could wait.

At least until after dinner.

NEW YORK TIMES AND *USA TODAY*
BESTSELLING AUTHOR

JACI
BURTON

"Jaci Burton's stories are full of heat and heart."

—#1 *New York Times*
bestselling author Maya Banks

For a complete list of titles,
please visit prh.com/jaciburton